## Haraak's Demai

"You will bring out enough gold to fill this pack!" he shouted as Kalie translated. "And you will bring out enough knives, axes and spearheads of copper to fill another of the same size. And food—since you have so much!" He laughed harshly at that and was joined by all his men.

Yelene nodded. "We have no axes of copper, and few spearheads, but we will give you the rest of what you ask," she said.

Haraak scowled again after Kalie translated. "Then make them, for we will not leave without them! And some of those strange hides that you wear."

"He means cloth," Kalie explained, but the others had understood.

"Yes," said Yelene, as eyes were raised in hope for the first time in many days. "All this we will give you, and your men, whom we have healed and nursed back to health, all if you will simply leave!"

"Gladly!" said Haraak, looking distastefully at the land around him. Yelene turned to her people and began directing people to gather up all the gold in the city and locate the smiths with the greatest skill, when Haraak added, "One thing more. Fifty slave girls. All comely."

At Kalie's translation, Yelene froze, mirrored by everyone on the roof. The feeling of hope, nearly palpable a moment before, vanished. As the last echo of Haraak's words faded, an idea took shape in her mind. "We will give you our answer tomorrow," she said. Then she turned to Yelene and the rest of the council. "Come, we have much to discuss."

Books By Sandra Saidak

Kalie's Journey
*Daughter of the Goddess Lands*
*Shadow of the Horsemen* (Coming in 2012)

# Daughter of the Goddess Lands

Book 1 of Kalie's Journey

By Sandra Saidak

Published by Uffington Horse Press
San Jose, California

CreateSpace Edition

Published by Uffington Horse Press, San Jose, California, USA

This book contains an excerpt from the forthcoming book *Shadow of the Horsemen* by Sandra Saidak. The excerpt has been set for this edition only and may not reflect the final content of the forthcoming edition.

ISBN: 978-0-9846991-1-7

Learn more at: www.sandrasaidak.com

# Acknowledgements

So many people made this book happen, I don't have room to thank everyone individually. Those who I never met but helped immeasurably include Jean Auel who started the genre, Marija Gimbatus who gave us a new view of history, and Rianne Eisler who made these new ideas accessible to the masses.

Thanks also goes to all the members of my first Writers Group, the Over-the-Hill Gang, who taught me how to write. Special thanks to the members of my current group: Gerry Nordley, Candy Lowe, Adrian Gormley, Mike Van Pelt, Jason Stewart, Loren Means, Sarah Stegall, Robin Riversmith, Valerie Frankel, and Dio Sanchez (of blessed memory) who gave hours of their time reading this manuscript from its earliest draft and making it better. Very special thanks to the wonderful community of Jean Auel fans on www.ecfans.com who convinced me that, yes, I could tell a good story.

More personal thanks go to George MacDonald, without whom this book would never has seen the light of day—for so many reasons. To Joann Daughtery, thanks for the support--and all those workshops you dragged me to. To my daughters, Heather and Melissa, thank you for being an inspiration—always. To my mother, Charlotte Fisher, thanks for the editing—and the arguments. Last and always, thank you to Tom, who kept the cats off of my keyboard, the kids out of my hair and was always ready to come to the rescue during a computer emergency (of which there were many).

# Prologue

Black Sea region, circa 4000 BC

She remembered faces.

No bodies; no voices. Just faces drifting in and out of presence, just as she drifted in and out of consciousness.

Then voices came and joined the faces, though sometimes they were just sounds. The loud, frightening ones that came from the faces of the beastmen always sent her into fits of moaning and thrashing.

After that, there came the gentle faces of women, and soothing words that she almost understood. Sometimes hands appeared and sponged her face with cool water, or gave her soothing draughts.

Sometimes hands grew from beneath the faces of the beastmen, and then she would scream until everything went black. Then, at least, she would rest.

"Her body is recovering, Helva." The voice belonged to the woman who had been caring for her.

"Yes, Orlia," said a new voice. "But her mind continues to wander. And we can find no head injury; nothing that would account for her state of confusion."

"But the injuries that we have found are troubling enough. The welts on her back? The bruising on her thighs? It's as if she were somehow forced into a sexual joining. Have you ever seen anything like that before?"

The woman on the bed knew she did not want to hear the answer, but she could not stop listening to the two women who spoke so calmly, and without any fear.

"The last part, yes, unfortunately. Near my home in the south, a man became unbalanced after his partner scattered their hearth. No one saw the warning signs for what they were, and one day, he followed her into the woods and forced himself on her. The village placed a brand on his face to warn others, and exiled him."

"Did that woman suffer in her mind, as well?"

"No, not like this. But another healer told me of a case in which a small child was abused in this manner, by her mother's own partner. I am told she never spoke again, although she recovered in other ways."

There was a gasp of indrawn breath. "How could such a creature exist? Or live with himself?"

"He didn't. He drowned himself in the river after his crime was discovered."

"A pity he didn't do that before he harmed a child."

"I have often thought that myself—"

Light spilled into the room, then, and a shadow leapt across the floor. The woman on the bed began to shake. One of the two speakers set a gentle hand on her shoulder, and the woman found herself less afraid, though she didn't know why.

"I was told that one of my kin might have been found alive," said a male voice.

Fear clutched her again, turning her insides to ice. But the women who had been caring for her welcomed him. They brought him close to her, yet warned him to stop just when she was about to start trembling again. That gave her pause. How did they know? And why did he stay back?

It didn't matter. For the moment, at least, no one was trying to hurt her, and things were becoming solid and familiar for the first time for as long as she could remember.

# Chapter 1

"Kalie?" the man was saying. "Don't you remember me? Can you tell me what happened to you? Where are Junie and Galev?

*Kalie.* The name was like a stone dropped into still water. It settled in her slowly, spreading out, touching other knowledge that might be memories. She looked into the concerned face of the man across from her. He was familiar; she was supposed to know him, though nothing like the certainty of her own name danced before her eyes. He was impatient, yet struggling to control it. He began to tap his foot, and then twist about on his cushion. When it seemed he would speak again, the gray haired woman beside Kalie leaned forward and put a restraining hand on the man's shoulder.

She is a priestess, Kalie thought. And this is a Temple of Healing. But not the one in my village.

How did I know that?

"Kalie?" said the priestess gently. "Are you starting to remember?"

"I remember that my name is Kalie," she said slowly. Slower still, she raised her eyes to the man across from her. "You are Joran!" The name slammed into her eyes and made her dizzy, so that it took a moment for his face to return to focus. Kalie turned her gaze to the priestess, but found her still a stranger. "Where am I? How did I get here? What happened to me?" Kalie asked.

"You are in the Temple of Healing in the village of Long Grass," said the priestess. "Some fishermen found you, nearly a moonspan ago, by Last Lake, a day's walk north of here." At Kalie's puzzled look, she added, "It is where the croplands end and the dry steppes begin; the last water for many days, although few people have traveled that far. You were starved and parched, and raving in a language no one could understand. As for what happened to you...we still don't know. Can you remember anything?"

Kalie shook her head quickly and, she noticed, more forcefully than necessary. She did not know why, but the priestess nodded, as if Kalie had just explained something.

"You and I live in the village of Tall Oaks," said Joran. "About six days from here. Early last spring, you left with my sister, Junie, and her partner Galev to travel east with some traders from the city of Gaea."

"I am a merchant?" Kalie asked, frowning. That didn't seem right.

"No, you're a potter." For the first time, Joran smiled. "And a very good storyteller. You had never been on a long Journey before; never traveled any farther than Gaea. You said you wanted to travel someplace new; someplace even experienced travelers hadn't seen, have an adventure and collect new tales before..." Joran faltered, looking uncertainly at the priestess.

Kalie pressed forward, unwilling to let the priestess decide what she should or should not be told. "What? Tell me!"

"Before you Joined with Bartev and settled down to raise a family."

Kalie stared at Joran. At the mention of pottery, she remembered the feel of clay in her hands, even a fleeting glimpse of jars and cups that she knew she had made. But Bartev? Her mind could bring forth nothing.

"Is he…Bartev here?" Kalie finally asked.

Joran shook his head. "He left for Gaea a few days before word reached us that someone from your party had been found. He hoped one of the priests could guide him on a spirit quest for you. Relatives of some of the others went with him."

Kalie absorbed this. More details of her life were coming back, but people remained missing. "Is there anyone else looking for me?" she asked uncertainly.

"Everyone in Tall Oaks!" said Joran. "We've been worried about all of you since you didn't come home at the end of summer." Kalie looked outside the open door of the temple. Late autumn sunlight shone in the courtyard. A few brown leaves still clung to the trees, while the rest swirled in eddies on the ground. It was nearly winter.

"I've been gone since spring?" Kalie looked from Joran to the priestess to the world outside the temple. How could half a year simply vanish from her life? And why did she fear to remember it?

The priestess settled on a cushion beside Kalie and took her hand, while Joran paced the small room. "Can you remember anything that happened? To you? Or to the others who were with you?"

Kalie closed her eyes and tried to remember. Junie? Garev? The names brought no faces to her mind, only a dark feeling that clutched at her gut and then vanished. She tried again—but not as hard as before. She remembered people screaming. She remembered a sick feeling of terror, and a glimpse of strange man-beasts with six legs and two heads and hair all over. Then everything went black.

Her eyes shot open and Kalie gasped as if she had been running. There was nothing there but the concerned face of the priestess and, farther back, the bewildered face of Joran, and the soothing calm of the temple courtyard beyond. She didn't know what had happened to her, but she did know two things. She was safe. And she didn't want to remember. Even if it meant having nothing to tell concerned families about their loved ones. Even if it meant never knowing who she was.

# Chapter 2

Kalie sat on a bench in the temple courtyard, staring at the stranger who gazed back at her from the depths of the polished copper mirror. It was a pretty enough face, she supposed, if still a bit gaunt. Wide set brown eyes set in a smooth oval face, accentuated with high cheekbones. Long brown hair, tending to curl at the ends fell past her shoulders.

Idly, Kalie twisted a lock around her fingers, then wondered if this was something she always did; something from her old life. They thought she was about eighteen summers. That seemed about right.

She set the mirror down carefully, and looked up at the snow-laden clouds in the winter sky. Swathed in furs, Kalie still felt the bite of cold, but preferred it to being indoors. Soon, it would snow again, and they would make her go inside. The healers had told her she was recovered enough to return to Tall Oaks. She didn't want to go there, but now that she was fit to travel, she had no excuse to remain in the temple. Of course, she didn't need one; she could simply claim sanctuary, or decide to dedicate her life to the Goddess, and they would have to let her stay.

But Orlia, the priestess and healer who had been with Kalie from the time she arrived, felt it was necessary for Kalie to return to her home, to see if familiar surroundings would help her regain her memory, or ease the terror that still clung to her, day and night. If it didn't work, she was always free to return to the temple.

At least all those people had stopped coming around, asking her questions.

She thought again of the anxious relatives who

had come to question her, wondering if she might have handled things better. Some had spoken at length of people Kalie only vaguely recalled. Others had just wrung their hands and wept. All had wanted to know what had happened, and Kalie had told them she didn't know. No one was satisfied with that; they just asked again, or launched into a heartwarming story of Junie's or Garev's or Tetie's childhood or the promising futures they all had.

Kalie had finally told them, as kindly as she could, that she thought all of them were dead. Then she added, as though speaking to herself, "They are better off that way." Then, at least, they left her alone. But they weren't doing it out of respect for her wishes. No one, it seemed, was comfortable around Kalie. She couldn't blame them. Her memory might be returning, but her skill with people was lost. Even those in the temple, who had compassion for that, were upset about the nature of her injuries, her odd behavior, her inability to explain it so they could at least know what they were dealing with.

Bartev had come to see her a few days after Joran left. At first Kalie was pleased, for she remembered him at once. He was a big bear of a man, warm and friendly and full of jokes. Kalie remembered that much of his humor stemmed from his many childish fears, which seemed so out of place in a man his size. She knew what it had cost him to travel so far from home in search of her. Yet from the moment he rushed to her bedside and yanked her into a fierce embrace, Kalie wished he had never found her.

She had shrunk in terror from his touch, and wept uncontrollably—though she had long since mastered her reactions, or so she thought—when the priestesses led him away whispering urgently to him. Kalie hated causing him pain. And hated her own helplessness even more.

Bartev was a physical man, who liked to stand close to people or throw an arm around their shoulders when talking with them. He didn't understand why he had to keep his distance from Kalie just to keep her from crying out in terror. Nor could Kalie enlighten him. Or tell him what had happened to her, or give him any idea of when they might be joined, when she wouldn't even let him comfort her with his body.

Kalie had finally asked Bartev to return to Tall Oaks without her. She promised to see him there when she was better. It had taken the insistence of the entire priesthood of the temple to make him comply.

Kalie had been relieved when he left. Now, however, sitting in the temple courtyard, knowing she would have to leave when the weather cleared, she felt only a nameless dread.

Orlia approached slowly, humming a soothing tune, and appearing within Kalie's line of sight from an impressive distance. She handed Kalie a cup of herbal tea, then backed up to perch on a bench several cubits away. Kalie smiled wryly. Oralia was a great healer, precisely because of this gift: she could put anyone at ease; make the most bizarre needs of her patients seem perfectly reasonable.

Kalie tasted the tea. Chamomile and sweet woodruff and something else. Lemon balm, perhaps? A relaxing combination, at any rate.

"Is it getting any easier?" Orlia asked. She did not ask if Kalie remembered anything more, nor did Kalie expect her to.

"Day by day, just as you keep saying."

"I thought we could play that word game again, it you're up for it."

"I'm remembering enough on my own, I think," Kalie said, not wanting to sound rude, just wishing her memory wasn't so important to everyone around here.

"We are all pleased that your memory of who you are and where you are from is returning," said Orlia.

"But you want me to remember what happened to me. And to the others who were with me."

"As a healer, I find myself in conflict there." At Kalie's raised eyebrow, Orlia continued. "You present the people here with many mysteries, Kalie. The answers are locked inside you. But seeking them causes you pain. As a healer, my concern is for the person I am caring for. If remembering causes you pain, I must advise against seeking to remember, and instead, search for ways to keep those memories buried. But also, as a healer, I am concerned for the peace of mind of the families that seek answers about their loved ones. Your memories may be the only key to that."

Kalie was about to retort that the concerned relatives she had met had lost far less blood and flesh than she had, and perhaps might require less attention, but she bit it back. Why was she intent on driving away everyone who tried to help her?

Then she noticed Orlia's intense expression, as if she had more to say, but worried it might upset her patient.

"What is it?" Kalie asked.

"It is the nature of your injuries," said Orlia. "As difficult as it is to believe, there can be no doubt that your...injuries...were caused by other people. But what kind of human could do that to another? If those who harmed you are still out there, they are a danger; a danger we can do nothing about until we know who and where and how many. No one wants to see what happened to you and your companions happen to anyone else."

*"Then why did it happen to me?"* Kalie cried. She froze, horrified at her outburst and nearly choking on the helpless fear that always brought bile to her throat. Orlia remained as calm and unaffected as ever. "Perhaps they are already dead," Kalie whispered a moment later.

"Perhaps. A man alone, gone savage for some reason, as animals sometimes do, would likely not live long. But I sense there is more to what happened to you than that. I fear you suffered at the hands of more than one man. You claim you think the others in your party are dead, and that they are better off that way."

Shame at her callous words washed over Kalie. "I don't know why I said that. I'm sorry..."

"Don't be. I have spent enough time with you to know that you are not, by nature, a cruel person. Quite the opposite, in fact. Those words tell me that you suffered something so terrible that to you, death would have been a mercy. But don't you see why that concerns us?

"And then there were the words you raved when you were first brought here; they seemed to be a language, but one no one who was brought to hear you recognized it. If there is a threat out there, we need to know what it is."

Kalie nodded, trying to hold back tears. "What do you want me to do?"

Orlia came closer and knelt beside Kalie. "There is a ceremony that might allow you to remember. Theron, my brother healer, has participated in it several times. I would be with you the whole time, but Theron would have to conduct the ceremony. It would require complete trust on your part. Could you do it?"

Kalie thought about it. Like most Temples of Healing, this one at Long Grass was presided over by a priest and a priestess, representing both halves of creation; the balance between male and female life forces. While she had seen Theron, and heard he was a gifted healer, Kalie had spent little time with him. She was told that she reacted violently whenever a man had attempted to care for her needs. As a result, the priest and male students had mostly kept their distance. Concepts like trust seemed far away from Kalie. She shrugged, affecting greater composure than she felt. "If you think it will help, then I will try," she told Orlia.

# Chapter 3

An acolyte brought Kalie a cup of something dark. Kalie sniffed it and wrinkled her nose. She took a small sip; it was just the right temperature for drinking, but bitter. She finished the rest in one gulp, wishing for water to wash away the taste. The room was dark, lit only by pinpricks of light from oil lamps arranged around the small enclosure. Orlia sat close to Kalie, while Theron and two acolytes sat against the opposite wall.

Also present was Helva, the oldest person in the temple. Kalie now remembered Helva as the other person tending to her when she first awoke inside the temple. Helva, a well-known healer, lived on the other side of the Black Sea, and was only by chance traveling through a town near Long Grass when Kalie was found.

Kalie handed the empty cup to the acolyte. "Now what?" she asked.

"First, remember, you are safe here," Theron told her. "Whatever memories may surface, they cannot hurt you now."

Kalie nodded, feeling her eyes grow heavy. She did not find Theron's words very reassuring. She leaned back into the cushions, suddenly disoriented. She reached out in near panic for Orlia, and felt the older woman grip her hand.

"I'm here, Kalie," she whispered. "I will keep you safe."

Theron began tapping a simple rhythm on a wooden drum. The acolytes followed with smaller, leather-covered drums. Soon Kalie was following the patterns of sound until that was all she knew.

"It's early summer," Theron began in a soft sonorous voice that matched the drums. "You're with friends, walking east, into the grasslands…"

At once, Kalie was there, gazing out over an endless sea of billowing grass. There were seven people with her: artisans and traders, even a musician who earned her keep by using her flute and voice to call forth the people of each town they came to, as Kalie told stories to entertain them when the trading was done. Junie thought they had reached the end of the world; she wanted to turn back. Selv, the leader of the merchants wanted to continue a little further. Then they saw a cloud of dust moving toward them from the east. Soon, they could make out strange creatures with two heads and six legs. Kalie cried out as recognition struck: they were people, riding on the backs of animals she knew were horses, although she had never known horses could be tamed.

That was the last coherent thought Kalie remembered.

After that, there was series of images that flew at her in no discernable order.

She remembered Garev disappearing beneath the legs of one horse, while a man's hairy arm reached down and grabbed her from atop another.

She remembered the screams of her friends, and the harsh shouting of the men above them.

There was the memory of pain as she was slung over the broad back of a horse and made to stay there for what seemed like forever, while the animal bounced beneath her. Then there was the pain of landing on her back on the hard ground and a man on top of her, touching her body in a sickening parody of love, with each touch bringing more pain.

She remembered a whole village of leather tents spread across a hot, dry, empty land of grass that stretched on forever.

There was thirst; raging thirst, and hunger too, although there were flocks of sheep and goats that stood by the tents and should have been enough to feed everyone. There was blood too, and the smell of blood seemed to fill the sweltering air, as if the very dust was filled with it.

There were human heads on sharpened sticks that stuck straight into the air, and one of them was Selv's.

Kalie came awake suddenly, her heart racing, despite the soothing potion and the gentle rhythms. "Water!" she croaked, for her mouth felt as dry as it had the day she woke up in this temple.

An acolyte hurried to bring her a cup of cool water, and Orlia helped her drink it. Everyone waited patiently until Kalie was ready to speak.

In halting, trembling speech, Kalie told the assembled priesthood what she had experienced, sometimes drifting into the speech she had learned from the horsemen, for there were no words in her own tongue for much of what Kalie had seen. She tried to explain what a "slave" was, that the men of the horse tribe were all "warriors" and while the women were herders who kept the flocks, most were also slaves.

At the end she was wrung out, but, as Orlia had hoped, most of her memory had returned, and she was coherent.

But no one could quite believe what happened to her. And no one listened when she told them the horsemen would be coming this way to invade a people who had no weapons, and no concept of warfare.

"Yes, of course, some of the things you describe really happened," Theron explained patiently. "As disturbing as it is for all of us—and most of all you, of course—it appears that somewhere to the east, there exists a band of unfortunate men, who have somehow fallen into savagery. They were undoubtedly cast out of their homes because of their violent behavior."

"And, much as I could wish otherwise," continued Orlia, "your account of sexual brutality is also true. All travelers must be warned to avoid the land to the east. Regardless of how few they might be, or how likely they are to be dead by winter's end, no one must go anywhere near that area."

"Their numbers are not small," Kalie repeated hopelessly.

"But they must be!" said Helva. "You described an entire city of tents; more people living there than in Gaea. And you claim all the men who live there are like the men who attacked you, and that all of the women accept it. Kalie, do you honestly believe that any woman would live with such deranged men? Or allow her children near such danger? If they could not prevent such behavior, the others of their tribe would simply have left such men to fend for themselves, and settled somewhere else. These 'memories' of yours, are more like nightmares. Visions created by a mind pushed passed its limits by violence." Helva sat back, smiling benignly, pleased that she had had been able to explain things so well.

"The women who live in that place are not like

us," said Kalie. "They think violence and fear are normal. They can't just take their children and leave because they have no place to go, and no idea homes like ours exist!"

Helva stared hard at Kalie. Finally, she said, "That is not possible."

"I know we would all like to think so," said Orlia. "None of us have ever heard of such things. Yet I fear we must accept Kalie's words as true. The evidence is too strong for all of it to be merely a nightmare."

Kalie sighed with relief. They couldn't change what happened, but at least someone here understood. As much as anyone in a sane world could understand madness. "We must do more than keep travelers away from the east," she continued. "We must be ready to defend ourselves when they come here."

Theron shook his head. "They are far away, Kalie. In another world, where strange gods rule and the Goddess holds no sway. If you had not, by ill chance, stumbled among them, they would still be unknown to us, as we are to them. You need only regain your strength and begin to heal."

"Your fear is normal, Kalie," said Orlia. "But you are safe now. As Theron said, they are far away, and do not even know where we are. Accept our gratitude for the warning you have brought, but your nightmare is over. Rest and get well." She signaled one of the acolytes to lead Kalie to bed.

Kalie made no protest. But as she left the temple she thought, I found my way here, on foot, with no food. They will come on horses, with supplies. And weapons. And what will happen to us then?

# Chapter 4

Kalie returned to her home in the village of Tall Oaks a few days past Midwinter.

She left Tall Oaks forever when the traveling paths were clear in the spring.

From the day she returned and attempted to resume her old life, it seemed to Kalie that nothing worked.

Tall Oaks was south of Long Grass, only two days walk from the warm waters of the Black Sea, so winter was milder here. The village, set in a clearing in the forest, consisted of about twenty beehive shaped houses, each containing an extended family of about eight to twelve people, generally related to each other through the mother who owned the house. Vegetable patches and workshops were scattered among the dwellings, while grain grew in cleared areas outside the village.

Kalie had lived with her aunt Arlie, a potter as her mother and sister had been, since Kalie's mother had died when Kalie was about ten. Some of this she remembered; some had been explained by others.

Arlie had welcomed Kalie warmly when she returned, as had her son and daughter who lived with her. Kalie's cousins were not yet joined with anyone, thus they lived with their mother, helping with her business, and caring for her through her bouts of arthritis, which grew worse each winter. Eventually, Selie, Arlie's daughter, would bring a mate to live with them, while Urev would leave to live in the house his mate shared with her female relatives.

It was assumed that once Kalie was back to her

old self, Bartev would move in as well, and soon there would be children to work the clay and stoke the kiln.

But Kalie never returned to her old self.

The nightmares might leave her in peace for a few days, but they never really went away. No one in the family, least of all Kalie herself, knew when she might wake up in the middle of the night, screaming about monsters and hairy men, or sobbing and begging them not to touch her.

She tried to take comfort in the familiar things she had enjoyed before, but the clay felt dead in her hands. She could shape only the most basic utilitarian vessels, and help with the menial tasks of stoking the kiln and sweeping out the shop. Once, she knew, she had shaped objects of elegant beauty: storage jars for grain with delicate patterns incised around them, perfectly balanced wine jars, ingenious grooved trays for husking grain, and even little toys in the shape of animals.

Now, as she swept the dust out of the workshop, Kalie found a broken pot, waiting to be swept out with the rest of the garbage. She gathered up the pieces and tried to fit them back together. It was no use: there were too many pieces, some were missing, and even with infinite patience and the strongest glue, the pot would never be functional again. Better just to throw this one away and make a new one.

Arlie entered the shop with a tray of cups for the kiln. Painted in stripes and chevrons of red and white and black, they were ingeniously made: when turned upside down, the random markings became faces. One could almost see the Goddess's All Seeing Eyes here, a nose there, even arms and hands. Arlie's work could be found in temples and household shrines all around the Black Sea, and even beyond. Until recently, it seemed Kalie was following in her aunt's footsteps.

Arlie's hands shook as she reached the kiln, and Kalie hurried over to help. After they had everything loaded inside, Kalie followed Arlie through the courtyard to the kitchen, which shared its back wall with the workshop. The heat from the kiln also fed the oven that cooked the family's meals.

Kalie went to the large storage jar that held the cracked grain and was about to begin work on the evening meal, but Arlie shook her head. "Sit and rest awhile, child. You work too much."

"It helps occupy my mind."

"Have some tea with me." Arlie took two cups from a shelf by the stove, and dipped out tea from the pot made fresh every morning, then kept hot all day in the coals for whoever wanted a cup. The cups, Kalie noticed, were of her own making. They were without any special adornment, but perfectly round and balanced, and glazed a rich, reddish brown.

She sipped silently. There was licorice root in the tea, covering the bitter taste of willow bark for Arlie's nagging aches and pains.

"Do you remember when you made this?"

Kalie looked up in surprise, angry with herself for letting her attention wander. Her aunt was holding up a small clay figurine of the Goddess in Her aspect as Mother. It was not painted and had only a hint of a face, with two tiny fingernail scratches for eyes and a pinch in the clay for a nose. The naked body boasted huge breasts and thighs, ample buttocks and wide hips made for bearing children.

"Not long after my mother died, I think," said

Kalie.

Arlie nodded. "It always seemed to me that you poured everything you felt into creating this statue. All your grief and anger, your need to understand why, all your passion. And I knew then that you had the power to work the clay. Not just work it; the power to put life into it."

Kalie stared at the tiny statue, seeking some connection with the strong girl who had made it. "The person who sculpted that Goddess no longer exists," she said.

Arlie shook her head. "She's lost, perhaps, but she's not gone. Our Goddess doesn't squander gifts on those who can't use them."

"Where was our Goddess when the beastmen took me?" Kalie asked bitterly.

"Maybe you fell out of the land of the Mother, and got lost in a place of different gods. Or demons. But She brought you back to us. You must know She still loves you."

Kalie was silent.

"What are you going to do about Bartev?" Arlie asked.

"What do you mean?" Kalie asked, puzzled by the sudden change in subject, yet knowing that it wasn't a change, not really.

"He loves you, and he's been waiting patiently all this season. I know you still love him. Why do you keep pushing him away?"

Kalie wiped away more useless tears. "I don't know. I only know that I can't stand to have him touch me. Not him; not any man."

"Does it still hurt? Joining, I mean?"

Kalie shrugged. "Not really. But I wouldn't

know. We haven't been able to…Anytime we try…I just…can't."

"Oh," said Arlie, trying to take it in. "That must be very difficult. For both of you. Have you spoken with the priestess? I'm sure she could help."

"I really don't like to talk about it, and neither does Bartev." Kalie stared out the kitchen's small window and into the courtyard. "He needs to find someone else. There are plenty of women who would gladly take my place. I wish he would stop waiting for me."

"That still won't solve anything for you," said Arlie. "If you don't want to join with Bartev, that's fine. But you'll need to join with someone, someday."

"Not everyone does," said Kalie. "Those in the service of the Goddess don't."

"But you have no calling for that life. And for as long as I've known you, you've wanted a large family." Arlie smiled. "I half think that was what attracted you most to Bartev: all his brothers and sisters, aunts and uncles—even his grandmother, still alive and into everyone's business at what? Sixty-five winters? A happy house, full of children. If you still want that, then you'll have to join with a man eventually."

Kalie could only shiver uncontrollably in the warm kitchen.

Things grew worse when spring arrived. As the anniversary of her ill-fated journey approached, Kalie grew increasingly skittish. She shunned the company of others, remaining alone in her room unless forced out. Even the simplest activities became difficult.

When the first clear weather brought people

out to their rooftops, Kalie joined them, determined to retake some of her life. As she stood on the roof of Arlie's house, watching butterflies cavort against a pale blue sky and savoring the warm breeze, fresh with new life, her gaze turned eastward to where the edge of the grasslands were just visible in the distance.

A cloud of dust blew out of the eastern horizon, solidifying before Kalie's horrified gaze into a horde of six legged beasts with two heads. Swiftly, they raced down upon the unprotected village. Kalie tried to utter a warning cry, but her throat closed in terror. She looked around frantically, only to find her friends and neighbors smiling and discussing the upcoming planting season, and planning the Spring Festival.

"Don't you see the danger?" she shouted. "Do something to protect yourselves!" But everyone continued about their business, not hearing her at all.

Then the village was burning, and men on horseback surrounded her on all sides, laughing and taunting her as she tried to escape.

Kalie began to scream as the smoke and darkness smothered her.

She awoke in the cool, dark recesses of Tall Oaks' Temple of Healing. Fighting off the gently restraining hand of a young healer, Kalie lurched from the pallet on which she lay and stumbled to the door and into the courtyard beyond.

The spring sunlight was blinding after the dim interior of the temple. Kalie blinked frantically, trying to see what had become of her home. A quiet peaceful village basked in the warmth of a spring afternoon. There were no smoking ruins, no corpses, no terrified children hiding in the wreckage.

"What happened?" she asked the concerned young man.

"You had some kind of fit," the healer said. To his credit, he covered his obvious discomfort well. "Sit down," he said, pouring her a cup of cool water from the jug on a shelf. Kalie recognized it as her aunt's work.

The priestess came in while Kalie was drinking the water and trying to sort out what had happened.

"How do you feel?" she asked.

Kalie shrugged. "Confused. Embarrassed. I guess I was only dreaming the attack on the village. But I was awake. And it seemed so real."

"That can happen sometimes," said the priestess. "Those Who Serve the Goddess often experience visions of things to come. But anyone can be touched by the Sight. It's just more frightening when you're not prepared for it."

That's certainly the truth, Kalie thought. She looked into the serene, lined face of the gray haired priestess. "Do you think what I saw will come to pass?"

"I believe that what you saw was memory, not future, combined with the fear that you carry in the present. I can give you a draught that can prevent it from happening again, if you like."

Kalie thought about it. Even now, everyone was trying to help. But this place was no longer her home. She was never going to go back to the way she was, and the people here were never going to understand what happened to her.

"Are there any visitors staying here who will be traveling west, soon?" Kalie asked the priestess.

Kalie left Tall Oaks a few days later, with a walking staff in her hand, and a pack of provisions on her back. The priestess had given her a pilgrim's beaded necklace as well, so that she would be received and sheltered at any temple she stopped at—no questions asked.

Kalie had objected at first, since she wasn't a pilgrim on any sort of religious errand. The priestess had disagreed, saying that Kalie was on a journey to heal herself, and that was as holy an errand as they came.

Her cousin Urev would escort Kalie as far as Gaea. After that she was on her own. She smiled her goodbyes to family and neighbors, and did a remarkable job of controlling her trembling. If anyone knew how afraid she was of leaving, they would have convinced her to stay. And, frightened as she was of traveling alone into the unknown—again—the only thing that frightened Kalie more, was the thought of staying here. Under the shadow of the beastmen.

While they were concerned for her, Kalie knew that most of the people of Tall Oaks were relieved by her decision. She was possessed by strange spirits now, and that frightened people. Only Bartev made any show of begging her to stay. Marlie, his new lover, waited at a respectful distance. Kalie thought she seemed nervous. Was she afraid Kalie would changed her mind at the last minute, and reclaim Bartev?

No need to worry, Kalie thought sadly. She wasn't jealous of Marlie for taking her place, nor angry with Bartev for finding someone new. But she felt pain as she thought of the life they would have together, and the confident, careless way they would approach it. Everything was theirs for the taking. There was no fear staining their souls; no thought that it could all be snatched away. Simple joys like laughing together over a shared joke, making love, having children and building a life; things that Kalie had once taken for granted, as Bartev and Marlie now did, were now out of her reach—perhaps forever.

She bade Bartev farewell, and set off on the road to Gaea.

# Chapter 5

The group walked south for two days, then turned west. Each night they found a likely camping spot by a stream or spring, or, in one case, a small farming village. There they were fed and housed by bored villagers eager for news and stories. Besides Kalie and Urev, the party consisted of two brothers with copper tools and bangles to trade, and a young girl traveling with her grandmother to one of Gaea's many temples, to see what the priestesses there could make of her strange knack for knowing things before they happened.

Kalie remembered that early in her last journey, she had talked and joked with her companions. Now she was silent, ignoring the conversations that swirled around her, and only occasionally joining in the traveling songs they others sang. At night, she rolled herself into her furs and willed herself to sleep, never offering a story, or listening to those being told. Urev had tried to get her to socialize at first, but soon grew to accept her silence.

On the fourth day, they passed a large party of travelers going the opposite direction. Some were pilgrims, the rest merchants from Gaea carrying salt, gold jewelry, linen cloth and seashells. Even Kalie came a little out of herself to admire the goods and try on a necklace of shells. Urev would have bought it for her, but she declined. Dressing up and ornamentation suddenly seemed like too much effort. The two copper traders had no such reluctance, and soon a lively bargaining was under way.

The two groups camped together that night, amid much storytelling and sharing provisions—particularly the jug of wine the traders offered. The next morning, Kalie warned the party about the dangers of the eastern steppes, but they said they would be turning south again before they got that far.

The next day the breeze carried the scent of salt and a rich, invigorating smell that reminded Kalie of wine. Soon the much-used trail led them to the steep cliffs overlooking the Black Sea. Kalie gazed down at the pounding surf, gleaming white sand, and the sunlight glinting on the endless waves. For a moment, she wanted nothing more than to sit down and stare at the clean, safe waters, so different from the parched grasslands of the east.

Urev pulled her along with the others, perhaps afraid she might throw herself off the cliff. Strange, considering how hard she had fought for life, that so many people now feared that Kalie was a danger to herself. She sighed. Another reason for her to leave—for everyone's sake.

They walked west along the coast for half the afternoon, then came within sight of the shining city of Gaea.

Built from varied materials, the houses and temples of Gaea were larger than any Kalie had seen. Many were two-storied and all were whitewashed, inside and out, creating cool, clean interiors, and uniform white exteriors that caused the city to shimmer in the sun.

Once within the city, the six travelers bid one another farewell, and went in search of their own varied pursuits: the brothers to the marketplace, the girl and her grandmother to the Temple of the Wise

Women and Kalie and Urev to the Temple of Healing. Urev offered to stay a while longer, but Kalie hugged him goodbye—once a simple gesture she made without thinking, now a frightening act she had to force herself to accomplish—and told him to enjoy the sites of the city.

Urev needed no further urging, and Kalie settled down in the courtyard to await the arrival of the priest or priestess. While she was waiting, Kalie heard a commotion from the docks far below. Not even the joyful sounds of laughter and cheering could keep her from wanting to bolt from the loud noise and find the nearest place to hide. Gritting her teeth, she made herself climb the ladder through the rose trellis that led to the temple roof and look down to see what was going on.

A big white sailed trading boat was gliding to the shore. Kalie couldn't tell how many people were aboard, or where they were from, but for a moment she felt the excitement of the woman she had once been, and wondered what treasures the merchants might be bringing. Dried fruits and obsidian from the peoples on the southern shore of the sea? Brightly dyed linen cloth from the west? Silver and amber and wine from places so far away she could only imagine?

A year ago, when Kalie had decided to make a journey, she'd had to choose between a voyage by sea or one on land. She had sailed along this very shore, on a boat just like that one, to get a feel for what days on the sea would feel like. Kalie had decided that the boat was too confining, and that being a passenger would not be as exciting as traveling on her own two feet, an equal to everyone else in the party.

So she had gone east into the grasslands

instead.

And now she stood atop Gaea's Temple of Healing, living within a waking nightmare, wondering just how different things might have been if she had chosen the sea instead.

Kalie stayed in Gaea for nearly two moonspans, discussing her nightmares with the healers, taking mud baths and enduring rituals that everyone hoped would help. She meditated alone in a whitewashed room, and joined in the singing and dancing with which the people of Gaea welcomed the summer and gathered the first of the harvest and she showed the potters of the city her technique for shaping and glazing tiny clay beads.

Then, after thanking everyone for their efforts, Kalie boarded a boat loaded with shells, jars of caviar and several other passengers and sailed south toward the marshy delta where a river – known simply as the Great River – emptied itself in the sea. She didn't really know why: one place was as safe as any other when the threat came from one's own mind. But some vague instinct told Kalie that putting distance between herself and the place of her attack might be a good idea. Since that was the closest she had to direction from the Goddess, Kalie headed west.

This part of the coast was thickly populated, so the boat put ashore each night, and its crew and passengers slept comfortably in the temples dedicated to travelers, while the merchants haggled in the marketplaces, and everyone enjoyed the new sights. When they reached the delta, Kalie bought passage on a fishing boat for twenty of her clay beads. Trade goods were hard for a lone traveler to carry, so Kalie, knowing her journey could be a long one, had decided early on to use beads, and had made a great many during her stay in Gaea.

This doesn't look much like a river, Kalie thought, gazing out across the morass of quicksand, marsh and little islands that seemed to float. Her guides, a brother and sister who knew the marsh, ferried travelers nearly as often as they caught fish, and guided the boat through treacherous marshland that had sucked more than one foolish sailor to its murky depths.

The folk who dwelt in the marsh were a small, shy people. They lived in tiny inter-connected villages anywhere there was solid, if soggy, land. Fish and ducks were plentiful, and everyone who lived here ate well. Living space was harder to come by than food, with a settlement on built on every island big enough to sustain one, and even on manmade islands, conjured from the water with logs, woven reeds and mud.

Kalie was passed from one boat to another, in exchange for beads or a day's labor helping with the nets. She developed skills she had never thought to acquire, as well as a pleasing strength in her arms and back. The marsh folk gave her a vile smelling paste to smear on her skin that kept the mosquitoes from eating her alive, and eventually, Kalie got used to the smell. She learned their songs and stories, and came to revere the river as they did.

One family invited her to stay with them, and she did for most of a moon span. The marsh was warm and enfolding and so very different from the steppes. Even if the beastmen traveled this far, their horses would be useless in the treacherous marshes, where land might turn to water at any moment, and quicksand could only be crossed one light and cautious step at a time.

But after a short stay, Kalie grew restless, and headed west again. The marshlands gave way to a seemingly placid river, nearly as wide across as the sea. People told her that the river began in the mountains so far to the west that it would take five years to journey to its source. To Kalie, that sounded like a fine plan.

The river narrowed when they came to a place where mountains reared up on either side. The land here was heavily populated, but it was the river that provided the only direct form of transportation. Boats were common and a place aboard easily secured. The strong current made travel eastward easier, while strong rowing and intense concentration was required for those, like Kalie, traveling west.

When the left bank opened into farmland dotted with villages and towns, Kalie left the river and continued her journey on foot. It was late summer now, and the easy rhythm of harvest and festival drew her onward. She began to look for a place to settle for the winter. She tried to take up pottery again, in a town whose master potter had died without leaving behind an apprentice. It was a quiet place, and though she had traveled so far that the people here spoke a different language, Kalie picked it up quickly.

She moved into the workshop, and soon met a man who offered to help her forget her painful past, and remind her of what the joining of man and woman was meant to be.

It worked for a while.

But then the nightmares returned, and Kalie never knew when her mind and eyes would grow dead in the middle of passion, or when she might start a fight with her lover for no apparent reason. Her partner ran out of patience, and Kalie ran out of hope, and the next thing she knew, she was moving west along the river again, looking for a place—and a Goddess—that she no longer believed existed. But moving felt better than staying still.

When the river turned south, Kalie continued west overland, heading toward a range of mountains so tall they brushed the clouds. The people who lived in this area told her that the snow on the highest peaks never melted, even in the hottest summers, and there were hidden caves within them, sacred to the Goddess.

Though she scoffed silently at the last part, reaching the mountains seemed like a worthy enough goal. Yet again and again as she traveled, Kalie met people who sought to convince her to stop, to try again with a new family, a new man, a new craft.

Nothing worked.

She stayed for a time in a lakeside village surrounded by a dense coniferous forest. There she met Analia, a young woman with brilliant red hair, who pointedly suggested that if relationships with men didn't work, perhaps it was time Kalie tried a woman. Analia was eager to show Kalie how it worked, and had a three-year old daughter, who would become Kalie's as well, so she needn't worry about finding a man to give her a baby.

Kalie's new lover had a brother who crafted metal in the village forge, and offered Kalie an apprenticeship. Everyone was impressed with the way she took to the difficult art of working copper—not least of all, Kalie herself. For a time, it seemed she had found a place to be. She learned the stories these people told, and shared with them those she had learned in her travels. Everyone enjoyed her stories.

After a while, however, the smith became alarmed at Kalie's growing skill--and interest--in making sharp objects—to the exclusion of everything else. While he made armbands and hoes and mirrors from the copper, Kalie set herself to forging a knife that didn't lose its killing edge and a new kind of axe that could take a man's head off. The day she proudly showed him a deadly little knife that was nearly all blade, and could be concealed almost anywhere on the body, the smith told Kalie her lessons were over—and so was her time at the forge.

Kalie flew into a rage that shocked and frightened her, but she couldn't stop it. From somewhere inside herself, she watched as people she had come to know restrained her as gently as possible, while a priestess from the temple hurried over with a clay cup and forced something laced with honey down her throat. She woke up later inside the temple, still unsure of what had happened, but very clear about the way people were looking at her.

Analia sat with Kalie, explaining over and over that she still loved her, but her loyalty had to be to family first; she couldn't allow herself to get caught between a lover and her brother—and there was her daughter's safety to consider. She wept, hoping Kalie could understand. Kalie did her best and thanked Analia for all she and her family and done.

No one asked her to leave, but Kalie did anyway.

Finally, she stopped at a small village in the foothills of the tall mountains, for no other reason than she was too tired to go on. It was just a quiet, dusty village, like countless others she had seen, its only extraordinary feature being pools of water that bubbled hot and steaming from a rocky outcrop. When the villagers proudly showed their guest this water, Kalie thought it smelled like rotten eggs and wouldn't get near it. Everyone laughed, for they were used to this reaction, and explained that the hot springs had healing powers that had brought cures to people who had been given up as hopeless by healers throughout the area. They were also, they told Kalie, a wonderful way to relax after a long day.

Kalie decided both uses suited her. While she didn't expect any miraculous cure for her ills, she got over her reluctance and found that bathing in the springs was one of the most delightful experiences she could remember. And while the village had no need for a potter, a smith, a fisherman or any of the other skills Kalie had picked up, the sick arrived almost constantly from everywhere, and the healers could always use an extra pair of hands.

Then she discovered that for many patients, a well-told tale could distract them—temporarily, at least—from their pain, or make the time of waiting for a miracle pass more pleasantly. Oftentimes, it was the relatives who brought loved ones to the temple, and now had nothing to do but wait, who came to hear her stories. They gave her gifts of food and furs and whatever else they had brought with them.

And while Kalie had never heard of anyone making their living solely by telling stories, and often felt she was living off the charity of the village, she enjoyed her work, and her new neighbors, enough to stay. For a while, she told them.

And so five years passed quietly.

# Chapter 6

"—and the magician turned himself into a huge beast, and all those around him quailed in fear. Many wished this stranger among would leave before she unleashed more of his anger.

"But Owl only beat her wings together as if impressed and said 'I have heard as well that you could even change yourself into the smallest of creatures, but this I do not believe.'

"'Oh, no?' bellowed the magician. 'A trick like that is nothing to one such as I!' And he turned himself into a tiny mouse."

The younger members of the audience broke into giggles as they saw what was coming. Kalie smiled, and let their anticipation build for just a few heartbeats.

"Of course, Owl swooped down upon the him and snapped him up in her beak. She only hoped he wouldn't upset her stomach.

"After that, the people were never again bothered by wicked magicians, or anyone else who might wish to rule them. They offered Owl many rich rewards, but she merely spread her wings, and flew to the next place she might be needed."

Appreciative whistles and hand clapping greeted Kalie, as well as requests for more stories.

"No more for today," she said firmly. "But I will be back here tomorrow."

"Kalie?" asked a little girl. "Can you summon Owl to this temple? Can she make my brother well again?"

Kalie's good cheer vanished as she looked into

the trusting cornflower eyes of the child. This was the part of her work she always hated.

Fortunately, she was spared from having to answer by Sylvan, the chief healer. "The Spirit of Owl is already here, within the healers of this temple, and within you, too, Mina," said the grey-bearded elder. "Just as your parents brought your brother here in search of a cure when the healers of your own village gave up, so too, do all of us here, carry on Owl's work, of looking for answers in unlikely ways."

Mina, now staring into the kindly hazel eyes of the old man, nodded gravely, and allowed her father to lead her away, with hardly a glance at Kalie.

Kalie sighed with relief. "Thank you, Sylvan. I never know what to say to things like that."

"And yet when you tell a story, the words dance from your tongue." They left the guest-house of the Temple of Healing and stepped out into the summer sunshine. Shadow was waiting for Kalie outside the temple, thumping his tail happily when he saw her. Kalie petted him absently as she thought of the rest of her day.

She had to check her snares and gather firewood. Then, a long slow afternoon of watching the eastern mountains and thinking of absolutely nothing. Perhaps a soak in the hot springs before bed. After all, the sun stayed late this time of year.

"There is a patient I would like you to speak with," Sylvan said. "After you've finished your solitary time and your meditations," he added quickly, as she went rigid.

"I don't come back to the temple until tomorrow," Kalie said, cringing at how petulant she sounded. But her routine was important. Sylvan, of all people, knew that.

"Perhaps I could bring him to you. Or perhaps you could meditate briefly and speak with him now. Accept food and wood from the temple this day. You've more than earned it."

"Who is he? Why do you want me to speak with him?"

"His name is Caiden. He arrived alone, two days ago." Kalie nodded. Of course she had heard of him; she heard everything in the temple. "He has a growth in his stomach that is poisoning his body. No potion made by mortals, nor even the Waters of the Goddess can cure something like that. The only hope is to cut into his flesh and remove the mass."

Kalie shivered. "Cara has done so many times; often successfully."

"She plans to do so for Caiden tomorrow. He is very much afraid, although he is a strong man, who made the journey here despite considerable pain and growing weakness. He heard your stories yesterday, and asked about you."

"What did you tell him?" Kalie demanded.

"That you were much like him: a proud spirit who has overcome great difficulty—and great fear. And I suggested the two of you speak."

"Come to my dwelling before sunset," she said reluctantly. "Share a meal with me. I will return here with you, and speak with Caiden."

"Will you wish to sleep in the temple tonight?" asked Sylvan.

"Most likely. And no, I will not ask for more poppy syrup in exchange for altering my routine."

"Good, since I would not give it to you anyway."

"Which is why I won't ask." With a whistle to Shadow, Kalie hurried to the woods.

In the five years since she had come to Hot Springs, Kalie had lived alone—close enough to the temple to run there during the night when evil dreams awoke her, far enough so she didn't have to be near anyone when she didn't want to. She had not lain with a man or a woman in all that time, nor had she lived with any of the extended families who dwelt in the wooden and wattle houses of the village—although several had invited her.

She lived cautiously, clinging to a routine that many people found odd, although of course, no one bothered her about it. Each morning she walked in the woods near the settlement, to gather food for herself or herbs the priests could use in their healing.

Kalie often marveled that in her quest to heal herself, she had learned nearly as much about medicinal plants and what to do with them as some of the healers. She knew, for example, which plants could bring sleep freely and gently, and which brought it at the cost of frightening dreams or sick feelings the next day. She knew that some infusions made her feel in control of her life, while others—which she avoided— brought what many people considered to be a joyous loss of control.

Her snares were empty, but Shadow flushed a rabbit from cover and Kalie killed it with a hard flung stone. Stew for supper. She was glad to have more than porridge to offer Sylvan. And she had mushrooms, turnips, and onions to thicken the stew. There was even salt, from a grateful patient who came from a land south and west of here, on the shores of a sea even larger than the Black. That was good, since most of the rabbit would go to Shadow.

Kalie had found the half-starved dog shortly after she and the people of Hot Springs had finished building her dwelling. Dogs were important to the village, as sheepherders, guardians and hunting companions, but often, as in most of the places she had been, there were more dogs than places for them. Usually, dogs without human families managed well enough, scavenging from the refuse midden at the edge of the village, or returning to the hunting ways of their ancestors.

Sometimes, however, a dog was born who forgot his ancient skills, as if domestication had reached into his very bones. Life could be difficult for such a dog. When Kalie had first seen Shadow, poking through the midden, but clearly having no chance at any of the choice scraps that the bigger dogs were quarreling over, she had gone to the temple for a bowl of rich broth—normally intended for the patients—and set it down as close as the dog would let her. After he lapped it up, the dog—hardly more than a puppy—had whined for more, so Kalie had beckoned him, not really expecting him to follow. But he had trotted after her, and been with her ever since.

Now Shadow was a sleek, healthy dog with a coat brindled black and amber. As they reached the hut, Shadow bounded forward, as Kalie had taught him to, and entered the hut first. If there were any danger waiting for her, he would find it first, and warn her. Of course, there never was any danger. Kalie was the only one here who ever thought of such things.

She set the rabbit inside, and then returned to the front of her hut to sit on the little bench beneath the oak tree which shaded it, and enjoyed the summer sunshine. Shadow rolled on his back, and Kalie rubbed his belly, as only she could. It was good to matter to someone, even if he was just a dog. Shadow's tail was thumping with pleasure. Then, in an instant, he was on all fours growling low in his throat to tell Kalie they had company.

She followed his gaze. Two runners were approaching the village from the east. Kalie shaded her eyes to see them more clearly. They were a man and a woman, dressed in identical loincloths and sandals, although the woman wore a leather band around her breasts. Both wore their hair short, and the bands that held their hair out of their faces identified them as temple messengers, which meant they were among the swiftest people on earth.

"Don't worry," Kalie told Shadow, rubbing his ears until he stood down. "They're not headed our way. Their business is with the temple. See?" The messengers reached the temple and were welcomed in with water and food and a place to rest. "Nothing to do with us." But even as she spoke, Kalie knew these people had come because of her. She considered that her years of peaceful anonymity were about to come to an end, and then decided that that was probably all right.

When the acolyte came to summon her to the temple a short while later, she was ready.

# Chapter 7

"You don't have to go with them," Sylvan said.

The messengers both glared at the old healer. "The Council is aware that you are the only person who has any direct experience with them," said the man. "And that, at one time at least, you could speak their language. Anything you could remember now would be of great assistance."

"Your safety will be guaranteed," said the woman. "When Aran and I left, there were only seven of them, all wounded, and under heavy guard. You won't have to be alone with them. Just help us to communicate with them, so we can put a stop to this madness and assure everyone's safety. Yours included!"

Kalie wanted to point out that no one's safety could be guaranteed any longer, but she discovered that, for several moments, she could not speak at all. Her nightmare had returned, as she knew it would, yet here she was, frozen. Unable to think of a single intelligent question. She glanced out of the open door, which faced west, then looked away. No, there would be no more running. "How many villages were attacked?" she asked. "How many dead?"

"At least forty dead when we left," Aran said through shut teeth. "Many others grievously wounded. Two villages burned and trampled before any survivors reached safety. The third place they attacked was a large town to which many of the survivors had fled. Sala was present for that." All eyes turned to the other messenger.

The question was dragged from Kalie's throat.

"How did you subdue them?

"Everyone was horrified by the victims' stories. Some had even gone to see for themselves what remained of the two villages. Everyone was afraid it could happen to us. So, when it did, I suppose we were better prepared. It was a hunter named Mara who saw the weakness. She realized that the horses' greatest vulnerability was their legs. The men's greatest vulnerability was, well, being astride horses. Horses that were on the ground with their legs all tangled up, that is. Once we had everyone who knew the use of a bola at work, most of the horses fell."

"And once the horses fell," said Aran, "their riders were much easier to restrain. Many were hurt when the animals fell on them, and needed medical attention. There were only about fifteen of these men in the attack, although many of the previous victims believed there were many more."

"There were many more," said Kalie. "They simply split into smaller bands when they saw what easy prey you were. My guess is that there have been other attacks since you left to find me."

Aran and Sala exchanged worried glances.

Kalie gripped the edge of the cushion on which she sat until her fists shook. "Seven years ago, those same healers and leaders who sent you here assured me that I was the victim of an isolated attack. They didn't believe a word I had to say! When I warned them this would happen, they offered me draughts to control my madness! Now that it turns out I was right, they want my help?"

"As they freely offered you theirs when you were in pain that no one could understand," Aran said softly.

Kalie blushed, but more with anger than shame. If they had believed her in the first place....She shook her head. There was no point in "what ifs"; she had always known the beastmen would come, and she should be grateful things had turned out the way they had. This time.

"What, exactly, do they think I can do?" Kalie asked, twisting her shoulders in a useless attempt to ease the tension cramping her neck and back. Sylvan moved beside her, and began to massage the pain away. She smiled her thanks, noting the surprised looks of the other healers. As far as they knew, Kalie never let anyone touch her. The messengers, of course, saw nothing unusual.

"Just try to communicate with them," said Aran. "There must be something terribly wrong with these people. All the Holy Ones and Council members want to do is fix what is wrong. But we can't do that without talking to them, or understanding how they think."

"I'm not sure they think at all," Kalie muttered. But no one here was going to understand that. Nor would anyone here understand that the beastmen were dangerous, soulless monsters.

But the people to the east...they had seen the monsters destroy villages and kill those they loved. Perhaps some of them had even suffered attacks of the kind that Kalie had...the kind that no one wanted to talk about. Maybe she could help them. Maybe they could help her. If nothing else, they would finally believe her.

Kalie turned to look at Sylvan. He dropped his hands from her back and met her eye. "You don't have to go," he repeated.

"Yes, I do." And though the words were for Sylvan, Kalie sensed relief from the messengers, and the others in the room. "We can leave in the morning," she said, wishing she could stay here just a little longer. As if five years of doing basically nothing with her        life        wasn't        long        enough.

"...And then I woke up in a temple of healing, far to the east of here," Kalie concluded her story.

"That's amazing," said Caiden, his own pain seemingly forgotten in the wake of Kalie's story. A story she had never told in full until this night.

"It's hard to believe..." he began, and then stopped. Caiden was a large, rather hairy man, although he had clearly lost a great deal of flesh recently. His clothes hung loose about his frame and his hazel eyes were big in a gaunt face. "I don't mean to say I don't believe it. It's just that...I've been so busy fighting this thing that's growing in me. When the healers of my village told me what it was, I shouted and cursed the Goddess for causing it until my own family drove me away for fear my sacrilege would bring greater harm upon us. If She has created men as well as illnesses that cause such horror..."

"I said the same things when I began to recover," said Kalie. "And I received many of the same reactions you did. I guess you could say that's what we're both doing here. But for every person who judged me, or feared to be near me, there were at least three who embraced me and sought to help. It's the same way for you, Caiden. All you have to do is let the people here help you."

"By cutting into my flesh in an operation that has a better chance of killing me?" The older man snarled, showing yellowing teeth. Kalie guessed he had been a hunter or woodsman of some kind in his old life.

"It is the only chance we have of saving you!" Kalie said firmly. "I can't promise there won't be pain, or that your life will be exactly like it was before. Goddess knows, mine hasn't! But life is better than death. I've come to believe that much, at least."

Caiden was gazing intently at Kalie. "Are you really going back to face those monsters?"

All at once she was very tired. "Yes," she said simply. "So you see, we both get a chance to face our fears—and maybe benefit from them. You need to sleep now."

At Kalie's signal, an acolyte came forward and helped Caiden to his feet and led him to one of the sleeping rooms. She was alone in the temple but for Shadow curled up by her side, and Sylvan waiting silently on the other side of the brazier that glowed warmly between them.

It was nearly midnight and Caiden wasn't the only one who needed sleep. Kalie was going to have to keep pace with professional runners in just a few hours. But it felt good to sit here with the ones she had come to love best in these last five years. And she needed to talk to someone, just as Caiden had.

"Do you think I'm being arrogant in going with them?" she asked the priest.

Sylvan's eyes flew open and he choked on his tea. "Arrogant? That's the last word I'd have thought to use for what you're doing. Why would you wonder that?"

"For thinking that I can save everyone by running half-way across the world and working some kind of magic? For thinking that this time, everything will be different? You know, there's a good chance that when we get there in, what?—half a moonspan at the fastest pace possible?—we'll find every village and town around the Black Sea laid waste, and beastmen ruling a land of slaves! And I think I can do something about it? Oh, forget arrogant! Maybe stupid is a better word!"

Sylvan stared at the woman across from him—then burst out laughing.

That took her by surprise. "You find this funny?" she asked.

Sylvan shook his head. "You're willing to return east and face a horror that you alone know the depth of, with nothing more than yourself as a weapon, when anyone else who'd been through what you have would probably be running in the opposite direction—and you're calling yourself names? Facing your greatest fears, and putting aside your anger at those who didn't believe you makes you many things in my light, but arrogant and stupid are not among them."

Kalie found herself pleased by Sylvan's praise, but still wary. "Don't start painting me as a hero from one of the old tales," she said.

"Why not? What are most heroes but ordinary people, thrust into extraordinary situations? I listen to your stories, Kalie. You favor the tales of cripples who triumph through strength other than physical-and answers that come from places most people would never think to look."

"Well, consider my audience."

Sylvan shook his head impatiently. "That's only part of it. You came here to heal yourself, and you have—as much as you can, here in the west. To complete the process, however, you're going to have to return to where it all started, confront your fears and overcome them. And that's what you've decided to do, whether or not you see it. But in doing so, I believe you will help a great many people; more, even, than those you've helped here these five years."

"I haven't helped anyone! Not the way you and the other healers do! Great Goddess, I've done nothing here but get older!"

Sylvan leaned over Shadow and stroked the soft fur around his ears. "I think many would disagree. This dog. The sick and dying to whom you gave hope and solace with your stories. The frightened, grieving relatives, whom you always listened to, and seemed to find just the right story for. That's more than many so-called successful people do with their entire lives."

"Thank you," Kalie said wonderingly, though privately she thought that helping distraught family members was the least she could do, considering how callous she had once been. Still, the thought that her life since the attack had not been wasted was one to cling to. "You know, Sylvan, there's a good chance I may just fall into a dead faint the moment I set eyes on the beastmen. And if they've escaped; if others have come in force…" She shut her eyes, clutching the copper knife she kept sewn into her shirt. "I won't let them take me alive again."

"Let's hope it doesn't come to that. I've never been one the Goddess chooses to speak through, but I sense that important events are about to unfold- and that you will be a crucial player in them."

Kalie shook her head. "More mysteries. Somehow, I don't think strength is what I'm known for in the Worlds Beyond Worlds."

"You overcame the grip of the poppy juice. Few people can do that, regardless of their reasons for beginning it, or how strong their desire to stop."

"I can sleep without your poppy syrup for no other reason than that I don't know how to make it! You never let me learn the secret. When I asked you to wean me from it, I had no way of knowing how strong the dose was any given night. So eventually, I just slept, regardless of what I was drinking. And if not for your patience, I doubt I'd be free of it now. I'd have simply found something else to be my crutch."

"You'd be surprised how many people do exactly that."

They sat awhile longer in silence. Then Kalie said, "I would ask one more thing of you, Sylvan. Keep Shadow for me."

The old priest raised an eyebrow. "He will want to go with you. And if there is danger…"

"If there is danger, he will die protecting me. I don't want that to happen. You and he are the closest I've had to family for many years. Whatever…lies in store for me, I'd feel better knowing you were both safe…and together."

Sylvan smiled sadly. "You still can't speak Her name, can you?"

Kalie blushed. Anyone else would have said, "Whatever the Goddess wills…"

Then her expression hardened, as she knew she must as well, if she was going to make this journey. "If the Goddess existed, we wouldn't be facing this crisis!"

"Are you sure?"

"If She let this happen on purpose, then She is evil, and no one should worship Her. If She lacks the power to protect us, then She is nothing more than—" Kalie bit off her tirade. "The night is too far gone for a discussion of this kind."

"One we've had so many times before," Sylvan agreed. "Still, I think that a part of you is still searching for a way to believe again. Perhaps, on this journey, you will find your way back." He put an arm around Kalie, inviting her to make it an embrace. After a moment she did. "I will care for Shadow, here at the temple. Go with the Goddess."

# Chapter 8

Kalie set out with the two messengers shortly after dawn. She wore a simple linen shift and sturdy leather sandals. She carried a change of clothes, comb and bedroll, but nothing else. As travelers on temple business, they would be fed and housed by anyone they passed. Aran and Sala were pleased that Kalie was willing to travel light. She learned they were afraid that she would insist on countless items that she simply couldn't do without. For her part, Kalie was dismayed that in seven years she had accumulated so little that meant anything to her. The only thing she wanted to take was Shadow, but she knew he was better off here.

It was amazing, Kalie thought, how much faster the journey east was, compared to the journey west. It had taken her two years to reach Hot Springs, yet less than one moonspan to get back to Gaea. Of course, traveling on temple business meant having nothing to do but walk or run along the best paths. Then, when they reached the river, it meant being given a place on the swiftest boats and not stopping for other passengers.

It was high summer now, and everywhere they went, people gave them the best of the harvest to eat as they traveled, along with loaves of fresh bread, dried meat, and sometimes, just garlands of bright flowers. No one stopped them, other than to wish the blessings of the Goddess upon their journey, but the blessings and gifts sped them on their way, and made the traveling easier.

Kalie had a strange sense that she should remember such things; that somehow, the world was changing, and the simple ways people cared for one another now would someday be only the stuff of legend.

It was not until they reached Gaea that the reality of the mission hit Kalie. The laughter and bustle of trade and festivals she remembered from her visit seven years before were gone. The temple where they stayed that night was buzzing with rumors of beastmen and violence. Everyone seemed to be afraid. Some were even shouting about the end of the world.

If the temple was boiling with people and fear, the rest of the city felt deserted. Kalie and her companions were told that nearly all of the city's leadership— Council members, priests, healers and those skilled in language—had gone to Riverford, the town where the beastmen were being held, and where many of the survivors of their attacks still lay in the temples of healing.

Everyone else seemed to be hiding indoors, waiting for word that the Wise Ones among them had taken care of the problems; that life could go on as before. Kalie felt like running down the streets yelling that life would never be as before, that even if a miracle happened, and the beastmen returned to their eastern steppes and never came back, the violence and fear that they had brought to the people of the Goddess would taint the land forever.

They left early the next morning for the last stage of the journey. They would pass close to Tall Oaks, but would not stop there, for which Kalie was grateful. She wasn't ready to see the village of her birth or any of the people she knew. It was hard enough to see the faces of strangers as they passed. For now, in addition to flowers, food and blessings, the people they met shared their fears--and their faith that the Holy men and women who had gone to manage this crisis would take of everything.

Kalie especially hated the way they looked at her: when she had left, she was a mad- woman possessed by evil spirits, running from something that didn't exist. Now, she was returning as the people's shining hope: *from out of the west came a mysterious woman. She alone knew the ways of the dangerous strangers...* Kalie could almost hear the tale being told around the fire. Had she not survived among them, once upon a time? Had she not warned the people of the east of this very attack?

If they only knew how much she wanted to be their savior. If they only knew how slim her chances of success.

They camped the last night in an isolated temple set amid rocky hills where the soil was too poor to support a farming village—or very much else. The temple was deserted but for an ancient priestess, who fed the travelers a simple meal of lentil porridge, barley bread and a strong flavorful cheese she made herself from the small herd of goats that were the only beings this land could sustain.

Kalie knew they were only one day's travel from Riverford, but was shocked when she realized that Long Grass was only two days to the north. If the beastmen had taken only a slightly different path, they would have hit the little village whose priestess had nursed Kalie back to health all those years ago. There was no way that tiny population could have mounted the kind of defense that Riverford had.

The sun was low in the sky when Riverford first appeared in the distance. As they approached the town, Kalie forgot, for a moment, the dire events that brought her here and simply stared. She had heard of this place, of course, but the tales didn't do it justice. Most of the buildings Kalie had seen on her travels were made of wood or thatch, or sometimes, stone. People lived in family dwellings that were round or square, sometimes close together, sometimes far apart. Only in cities like Gaea did they have more than one story.

Riverford rose up from a treeless plain, with homes that stood shoulder to shoulder, and piled on top of each other, made entirely of mud bricks. The rectangular warren of houses showed a blank face to the outside world, for the doorways were on the roof—protection against seasonal flooding.

But today Kalie saw, as Sala gave a sharp cry, and pulled both Aran and Kalie to the shelter of a small outcrop of rock, the town's strange architecture provided protection against something else.

At least two hands of horses, each with a man astride it, rode back and forth outside the walls of Riverford. Others were camped nearby. The ladders that usually leaned against the walls had been pulled up. The crowds of townsfolk who would normally be found on the rooftops, bartering, gossiping or working at various crafts were nowhere to be seen. Only about a hand of people, young men, from what Kalie could see, stood on the roofs, keeping watch on the beastmen.

"Those would be the beastmen who split off from the group that attacked the villages," whispered Kalie.

"They must have arrived after we left to find you," said Aran.

"What are they doing?" Sala asked.

Unbidden, Kalie's mind supplied the word. "*Siege*." At her companions' blank look, she explained further. "They have surrounded the city, and will probably attack anyone who tries to leave."

"But...why?" asked Aran.

"They must want something," said Kalie, trying to remember what she had once known of... what did they call them? Strategies? Tactics?

"What could they possibly want, aside from their own people?" snapped Sala, almost forgetting to whisper. "And surely, by now, those would have been sent forth from the city with gratitude and relief!"

Kalie felt the bile rise in her throat as she thought of the number of things the beastmen might want from a place like Riverford. And how easily just four hands of beastmen could keep countless times their number hostage inside a city that must soon run out of food.

Kalie glanced behind her, at the fiery sunset that, for the moment, shielded her companions and herself from the beastmen's far too keen sight. "We must find a better hiding place before the light changes," she said. "And I must return after dark."

"Are you sure about this?" Sala asked. The moonless night was almost pitch dark. Lights showed through the outer windows and inner courtyards of the city, but in a random pattern that the beastmen were not used to, and thus served to disorient them even more than the strange landscape they found themselves in. Their small numbers would help Kalie as well. From her observations of their camp, many of the beastmen were wounded. Thus only a few tired warriors were awake, maintaining the siege.

Or so she kept telling herself.

Aran had crept to the city walls under cover of first darkness and flung a rock wrapped in hide to the watchers on the roofs. The hide was covered in the esoteric markings that the priests used to communicate, and could be read by those similarly trained within Riverford.

Kalie's respect for her two companions had grown considerably. Until now, she had thought that messengers were just people with good memories and strong legs.

The three watched in silence, cloaked in darkness, the darkest corner of the city. Kalie would have about sixty heartbeats to run to that corner, climb the rope that awaited her, and disappear into city without the beastmen knowing.

"Are you sure?" Sala repeated.

Kalie turned to her. "I am sure that I can do no good out here. If I'm to be any use at all, it's in *there*." Her dry throat could barely bring forth the words.

"We promised to keep you safe," Aran protested. "The situation has changed since we were sent—"

An owl hooted.

From inside the city.

"That's the signal," Kalie whispered through dry lips. She watched the beastman who kept watch on this part of the city ride into the darkness and disappear, counted ten heartbeats, then raced across the open space toward the wall, leaving her would-be protectors behind.

How did the city get so far away? Kalie had the terrifying sense that her goal was moving away from her, and that any moment the pounding hooves and hot, stinking breath of the beastmen would be upon her.

Then she was panting against the loam-scented bricks of the city, a slender rope, nearly invisible against the dark wall, hanging just within reach. Kalie grabbed and jumped, bracing her feet against the wall. Strong arms hoisted her upward, even as she began to climb. Those final moments on the wall were even more terrifying than the run across open space, for she imagined a spear in her back the whole way up. Just when the fear became unbearable, Kalie reached the top, felt herself pulled over and down to a rooftop courtyard.

"You're safe now," said a young voice, and Kalie couldn't tell if it belonged to a boy or a girl.

"Or as safe as anyone can be with monsters riding in circles around our city," snapped a gruffer one, definitely female.

"I must speak with your leaders," Kalie said before she could even see who or how many she was talking to.

"The council was assembled as soon as we deciphered your message," said a third voice, this one male. "Follow me."

A torch flared in the darkness, and Kalie could at last begin to make out her surroundings. She looked down over the ledge she had just climbed over. That turned out to be a mistake, for the earth was so far below it made her dizzy, and at that moment, the beastman she had just evaded swam into view.

"Careful." The gruff sounding woman had Kalie by the arm, and was pulling her away from the edge. "It's always a bit disorienting the first time."

Then there was no time to see more, because they were leading Kalie to a ladder that poked out of a hole in the roof. The man and woman who had met her hurried down the ladder, leaving the young person—a girl, Kalie had decided—to hold the ladder and offer encouragement while Kalie carefully descended.

# Chapter 9

When she reached the bottom, Kalie found herself in a spacious room with whitewashed walls painted in spiral designs of red and black. Oil lamps set in wall niches provided enough light for her to count about three hands of people. Most sat on cushions of brightly colored woven cloth or on clay benches cunningly attached to the walls.

The man and woman who had guided her here led Kalie to a small alter against one wall. It held a finely wrought statue of the Goddess in her form as wise-woman. Beside it, on an embroidered cushion sat probably the oldest human being Kalie had ever seen. Wisps of white hair were caught into a bun on top of her head. Her face was a map of wrinkles, stretched tight over high cheekbones and a mouth missing several teeth. But her flint-like eyes shone with wisdom and power.

"Yelene, High Priestess of Riverford," announced the man who had brought Kalie to the room.

"Welcome, Kalie of Hot Springs," Yelene said in a strong voice that belied the frailty of her body.

A young man brought Kalie a bowl of water and a thick cloth to wash off the dust of the journey. A young woman gave her a cup of clear water to drink. Yelene poured a libation of wine over the statue beside her. Despite her lack of faith, Kalie felt a stab of hope. Wisdom was sorely needed here today.

Yelene addressed Kalie, but her speech carried throughout the spacious room. "Forgive our lack of hospitality. We cannot offer you the delicacies for which our city is famous, nor even simple bread and fruit. For as long as the strangers guard our city, preventing anyone from entering or leaving, our food must be rationed."

Kalie nodded. "What of the water?" she asked, fearing she had just washed her face and hands with someone's share of drinking water.

"There is a spring below our city that serves us well. Water is not a concern. Yet. Let me introduce our council—or at least what remains. Two of our wisest members are dead now. Killed when they left the safety of our walls and sought to speak peace with the strangers."

Yelene pointed to a man nearly as old as herself. "This is Karnac, who helped build our city. Valen," Yelene indicated a man only a few years older than Kalie, "a priest skilled in languages," she explained. "Maris," she pointed to another elderly woman, "is a wanderer, and makes her home with us until the crisis is resolved."

Despite the seriousness of the situation, Kalie was momentarily delighted. She had heard of Maris: a healer who traveled the world, calling no place home. She had probably seen more and learned more than anyone Kalie had ever met, and she hoped to have a chance to speak with her. "And her apprentice, Alessa," Yelene continued, smiling at the young woman, about Kalie's age, who sat beside Maris

"When did the siege begin?" Kalie asked, and then had to explain the term.

Yelene grasped it quickly. "Twelve days ago. They rode out of the east, making the most appalling noises. Then they formed a tight group on our northern side, and one man—their leader, we presumed—began shouting up at those gathered on the rooftops in a language no one could understand."

"Has any progress been made at communicating?" Kalie asked.

"Very little," replied Yelene. "Your arrival has brought us hope."

Kalie tried not to cringe, just as an elderly man spoke up from across the chamber. "We thought they only wanted their countrymen back. Since most were well enough to travel by then, we brought them to the roof, and lowered a ladder that they might leave us and return in peace from whence they came."

"What happened?" asked Kalie.

"As soon as the ladder was lowered, several of the...beastmen, rushed toward it, waving their weapons."

"Others," said Karnac, "shot arrows at the healers who stood with our uninvited guests. They were trying to help them down the ladder!" His voice shook.

"It was unbelievable!" cried a woman, whom Kalie suspected was one of those healers. "It was like something out of a nightmare! Nothing they do makes any sense! Since that day, they have attacked anyone who tries to enter or leave the city. We are trapped in our homes while the crops rot in the fields, and if we do not soon leave our walls to plant the winter crop, that, too will be lost!"

"How much food is left inside the city?" Kalie asked.

Yelene looked toward the statue of the Goddess before answering. "If we eat everything including our planting seeds and trade goods—honey, dried fruits and wine—four or five days. After that, we could feed the children for two or three more."

Kalie looked at each of the anxious faces surrounding them. She knew that they were experiencing something even worse than she had. From the moment Kalie had awoken to even partial awareness in the village of Long Grass, she had been free to leave the place of her attack, to run to the ends of the earth if she chose. And she had.

These people were trapped. It was maddening. Yet she knew she could not rush into a meeting with the beastmen. Information was vital to their survival.

"If you would, please, before I attempt to speak with the beastmen, tell me everything that has happened, from the first attack to the present." She glanced around the room. "Was anyone here present for the first attack?"

"I was," croaked a voice. Kalie turned, along with everyone else in the room, to the sound. At first glance, she saw an old man sitting on a cushion by the far wall, with one leg propped in front of him, supported by a larger cushion. As she directed her full attention to him, however, Kalie realized he was not much older than her, yet his thinning hair was white, and his hands shook with a palsy often associated with age.

"This is Camus of the village of Pinewood," said Yelene.

Everyone waited politely for Camus to begin. After several attempts, his quavering voice carried his tale. "Our village lies between a forest and the open plain. Everyone was in the fields, planting wheat for the late harvest, or keeping birds away from the first.

"When we first heard the noise...I remember looking up, puzzled that there could be thunder when the sky had barely a cloud. Then…maybe I was slower than the others to realize…I looked to the east—I had to shield my eyes from the morning sun—and there they were!" Camus began to cough. One of the priestess's attendants brought him water in a ceramic cup. Camus sipped, trying to keep water from sloshing out over his shaking hand. After a deep, shuddering breath, he began again.

"They had two heads and six legs." He looked around defiantly. "The folk here tell me they were only men astride horses. They were not men! Men could not do the things those creatures did!

"They came like a skein of geese: one in front, a line of others falling away from him on either side. They rode across our fields! A whole season of food, just…gone. By the time they reached us, most people were running; screaming. I just stood there, frozen. The noise was…I thought my head would split open from the thunder they made.

"Then, I saw a child running across the field, probably looking for his mother. For a moment I thought…Goddess help me, I actually thought, 'ah, good, they will have to stop, now.'" Camus made a sound like a hic-up; a cross between a laugh and a sob. "One of the creatures just…rode over the boy. His body split as it fell." Camus began to shake his head. One of the healers, a large woman in a white robe went to his side, whispering soothingly.

Camus pushed her away—with more force than necessary, Kalie thought—and almost shouted, "I will continue!" Then, more quietly, "Two of them rode past me. One on each side, as if I were a tree. Still, I could not move. I suppose one more came up from behind, but the beast only caught me a glancing blow.

I don't remember anything after that.

"The next thing I knew, I was waking up in the ditch that ran along the edge of the field. It was late afternoon, and I didn't know how I'd gotten there. One of the others thinks I was knocked into it by one of the beastmen, and that is why I still live. I tried to climb out, but one of my legs was broken. I crawled with my arms and one good leg as best I could, until I could look out, and see what was going on.

"Where our village had been was a dying bonfire. Nothing was left but charred wood, ashes, guttering flames. The bodies of my friends, neighbors, my mother..." He was crying now. "The few that were able to walk helped gather together the rest of us. Someone set my leg. Some wanted to stay and burry the dead. Some just ran—or staggered—as far away as they could. Someone whose wits weren't shattered like mine, ran all the way to Riverford, and brought back healers, and a priestess to help with the dead. Then we salvaged what we could and came here."

There was a moment of silence. Even those who had doubtless heard the story before looked saddened or angry. Finally, Kalie said, "You could not have saved them, Camus. And you will do more good by living. You already have."

Camus stared at her. "How did you know...?"

"The same thing happened to me. I was captured by beasts like these. I think I lived with them for a time. The merciful Goddess—" Kalie nearly choked on her own hypocrisy, but knew it was necessary—"has clouded my memory, but now, if it might help prevent what has happened to you from happening again, I shall ask Her to restore it." Kalie turned back to Yelene. "But what happened here? You say you are holding some of the beastmen prisoners. How, exactly did that come about?"

"Yes, that," said Yelene. "It was actually several things that made the outcome here different than that of Pinewood." The priestess glanced at a young man about Kalie's age, who wore the white robe of a priest. "Valen was drawing water from the river when they arrived, and has since spent much time with them, trying to learn their language. Please, my son, share what you know, again."

"It seems we were fortunate in many ways," the young man began, much more comfortable addressing the crowd than Camus had been. "From what we could learn, more than six hands of riders came into our lands, and attacked the first villages. After that, they split into two groups. Thus it was only about three hands of men that brought their violence to us."

"It was more than enough!" spat a woman near the ladder.

Valen smiled grimly. "Indeed. And they rode through the little fisher-village across the river just as they had the others places, bringing pain and death and fire. But when they wanted to cross the river to reach the town, there was only the narrow bridge. I think perhaps, these people have never seen a bridge before. It took time for them to decide to try it, and then they could only cross one at a time. By then, everyone had gathered inside the town, and pulled up the ladders, denying them entrance."

"Such a thing has never happened in my lifetime!" said a man who looked nearly as old as Yelene. "Always has the city of Riverford stood open to all who pass by; her shrines and markets welcoming everyone. And now look at us: huddled inside, afraid of each passing shadow. May this dark time past swiftly and never return!"

Many in the room echoed this sentiment. Kalie felt like shouting they had better remember the old days; they weren't coming back. But it was Riverford as it was now that gave her hope. Though not designed as a fortress, the city had become one. If others could be built this way...

"Yelene tried to reason with them from atop the roof," Valen's words brought Kalie back to the present. "But the men only flung spears at her, and began to beat upon the walls, as if they wanted to break apart our entire city. We were still trying to decide what to do, when a group of survivors from the fisher-village—mostly young children—tried to cross into the safety of the city. When some of the men turned their beasts to attack them...well, we had to do something."

"We began throwing anything we had at them," said a burly woman with the muscles of a smith. "Pots, dishes, loom-weights, anything that came to hand."

"It was a party of hunters who had come to trade fresh game and hides and feathers who found the answer," said Valen. "They felled three horses with their bolas, and struck one rider from his beast with a spear. At once, those still mounted turned their horses and fled across the bridge."

"But the bridge was not built to take such weight," said the smith.

Valen nodded. "Three or four made it across. After that, there came an earsplitting roar, and the sounds of men, horses and wood crashing into the water. Those who remained on this side of the river became quite crazed."

"It became necessary to subdue them for their own good," said the priest who sat beside Yelene. "They attacked everyone who tried to help them. Even the ones trapped beneath their own horses, who must have been in considerable pain, fought the healers."

"One of them kept spitting out the poppy syrup I tried to give him for the pain," said one.

"We had to create a separate healing place for them, deep within the town, both to keep them confined, and to spare their victims the grief of lying beside them while they all recovered," said the priest.

Kalie was trying to keep the numbers straight in her head. "How many do you think escaped?" she asked.

"Three or four, perhaps," said Valen. "We had…let me think…nearly three hands with us at nightfall." He held up the fingers of both hands, then put one hand down, and held up two fingers with the remaining hand.

"Twelve," said Kalie, trying to remember the number words beyond ten. "What happened to them?"

"Two were already dead," said Yelene. "Two others injured so badly we could only give them the Mother's Mercy. One died of his injuries a few days later."

"So you have seven of…them…here?" Kalie strove to keep her voice steady.

Valen nodded. "Their language is strange. We have tried this whole turn of the moon to communicate with them, but it has been difficult."

All eyes seemed to be on Kalie.

"It is more than their language," Kalie said. "It

is their way of thinking."

There were nods and startled looks from those assembled. "Yes," said Yelene. "That has become clear. You have not so much as looked upon them, yet you know this. Perhaps with your help, we can find a way to make peace—or at least discover what it will take to make them leave."

Kalie took a deep breath. "I will do all I can."

"We shall meet again in the daylight," the high priestess said. "A chamber has been prepared for you." At her nod, one of her acolytes rose and went to Kalie.

"Thank you," said Kalie. "But I would prefer to go now to speak with the beastmen."

Yelene looked at Kalie. "When did you last sleep?" she asked.

Kalie had to think.

"Rest," the priestess told her firmly. "The night is nearly spent and all are weary. In the morning we will go to them together."

Yelene left the room, leaning heavily on the younger of her two acolytes, while Valen held her other arm. The room emptied behind them. No one looked at Kalie. Having no choice, she followed her guide.

"How do you find your way around this place?" Kalie asked as they made their way through the maze of passageways, some of which opened onto torch-lit courtyards, while others were dark caves.

"Practice," said the girl, with a note of laughter in her voice. "I've lived here five summers, and I still get lost."

"That's comforting."

"Don't worry. I'll make a special effort not to lose you."

"What is your name?"

"Daleen. From the village of Swiftwater, now in the service of the Goddess. Here's were you'll be staying."

Daleen pulled aside a soft blue curtain that hung in a doorway—just like any other doorway, Kalie thought—and ushered Kalie into a richly appointed room. Smaller than the shrine they had just been in, this chamber was designed for living—and living well.

A wooden bed platform stood against the opposite wall and was covered in sheepskins and red and blue striped woolen blankets. A fine blue glazed ceramic jug stood between a pair of matching cups. A matching platter stood empty beside them. Kalie guessed that under different circumstances, it would be heaped with delicious food.

"I would offer you a bath," Daleen said. "But all our water must be saved for drinking." Kalie saw she was pointing a square tub sunk into the floor opposite the bed. Built of the same mud bricks as the room, the tub had a drain built into it which could be closed with a piece of cork to hold water, or opened to draw the water away. Kalie had never seen anything like it before. Someday, she vowed, she would return and find out just how it worked

The young priestess smiled sadly. Clearly, she enjoyed offering visitors such amenities.

"Thank you, Daleen," Kalie said. "I think I'll just rest now." The girl nodded and left. Kalie sat on the bed, then stretched out awkwardly. She didn't think she would sleep in this strange place, despite being exhausted. But the fur-covered bed was deliciously soft and the gentle sounds of human activity in the rooms above and below blended into a kind of lullaby. I'll just close my eyes for a moment, she thought...

When Kalie awoke, she felt disoriented. The only light in the room came from an oil lamp on a shelf by the bed; no sunlight came into the room to indicate time of day. She got up and found a robe of fine white linen at the foot of the bed; the kind the priests wore. While pleased at the honor they were showing her by dressing her as one of their own, Kalie was troubled by the thought that someone had entered the room to deliver it, and she had not awoken.

Dressed and composed, Kalie drew aside the curtain and looked around. She heard people singing as they worked, children shouting as they played, and the whispers of many quiet conversations. Light streamed into the corridor from a courtyard farther down. Kalie headed in that direction, flattening herself against the wall as a herd of small children ran past her.

She nearly collided with a woman walking around a corner. "Oh, Kalie, I was just coming to get you!" It was another of Yelene's acolytes. "The council is already gathered in the place of the horsemen. Are you ready to speak with them?"

Kalie wasn't sure if the girl meant speak with the horsemen or speak with the council, but she nodded and followed as calmly as she could.

They went through yet another maze of corridors and ladders, eventually ending up in a ground floor courtyard deep within the city. "The horsemen don't like being indoors," her guide whispered. "They spend most of their time out here, under the sky. And they don't like that much either, because they're always surrounded by walls."

Kalie paused for a moment, thinking that was strange, for did she not remember the beastmen living in dark tents, more closed off from the sun than even this place? Then she had no more time for thoughts or anything else as they stepped outside into one of the largest courtyards in the city.

Clay benches jutting from walls that formed the yard were filled with solemn looking people. Kalie recognized several from the meeting the night before. Yelene and her acolytes were seated beneath a rose trellis, while others had found what shade they could. Many wore hats of woven reeds to escape the glare.

And in the center, standing or squatting on the hard dirt, were seven nightmare visions from Kalie's past.

# Chapter 10

Kalie's first reaction was that they weren't as big as she remembered, but perhaps that was because they were looking at her from the ground, rather than from the back of a horse. Still, they were big enough. Blond where her people were dark; muscular where the people of the Goddess were more slight and wiry. They were dressed mostly in dark leather, but three wore cloth shirts of what seemed to be local weave. None were what she would have considered terribly clean.

Three squatted around a dice game. Two lazed in the dust, staring morosely around themselves. Two others sat on a bench carving pieces of wood.

Kalie's head whipped back to the two carvers. "Why do those men have knives?" she asked, not even looking to see who might be close enough to answer.

"Both knives belong to Narin, the one who's teaching the horseman." It was Valen who spoke. "Don't worry. He'll take them with him when he leaves."

It was then that Kalie realized that one of the men, slightly built with long black hair tied back with a leather band, was a resident of Riverford. The other, brown haired and muscular, was concentrating on the carving he was making—a horse, she noticed. It was really quite good. She wondered if he had ever carved wood before, as it was rare on the steppes. But if he had become this skilled in the short time he had lived here…that was impressive.

Counting strangers again, Kalie was about to ask where the seventh beastman was when the question was answered. He emerged through the corridor opposite her, followed by a young woman. The satisfied expressions on both their faces left little doubt as to what they'd been doing.

At Kalie's shocked expression, Valen smiled. "Given the beastmen's behavior, few women have wanted to join with them. But Maylene..." He indicated the young woman who couldn't have been more than fourteen, "thinks we can begin to reach them by showing them the proper way to honor the Goddess. Maris is trying to do the same by learning their games of chance, and Narin, by teaching the one who's interested, to carve."

Kalie shook her head. Maybe her people knew what they were doing after all.

Yelene motioned for Kalie to join them under the trellis. Kalie nodded and took a deep breath. Surrounded as she was by people she could trust, walking past the beastmen was still an ordeal. She touched the fold in her robe where her flint knife was hidden, then the copper knife bandaged to her right thigh. Head high, she made her way across the courtyard and took the seat the high priestess indicated.

Woven mats were being set out for those who could not find a place on a bench, or who preferred a mat. The early morning sun left much of the courtyard in shade; for now, the place would be pleasantly cool, despite the number of bodies. At Yelene's signal, small portions of flat bread and dried meat were distributed to everyone—including the beastmen.

Kalie's stomach was roiling sea. She knew she would eat nothing this morning, but had brought her clay cup, as did most of the others present. She would drink enough water to keep her tongue working, but that was all. She waited in respectful silence while Yelene invoked the blessing of the Goddess on their endeavors, and poured a libation over the large statue in which the Goddess, in her aspect as Mother, watched over the proceedings.

As the simple meal was consumed, Kalie watched the beastmen carefully. Throughout her long journey, she had made no effort to recall any long-buried words of their tongue. If she had, she would have been a quivering wreck long before reaching Riverford. Her only hope, it seemed, was to trust a Goddess that she no longer believed in that all would emerge when she needed it.

That was more or less what happened.

While the two groups ate, Kalie watched, and listened. She noticed the way the beastmen touched each morsel of food with their tongue, then wolfed the rest down after a few moments pause. Some sort of ritual? Nothing else in the rough way they grabbed at food, licked their fingers or jostled each other wile they ate carried any sense of purpose or solemnity.

While Kalie was not close enough to the beastmen to be considered seated among them, she had no trouble hearing them, despite the babble of voices in her own tongue. Every word they spoke in their harsh, guttural tongue was loud; louder than the familiar speech behind her.

Meanings of words emerged as Kalie listened. Some of them brought memories, but she kept her reactions under control. Finally Kalie felt she was ready to begin. She glanced at Yelene, who nodded, and gave a soft command that silenced all of her people. It took longer for the beastmen to fall silent, but eventually, they realized that something had changed, and turned their attention toward it.

"We talk," Kalie said in the strangers' tongue.

Instantly, she had the attention of all seven men.

"I speak…some of…beastman tongue…" Kalie felt a bit of satisfaction. They could tell her their name for themselves if they chose; in the meantime, let them know how their enemies viewed them.

There was a babble of voices as all of the visitors from the east tried to ask questions or issue orders at once. Yelene leaned forward and spoke to Kalie. She nodded and waited them out. When the men fell grudgingly silent, Kalie pointed to Yelene and said, "Yelene. Leader." The men cast confused looks between themselves, but Kalie knew she had the right word. She tapped her chest. "Kalie." Then she pointed at each man in turn, a questioning look on her face.

They introduced themselves. The man who was learning to carve was Riyik. The one had arrived late with the local woman, hardly more than a boy, Kalie thought, was Kariik. Another was Garaak. Kalie just nodded, as all were named.

Yelene spoke again and Kalie translated. "Yelene asks if one may speak for the others?" When that only seemed to confuse them she tried the word for "leader" again then, remembering, added, "Strong Man?"

There seemed to be some kind of silent communication among three of them. Finally Riyik stood. Yelene was about to ask another questions, when Kalie shook her head. "He is not their leader," she whispered, as more memories of her captivity among the beastmen tumbled through her head. She didn't know why he was doing it, but Riyik was taking the place of the person who was the official leader of the expedition—and strangely, none of the others were attacking him for it.

She pointed to Riyik's face, wind-burned, and unadorned but for a triangular tattoo on his left cheek. All of the men were tattooed in some fashion, but Kariik, the youngest, had the most elaborate one. The entire left side of his face was marked in black lines and swirls. "He is leader," she said firmly in both languages.

"But he is too young," said one of the priests. Others were making similar comments, while still others asked, "why the deception?" However, it was the beastmen's reaction that Kalie found the most interesting: they stared at her as if she hadn't existed a moment ago, but now was something important.

Kariik stood and approached with a swagger, but he seemed frightened. He spoke a stream of words out of which Kalie caught about one in three. Then she heard the word "Ahnaak." Memories and words flooded her mind almost faster than she could keep up. After several more exchanges, Kalie finally got the gist of it. As she turned to Yelene, she felt a strange combination of fear, hope, and satisfaction.

"I think I understand what is going on, now. Why the beastmen are camped outside, and why Kariik tried to hide his identity." Within the courtyard, silence ruled.

"This youth, Kariik," Kalie pointed, "is the son of their tribe's king." She did not try to explain what a king was. "The warriors outside the city fear to return to their homeland without their prince. They will not leave without him."

"But we tried to return him!" cried Yelene. "The others as well!"

Kalie sighed. This was going to be the hard part. "I told them that. They do not believe it." She looked from one confused, disbelieving face to another, seeking just one who could have somehow figured it out. But of course, they could not. And Kalie doubted she had the power to make them understand.

"When you brought their men to the rooftops, these creatures," Kalie pointed toward the warriors gathered outside the gates, "expected one of two things. That you had kept them alive only to slay them in front of their fellows, or that you would demand ransom for their return."

"What is ransom?" asked Yelene.

"Goods, things of value, given in exchange for one held prisoner. The beastmen thought that when you learned you held a king's son, you would demand gold and horses for his release. That is why the ones within the city tried to hide Kariik's identity. They feared you would demand more than the others could pay. Or, if I understood correctly, that you would sacrifice him to your gods, since royal blood—"

"This makes no sense!" cried Yelene. "We would do nothing of the kind, and these men must be sick indeed, if they think anyone would!"

"These men are sick," said Maris, speaking for the first time. "Sick in a way none of us could have imagined. That is what Kalie has been trying to explain for all these many years." She turned to Kalie. "If that is what they expect, can we not simply play along with this notion of ransom? Tell them they may have their men back for, say, one of their horses for each man? Or a few pieces of this gold they value so much?"

Kalie decided she liked this woman. "That might have worked at first, Honored Mother. But I fear they have been here long enough to learn about us, as we learn about them. They have seen we are not warriors; that we are not a threat to them."

"Turn it around, then," suggested Valen. "Offer *them* items of value if they will just take their people and leave!"

Kalie felt a rush of hope. "Yes! I was just getting to that. Kariik said…well, he implied that if we were to acknowledge his father as king over all, and send appropriate tribute, they would forgive the insult of holding warriors of Aahk prisoner—"

"Prisoner?" cried one of the healers. "Forgive us? We saved their lives after they tried to kill us! What's wrong with these people?"

"More than I could possibly explain," said Kalie.

"But it *does* appear that we finally have a way of bargaining with the beastmen outside," said Maris. "It matters little who pays who, as long as it means that our 'guests' depart safely, and the ones who keep us trapped agree to return to their homes without hurting anyone else. What will it take to make them leave?"

Kalie turned to the prisoners and translated the question.

The beastmen began looking about the courtyard in an appraising manner. She saw the light of greed in many eyes, but Kariik looked suspicious. Then Garaak began listing all sorts of items, many of which did not even exist within Riverford, such as horses and cattle, and foodstuffs that had long since been consumed. Another one began to speak of copper knives and arrowheads, while another shouted for gold, spreading his arms to indicate how much. It soon degenerated into incomprehensible noise, and Kalie turned her back in disgust. Kariik called for silence, but after Kalie's gesture, it came across as weak.

"I believe we must speak with whichever monster leads the pack outside," she told the elders, keeping her back to the beastmen. "It should be easier to bargain with just one. But we will have to think of a way to return the seven inside without making ourselves vulnerable to the others."

"We could try pushing them off the roof with long poles," muttered Karnac. Kalie was delighted with the suggestion, but could see that Yelene and Maris were not.

"Please ask them," said Yelene, "Why they have come here. And why they have hurt those who have never done harm to them."

Kalie did so, curious herself as to how they might respond.

After Kalie's first attempt, the seven beastmen looked at each other in confusion. A second try caused most of them burst out laughing. The carver looked thoughtful for a moment, and then he shrugged and remained silent.

Finally, Kariik spoke. "Does the goat ask the wolf why he hunts? Does the mouse ask the falcon? It is simply the nature of things."

"That appears to be all the answer we shall receive," Kalie said after she translated Kariik's words.

Yelene nodded slowly. "Let us go to the roof of the city. While we may get no better answers from the horsemen outside, perhaps we can strike a bargain that will free us of their presence." She rose, and walked with great dignity to the nearest ladder. To Kalie's relief, several hunters, armed with bolas and spears followed.

# Chapter 11

By the time Kalie and the council arrived at the roof of the city, the place was crowded with as much of the population as could fit. They were tense and silent, keeping themselves out of range of the beastmen's spears, falling back to give the best view of those waiting below to the priestess, her retinue and her guards.

Kalie looked down. The distance did not seem as frightening as it had the night before. But the armed beastmen put back much of the fear that had gone. Yelene walked to the edge. Kalie moved forward cautiously to stand beside her.

"Tell them you speak with the voice of all Riverford," said Yelene.

Kalie called out to the men below. "I speak for the city of Riverford!"

A man rode forward. He was probably the biggest warrior of the bunch, and his black horse was probably the largest mount.

"I am Haraak!" he shouted through a tangled red beard, his face seamed with scars and tattoos. "It's good to know one of you barbarians knows how to talk, but I will not lower myself to speak with you, woman! Bring me the man in charge!"

Kalie considered several answers, and then smiled. "I am the only one here who knows the little pig-grunts you animals call a language," she shouted. "But I will translate for our leaders!" With that, she beckoned Yelene, Maris and Karnac forward. Haraak stared in disbelief at the two women and one man, all of them probably older than any people he had ever seen.

While Haraak and his men began muttering to each other, Kalie whispered to Yelene. "What have they been eating all these days they have been camped out there? I see animal bones, and a few strips of meat over one of their fires, but nothing else."

"They had apparently slaughtered a flock of sheep that they found before coming to find their fellows here," said Karnac

"They've probably eaten most of it," said Maris. "And they've made no move to harvest any of the grain that survived their trampling. Nor even the vegetables on which they have camped nearly on top of."

"Nor fish from the river," said Yelene.

"They do not recognize that as food," Kalie explained. "They live almost entirely off of meat and milk—"

"The ones inside enjoy the bread we give them," said Yelene. "And seem familiar with it."

Kalie considered this. "But they do not grow the means to make it. They may not know it in the form it is in now. All that you grow is foreign to their eyes. They will not trust it to be safe to eat. And I see no flocks anywhere."

"We are growers and fishermen and crafters," said Karnac. "Most of our meat comes from trade."

Kalie grinned as a sudden idea took hold. "Bring me meat!" she whispered urgently. "A whole animal part, if you have any left."

The others shook their heads uncertainly. "I don't think—" Karnac began.

"Find one!" snapped Yelene, pointing to two acolytes who stood nearby, listening intently.

At that moment, Haraak began shouting from the ground. "I will allow you to translate, woman! You may convey my words to the man beside you. Tell him that in the name of Ahnaak, King of the Twenty Clans of Aahk, we demand the release of our noble warriors, and fitting tribute to your new king, to whom every man of this…rabbit warren must swear allegiance!"

A girl arrived, carrying a hind leg of deer, which had probably been pulled from a stew-pot.

Kalie took the meat and threw it over the wall to the ground by Haraak. "You are nearly out of food, Haraak. Yet as you can see, we have plenty. So I think you need to be gone from here even more urgently than we wish you gone."

Before Haraak could stop him, one of the warriors snatched up the meat and began to eat, proving Kalie's guess correct in front of everyone.

"So I think we must bargain, and quickly," she continued. "You may have the cowards who came to murder those who greeted them in friendship—provided you take them and leave our lands without harming anyone else—"

"You will die for those words, slut!" screamed Haraak. Many of the warriors near him grabbed for spears or strung their bows, but Kalie sensed a weariness in them. They were tired of breaking their flint spearheads against walls of sun-hardened mud, and tired of losing their arrows to an enemy who never fired them back.

The people near the edge of the roof backed away, but Yelene stayed where she was. Pulling a golden necklace over her head, she held it high so that sunlight struck it and gleamed into the eyes of those below. "Perhaps there is another way!" she shouted.

Kalie translated her words.

Hesitantly, the warriors lowered their weapons, glancing at Haraak for direction. The big man's scowl was replaced by a calculating interest. "Throw that down here, and we will talk!" he commanded, pointing at the necklace.

Kalie was about to refuse, but Yelene dropped the necklace without a word. Several warriors raced for it. The one who reached it first grabbed it from the hard earth and ran back to Haraak, handing it up to him respectfully.

Haraak took his time examining the piece, tilting it this way and that in the sun, counting the tiny gold plates cleverly strung on linen thread. He shouted an order to one of his men. The man dragged over a large animal hide, dumping out the gear that it held as he brought it to his chief. He spread the hide out on the ground, and Haraak dropped the necklace in the center.

"You will bring out enough gold to fill this pack!" he shouted as Kalie translated. "And you will bring out enough knives, axes and spearheads of copper to fill another of the same size. And food— since you have so much!" He laughed harshly at that and was joined by all his men.

Yelene nodded. "We have no axes of copper, and few spearheads, but we will give you the rest of what you ask," she said.

Haraak scowled again after Kalie translated. "Then make them, for we will not leave without them! And some of those strange hides that you wear."

"He means cloth," Kalie explained, but the others had understood.

"Yes," said Yelene, as eyes were raised in hope

for the first time in many days. "All this we will give you, and your men, whom we have healed and nursed back to health, all if you will simply leave!"

"Gladly!" said Haraak, looking distastefully at the land around him. Yelene turned to her people and began directing people to gather up all the gold in the city and locate the smiths with the greatest skill, when Haraak added, "One thing more. Fifty slave girls. All comely."

At Kalie's translation, Yelene froze, mirrored by everyone on the roof. The feeling of hope, nearly palpable a moment before, vanished. Kalie, briefly surprised that Haraak could even count as high as fifty, turned her back on the confused whispers and shouting behind her and gazed calmly at the beastmen below. As the last echo of Haraak's words faded, an idea took shape in her mind. "We will give you our answer tomorrow," she said. Then she turned to Yelene and the rest of the council. "Come, we have much to discuss."

"Yes, we do," said Yelene, leading the way down to the city.

# Chapter 12

"But what does he mean?" asked a young woman, whose plaintive tone reminded Kalie of a sheep. "People cannot be owned! Women or men, it makes no difference. Can't you just explain that to him?"

Kalie sighed, tired of answering the same question, no matter how many different ways it was phrased.

"Well?" demanded the man seated next to the speaker, his arm around her. The meeting was being held in the largest shrine in Riverford, much larger than the one Kalie had met them in the night before. Perhaps eight hands of people were crowded inside, with several times that number waiting anxiously in the courtyard outside.

Kalie looked at the young couple, afraid that if she tried to explain yet again, she would say something that she would regret.

She was spared having to answer by Maris. "Whether we like it or not," the ancient healer said in a voice that belied her age, "we have been called to deal with people who are entirely different from any we have ever encountered. Or imagined. Kalie has explained this notion of 'slavery' to us. Refusing to believe it will not change the fact that it *is*."

"I will gladly hand over the gold and cloth," said Yelene. "Even weapons of metal, though I shudder to think of those tools in the hands of such creatures. And as for food, I say give them our honey and wine and every bit of seed grain we have. All of that can be replaced! But I cannot give them human beings! I cannot ask any one of us to even consider such a sacrifice."

A heavy silence settled over the room. Kalie knew it was now or never.

"There may be a way," she began. "Yelene is right when she said that material wealth can be replaced. But now that they know of us—of great wealth in the west, held by people who know nothing of war—they will return, and in greater numbers. If the lands of the Goddess are to survive, I believe that the answer lies within Haraak's demand for slaves."

There was a roar of protest, but Yelene silenced it with a glance. "How?"

"What I am going to suggest will sound like madness—and it may very well be." She faltered, suddenly unsure of how to continue.

"It's all right, child," said Maris. "The words are in you. Just let them out." She whispered to the apprentice beside her, and the young woman brought Kalie a cup of something steaming. Kalie thanked her and sipped carefully. A rich, flowery tea greeted her tongue, and while she was trying to guess the ingredients, inspiration struck.

"There is a story I learned while I lived with the healers at Hot Springs." Kalie's voice took on the cadence of a storyteller. "Far in the north, where the snow never melts, there lives a bear that is pure white. When it stands on two legs, it is the height of three men, and no spear or arrow made by the hand of man can kill it. But the people who share this bear's domain have developed an unusual weapon, for such times as when a bear ravages a village, or when hunger makes the people desperate.

"They take a ball of fat, softened by fire, and

into it they slide a double bladed knife, folded together, and held in place by the fat as it hardens. They then leave the ball by whatever water source the bear drinks from. The bear usually swallows the ball whole, and goes on his way."

"And when the fat melts inside his stomach…" Maris took up the story. "The knife springs open and kills the bear—from the inside."

"A rather cruel way to hunt," said Yelene.

"Killing is often cruel," said a man across the room. "As much as we might seek to make it otherwise. But when threatened, all creatures will use whatever means are available to be the one who survives, even if another must die."

Yelene fixed Kalie with a piercing gaze. "What do you have in mind, child?"

"Haraak has demanded slaves. I say we should give him slaves. Women, willing to sacrifice their lives to save our world from his. We will be the knife swallowed by the bear. We will destroy their world—from within."

Where there had been painful silence moments before, the room was now in uproar. And while many shouted down her idea as impossible—or wrong—others wanted to know the details of her plan, and, to Kalie's surprise, many were volunteering to be part of it.

"I do not know exactly what can be done," Kalie said when order was restored. "Or what things people might be willing to do. We should make several different plans, and recruit those with as many different skills as possible. I know the tribe these beasts belong to is probably the largest of its kind. It is ruled by a man named Ahnaak. When that king learns of our land; of what we have…"

"He will send more of his warriors to ravage our homes," Karnac finished.

"Or he will lead them here himself," said Kalie. "And perhaps this time, they will decide not to leave at all."

Her words brought a new kind of fear to everyone in the room.

"I would risk my life for such an undertaking," said Valen. "But what, exactly, is it that you think we can do?"

"First," said Kalie, "our party must consist only of women. Any men we send would be killed immediately." Before Valen could protest, she continued. "And I think we must remain there for many moonspans, to learn all we can of our enemies; find their every weakness. It may be that simply by killing their strongest leaders, we can sew enough chaos to keep them from our homes for many years."

"And how are we to kill them?" asked a young woman. Kalie remembered her name was Marika, a refugee from one of the burned villages to the east.

"As slaves, we will prepare much of the food that the men eat, as well as making their clothing. There are poisons that can be added to food, and rubbed into cloth—"

"You are suggesting we ourselves become as these monsters?" a young man asked.

"Only those who are willing," said Kalie. "And only those who understand the risks: as slaves, our lives will be filled with pain and degradation. We may die in that land without accomplishing anything. I want no one on this mission who cannot fully accept what it means. It may be that I myself am the only one who qualifies."

"We would not let you do this alone, Kalie," said Yelene.

"Even if we wanted to, those men will not leave without many more than just you," said a young priestess. "And now that we have seen for ourselves what is at stake—"

"I will go," said the young woman beside Maris. "I cannot promise to kill anyone, although I fear Kalie may be right when she says it is necessary. But I will do all I can to bring the light of the Goddess to these men, and to show them that there is an alternative to coming to our land as enemies."

Maris smiled at her apprentice. "My young Alessa speaks the truth. These men are sick, in their minds and in their souls. Yet in demanding slaves, they have given us the key to our salvation—and possibly theirs as well."

Alessa smiled. "They did insist that we come with them," she said softly. "So it could be argued that any…change…we bring to their land was at their own request."

"They are not inviting us to come as teachers!" Kalie said pointedly.

"True," said Alessa. "But it may happen anyway."

"We must go to their land to destroy them!" Kalie struggled to keep her voice soft; her tone reasonable.

"I would be willing to slay them," said Marika. "After what they did to my village and my family, I truly believe, the best use of our lives is to slay their leaders while they sleep—if they are truly foolish enough to sleep beside women they have violated and named 'slaves'?" She looked at Kalie for confirmation.

"They will do so," Kalie insisted. "They will do it without fear that a woman could strike back—or even imagine it." She stood and addressed the room. "What I am suggesting could well mean death for all who come with me. But it may be our only chance to stop these beastmen from destroying the Land of the Goddess! From doing to every village and city what they have already done to—"

"And I believe," Maris spoke softly. "That our greatest chance lies not in slaying these beasts, but in transforming them." She smiled at Kalie. "You speak of tricking a beast into swallowing the knife which will kill him. I speak of tricking that same beast into swallowing medicine that will heal him. Yet in either case, it is the women of the Goddess who must be swallowed by the beast for the change to occur. And the future of our world—and perhaps theirs—depends on that transformation."

"And all the while, we must seek to reach the women among them," said Alessa. "For they seem to be victims as well."

"Then why do they stay with such men?" demanded an exasperated priestess.

"That we shall learn when we are there," replied Maris. "And perhaps, teach them that they do not have to."

It was then that those assembled in the temple realized that Maris intended to go with them. "Good Mother," Valan said slowly, "these men have demanded young women…"

"And they have demanded fifty as well," said Maris. "Yet when the time comes, I think they will take what they can get and leave."

"And what, exactly, do you expect the rest of us to be doing, while you risk your lives on this deadly expedition?" demanded a young man, one of the few survivors of the village of Three Hills, two days to the east of Riverford.

"Pray," said Maris. "And bring word of this threat to all who live in this land. And to prepare some sort of defense in the event that we fail."

"Perhaps other cities could be rebuilt along the lines of Riverford," suggested Valan.

"Our city was built this way to keep out floodwaters!" cried Karnac.

"But it has effectively kept out the beastmen as well," said Yelene. "Perhaps the Goddess guided the hand of those long ago builders, knowing this day would come."

"If Maris is to go," said another priestess. "I would ask that Kalie step down as leader, and not go on this journey."

Kalie's jaw dropped. "I make no pretensions of leadership," she said quickly. "But I must make this journey! I am the only one among us who has lived with these beasts! I speak their tongue, and am the only one who can prepare the others…"

"I was told that when you stumbled into the village of Tall Oak seven years ago, you did not even know your own name!" the priestess interrupted. "Even now, I understand that you suffer from nightmares; that you have never fully regained your memory. To subject yourself to these horrors a second time is more than even the Goddess Herself would ask."

Yelene nodded. "Truly, Kalie, you have done

enough. Remain with us, and complete the Healing you have sought for yourself these seven years."

Others in the room nodded. Kalie was touched by their concern, but knew she could not remain safely behind in Riverford while others laid down their lives at her urging.

"Kalie must come with us," said Maris. "As must my own apprentice, Alessa."

No one seemed willing to argue with Maris. A new energy filled the people in the shrine as, for the first time in days, they had something to do. Under Yelene's direction, they broke into groups. Some were charged with gathering the ransom goods, while Kalie met with the volunteers willing make up the group of slaves.

Several she rejected at once as too young, too frail or lacking the patience to endure all that slavery would mean. But in the end, she had to accept most who offered, and they still had only thirty women.

When everything—and everyone—was assembled on the highest rooftop, Yelene gazed down at the beastmen, then turned to address those who were about to leave their home, and their world, for possibly the last time.

"Of all the blessings that the Children of the Goddess have known and rejoiced in, going back to First Woman and First Man, perhaps the greatest gift is the power to make our own choices. The strangers who have come to our land, bringing death and pain, live in ignorance of that gift. I can see that now when I look at them. They do not think that we have the power to make choices, once they believe they have made those choices for us. Perhaps that will turn out to be their greatest weakness: they underestimate what free women are capable of."

Kalie began to feel better than she had in a long time.

# Chapter 13

The tall brown grass went on forever. Above it, blue sky, unbroken by even a single cloud reached down to meet the grass at the distant horizon. Grass and sky; Kalie was beginning to feel like nothing else had ever existed.

She tried to conjure up memories of the various places she had lived in her life. The sound of falling water; the damp touch of moss-covered stones; the woodland smell of ferns and mushrooms; the sap rising beneath the bark of towering trees…

Dust kicked up by the horses' hooves filled her nostrils, bringing a coughing fit to Kalie, and much amusement to her captors. Her pleasant memories faded.

Larren quickened her pace until she walked beside Kalie. "How much longer, do you think?"

Kalie glanced with concern at the younger woman. Her once-lovely face was more battered than any of the others; her creamy skin covered in bruises. Kalie suspected Larren had at least one broken rib, suffered in the latest round of what the beastmen thought of as mating. "Tomorrow, I think," she told the struggling woman.

That brought a fleeting look of relief to Larren's pale face. Sahrene moved up, offering her strong shoulder for support. Alessa fell back to Larren's other side, offering her assistance as well.

Kalie drifted on by herself. She was relieved they had made it this far without sinking into despair, as she had feared they would. Of the thirty women who had left Riverford with the beastmen nearly a moonspan ago, little more than half still lived. Her eyes strayed to the men mounted upon horses: large, powerful brutes, like the animals they rode. There would be no mercy from them—no slowing of the pace the women were forced to walk.

Finally, Haraak called a halt. The women sank gratefully to the hard ground, while the men laughed, leaping from the horses, stretching and walking with that curious manner of theirs, as if they owned the earth and everything on it. They fed the horses water from leather bags, as this part of the world held no water.

An angry curse told Kalie that rest time for the women was over. She hauled herself to her feet, flinging back her long brown hair, now filthy and matted, and joined the other women by the fire one of the men had built.

Alessa and Larren were preparing a meal of fresh meat from a wild goat the beastmen had killed and bread made from the grain, honey and fruit they had taken from the city. The men were shouting for water, and that other thing they drank, made from fermented mare's milk. Larren started to rise, but Kalie shook her head, and Sahrene set a restraining arm on Larren's. "I'll go."

Since bringing the men their drink usually meant being pulled down and mounted by each one of them, it was not a task any of them undertook willingly. But Larren, a "favorite" of the men according to their rough speech, wouldn't survive much more and all the women knew it. Sarhene, with her burly manlike build, and her slightly skewed face —as if the two sides were made separately and didn't quite join right—was occasionally considered ugly enough to be left alone.

"The one I feel sorry for is Maylene," said Traea, turning the cakes of bread on the flat stones with one of the few copper tools they had been allowed to keep. "We at least have each other, while she is kept apart, and made to wear those heavy wraps in this unbearable heat. Does their cruelty have no end?"

Kalie followed the younger woman's gaze to where Maylene, the youngest of them, sat with the beastmen. Unlike the other women, whose clothing was reduced to fraying rags, or the men who wore sturdy shirts and pants made of leather, Maylene was swathed in black felt, her long red hair and budding woman's body invisible to any who might be looking She was also allowed to ride on a horse behind one of the men, and given as much food and drink as the men themselves partook in.

"In that, at least," Kalie said, "they are not trying to be cruel. Kariik has claimed Maylene as his. That is why only he is allowed to force himself upon her, and why she eats better than we do, and rides instead of walking."

"But why do they torture her with heavy clothing in this awful heat?" Traea asked.

"From what I can tell, it is actually a form of respect. Women of rank dress like that."

"I can't imagine why," said Traea. "In a land this hot, the dress of the men makes more sense. Why don't the women just dress the same?"

Kalie shrugged. Soon her companions could ask the women themselves. Maybe they would have better luck than she did in understanding why the women put up with what they did. In spite of—or perhaps because of—what they had learned of the men of the steppes, many of the women who had followed Kalie into slavery believed that the hope for their mission lay with the women they would soon meet and form alliances with.

Kalie did not bother shattering their illusions; they needed any hope they could hold onto at this point. Things had been more difficult than even Kalie had been prepared for. For one thing, the initial pace set by the nomads was too hard for city women unused to constant travel. Several women died before Haraak realized he would have to slow the pace and increase the captive's rations if he was going to have any slaves at all to give his king.

Then as well, despite Kalie's warnings and preparations, some women simply could not submit to abuse without fighting back. Many of the warriors found their struggles amusing, and were not inclined to kill them for it—although a few died from what the men viewed as "discipline", necessary to teach the new slaves how to behave. Then a woman named Shara had blinded a warrior with a sharp stone while he lay grunting on top of her. Shara had been on her way to gelding him as well when his friends came to his rescue. Kalie smiled at the memory—until she remembered what the men had done to Shara afterwards.

But it was Maris's death that bothered her the most.

The revered wise woman had been largely ignored by the beastmen, other than their occasional grunts of surprise that she could keep up better than many of the younger women. They never molested her, nor—to Kalie's surprise— prevented Maris from using her store of medicines to treat the captives' injuries.

The great healer's faith held the women together better than Kalie's knowledge and experience ever could have. As Kalie began to believe that Maris might make it to the beastmen's home alive, she began for the first time to feel hope: hope that if anyone could reach the women of that Motherless land, Maris could.

Then one night, during one of the many sex games the beastmen liked to play, Kestra and Loeen, two of the younger women bolted in fear and began to run. They ran west, toward home, not that it really mattered: on a flat landscape of grass with no place to hide, men on horseback could easily catch fleeing women whichever way they ran.

Yet Maris had leapt to her feet and placed herself between Haraak and the fleeing women. He rode her down without even trying to turn his mount, killing Maris instantly. She had not been the first to die, nor would she be the last, yet it struck Kalie and each of her followers harder than the rest.

It had been so pointless. Kestra and Loeen and been recaptured; nothing had changed among the monsters who carried them east. Kalie had expected Maris to die on the grueling journey, but she had hoped, at least, that somehow, by some miracle that Maris still believed in, even if Kalie did not, her death would have meaning. Given strength to those she left behind, created hearts in the breasts of monsters who had none…something!

"We cannot say yet that her death is without meaning," said Alessa, coming to walk beside Kalie, and knowing her thoughts, as she always seemed to.

"This journey has just begun. Who knows what seemingly unimportant events will shine like beacons for us before the end."

Kalie managed a smile. "Maris chose well when she chose you, Alessa."

Although they had all worried in the first days after Maris's death that they had lost Alessa as well. She had shut down completely; not even arranging her mentor's body or speaking prayers over it—not that the beastmen had given them much time for any of that. It was Kalie who gathered up the old healer's medicines and tools. She carried them still, and would do so until at last Alessa was ready to take them.

And although Kalie had said nothing aloud, she feared that to lose Alessa would be to doom them all. The apprentice had much of her mentor's knowledge and faith but, more importantly for where they were going, she had beauty and youth and spirit. Unlike Maris, Alessa could capture the balls of a powerful man, or simply get close enough to kill him. Their mission depended on it.

She wanted to ask if Alessa blamed Kalie for her mentor's death, but kept silent. In a place where despair and death were never far away, some questions were better left unasked.

That evening, Kalie called a meeting. The men's exhaustion from the long journey and their eagerness to be home worked in the women's favor. With Kariik busy in his tent with Maylene, and the other men busy ravaging Larren and Kestra, none of them paid much attention to the rest of the chattel. All of the other women were able to meet undisturbed in the shadows beyond the men's campfire.

"This may be our last chance to speak

together," Kalie said. "For a while, at least," she added quickly. No point in making her brave companions feel more frightened and hopeless than they already did. "We will soon reach the beastmen's home. Once there, it is likely we will be separated; divided up among the clan chiefs and the warriors the king wishes to reward."

"I have a reward in mind for whoever thinks he's going to own me," said Sahrene, her already skewed face twisting even more with hatred.

"And you might well have that chance," Kalie said softly. "If you keep your head and think before you act." Sahrene looked chastened as she remembered the promise she had made when volunteering for this mission. "We need a plan," Kalie continued.

"We need several plans," said Traea. "I know it seemed simple at first—to me at least. Just kill their king and their chiefs, and do whatever we could to get them to fight among themselves. But now…" Traea looked over to where the men were, and fear shone in her eyes.

"There is nothing simple about killing," said Alessa. "And no guarantee that killing their leaders will cause this…this…civil war that we hope for."

"I agree," said Kalie. "But I believe that killing the king should be out first step. I have heard them argue over which of us is fine enough to be given to King Ahnaak."

Dara nodded eagerly. She, as well as several others had already learned much of the beastmen's tongue. "Haraak wanted to give him Maylene, but Kariik won't give her up. Another suggested Larren, but I think Haraak wants to keep her for himself."

"Can we agree that whoever goes to the king's tent will simply kill him at the first opportunity?" Kalie asked. She gazed at each of them in turn. One by one they all nodded their heads. Alessa was the last to do so.

Kalie felt tension she thought would never ease slowly unknot itself. They had a plan. Whether it would work or not was anybody's guess, but at least they had something to work toward.

"What about killing the chiefs as well?" Traea asked.

"That might be harder," said Kalie. "And perhaps not in our interest. Once the king is dead, it must be the chiefs we rely on to fight each other, or spend their strength helping the king's rival sons fight each other."

"I would like to suggest another plan," said Alessa. "If slaying the king fails, we should use our knowledge of healing and cooperation to open the eyes of the women." She turned to Kalie, smiling shyly in the dim light. "I believe you have something for me?"

Kalie took the bundle of herbs and tools that had never been out of her sight since Maris died and slid them to Alessa. "I'm glad to hand them over to one who can use them," she said.

Alessa was about to say more, but a harsh shout that it was time to sleep, sent the women scurrying to relieve themselves at the designated area away from camp, then back to the sleeping area where they huddled together like herd animals against the cold of night in the dessert. The guard posted nearby prevented any further discussion.

# Chapter 14

The next morning, a new energy filled the men. Even the horses seemed to have it. There were no morning rest breaks; even food was taken on the move. The men did not even stop to molest the women. All their focus was on the eastern horizon to which they journeyed.

Early in the afternoon, the men began shouting and pointing, increasing their pace yet again. The blazing sun behind them lit up what at first appeared to be only a dark smear on the horizon. Slowly, it changed into a huge cluster of black tents with people moving among them. Beyond the tents were flocks of sheep and goats, and—numbering more than the other two combined—horses.

It was, Kalie reflected, glancing back at the lowering sun, which had set earlier each night of their journey, the first full moon of harvest season. But in this land, there were no crops to harvest, no brilliant turning of the leaves, no resting from the day's labors under leafy canopies. There was only dull brown grass, ugly black tents and heat that showed no knowledge of a thing called autumn.

As the party approached the sea of tents, they were greeted by a cacophony of sounds. Dogs barked, women shrieked and men rode toward them in a clatter of hooves and weapons. Haraak rode up to meet them, nearly dragging Kariik along behind him. Words were exchanged too rapidly for Kalie to follow. Then, noise of a different kind engulfed them all as they were swept forward into the camp. Orders were shouted, women shrieked from tent flaps and men greeted each other with shouts and much thumping of backs and shoulders.

After the silence and open spaces of the past moonspan, the noisy crowds terrified the captive women. They huddled together, even Maylene, who wept with relief to be back among her friends.

Scowling women, all of them dressed in black felt like Maylene wore, peered from tents or strode boldly forward to spit at the foreigners, hissing angry sounding words.

Traea clung to Kalie. "What's going on?" she shrieked in her ear. Kalie could only shake her head, and keep walking, certain she would be trampled to death if she slipped. *I can do this*, she told herself, as memories buried for seven years collided with the solid, terrifying reality of the nomad camp. *When I first came here, I was a child; an innocent trapped in a nightmare. I return here a woman, willing to kill and die for my people. I will not be afraid…*

Finally, Haraak's voice boomed above the chaos. A relative silence fell. Then a group of shrouded women pulled Maylene from them and dragged her away. The rest were divided into two groups. Haraak led Kalie's to one of the tents, ordered them inside, and closed the flap firmly behind them.

They found themselves in utter darkness. But at least the noise was muffled.

Slowly, as her eyes adjusted, Kalie saw that the tent was empty but for the captives. It did not seem to have been used recently as living quarters. Scraps of leather, broken baskets, things she could not identify but seemed to count as rubbish were pushed against one side. There was no sign of a hearth, but then, how would one light a fire in a tent made of a thing that burned as easily as animal hair anyway?

A wave of exhaustion washed over her, but Kalie fought it. She looked at her companions: Alessa, Traea, Sahrene, Larren, Kestra, and Dara. Motioning for silence, though she doubted they could see her in the darkness, Kalie pressed her ear against the flap that covered the one opening in the tent, now tied securely shut from the outside. Snatches of conversations were brought by the wind, and taken away just as suddenly. But some things were clear to her.

Stories of an unbelievable land to the west were spreading through the camp. A land of gold! A land of endless water and green pastures for horses; where food and wine were as common as dust and grass on the steppes! Best of all, a land where men were so weak they bowed to women. Conquest would be easy, and then this fine land would belong to the Chosen of Aahk.

Kalie looked toward the women who had followed her into this nightmare. "The battle is joined," she whispered.

"What if...our plan fails?" asked Larren. Even speaking their own tongue, all of them, Kalie included, feared to speak aloud anything of their plan to murder a king.

"We will have time to construct a new one," said Kalie. "Many new plans, if need be. Winter will be here soon. Winters last much longer here than in our home and no one can travel while the ice holds the land in its grip. The soonest they can attack the west will be late spring. Maybe even summer. We have until then to lay our trap."

"That long?" Dara said slowly, as the full understanding of how difficult each day would be finally struck her. "We're going to have to stay here for a full turn of seasons?" The normally pale, blond girl looked like she was about to faint.

"We knew this would be a long journey when we agreed to come here," said Alessa. "We also knew we might never see home again. But the Goddess has blessed this work we do, and She has not forgotten us."

"And will She protect the one of us who kills these monster's king?" asked Kestra.

All of them listened in silence to the blood-chilling shrieks of laughter and the deafening roar that was simply life in this land. Whoever killed their king would die—quickly if she were lucky.

Then Alessa asked the question that all of them were thinking. "Do you think they might kill all of us, for the crime of one of us?"

"That's ridiculous!" Kestra said, but her voice shook. "Why would they—"

Silence reigned. Each of them had had nearly a moonspan to observe their captors. Based on what they had seen, they knew it was possible.

This was their first test, Kalie saw. Fear gripped every one of them. In the face of the enormity of this place; of what killing a king would mean here, they were all ready to abandon their only solid plan. And if they did that...If they did that, there might never be another plan, other than Alessa's idea that a lifetime of slavery for all of them would somehow lead to the conversion of the people who lived here.

Everyone was looking at Kalie, waiting for her to lead them. *Well, this was all your idea in the first place*, she reminded herself.

"I think," Kalie said slowly, "that we should

wait for a sign. If one of us is given to the king, it will be the Goddess telling us to move quickly and ruthlessly. If none of us are, it is a sign that we must proceed slowly and seek another plan."

"And until that time," said Alessa, "we must not fight back at all, no matter how hard that is."

"You don't need to tell us that, Alessa," snapped Kestra. "Those of us who are left all saw what happened to the ones who fought back on the journey."

They bowed their heads in silence, as each thought of the friends they had lost on the long road from the Land of the Goddess to the beastmen's Hell. Kalie briefly promised herself another look at the bandaged face of the beastman Shara had blinded before she died. She knew each of the women with her were making similar deals with themselves or their Goddess; something that would keep them focused on their goal, until they freed their home of the beastmen's threat.

Even if none of them ever saw that home again.

"We must watch and learn," she told the others softly. "As you begin to master their tongue, you can ask questions. Or, if it seems best, pretend you have not yet learned it, and see if they will speak more freely in front of you. We can learn a great deal that way, especially from the women."

"And you believe the women will not help us at all?" said Larren.

Kalie shook her head, wishing she could explain, when Kestra changed the subject with a question of her own. "Have any more of your memories returned? Now that you are back, surrounded by their language and their homes and their…smell?"

The door flap flew open, flooding the tent with light. Three women crawled inside, each carrying various strange objects.

Kalie and the others squeezed together to make room for them in the already crowded tent. The new arrivals settled down in the cramped space with the ease of long practice. One of them set a small object in the middle of the tent, which came alive with light a moment later.

"A brazier!" exclaimed Sahrene, as they all stared at the clay sphere perched on a tripod. "That's how they can have fire inside a felt tent. I was wondering about that…"

"But what is it burning?" asked Kestra. "It smells like dung!"

"I think it is dung," said Kalie, staring through the acrid smoke to the brightly burning lumps within the brazier.

While the western women exchanged disgusted looks, the local women cast aside their veils and regarded the strangers through slitted eyes.

In the improved light, Kalie saw them for a moment as a maiden, a mother and a crone—the Trinity of the faith in which she had been raised. Then as her eyes adjusted further, she saw them only as two worn and old looking women, who were probably little older than Kalie herself, and a younger one, about Maylene's age. It was difficult to tell more than that, for they were still wrapped in bulky robes, which must be unbearable in this heat.

There was silence as the two groups of women regarded each other.

Finally, Alessa spoke in the beastman tongue. "We mean you no harm. We are…" she searched for the words… "captives; brought here against our will. Perhaps we can help one another."

The women's eyes widened. Kalie guessed not many foreigners arrived knowing the local language. They whispered to each other in animated tones, but ignored the newcomers.

Alessa was not dissuaded. "My name is Alessa." She pointed at herself. "These are my friends: Kalie, Dara, Sahrene…." She pointed to each of the others, naming them as she went. "What are your names?"

The whispering turned hostile. The oldest of the three finally acknowledged the other seven women with a hate-filled glare and a hiss, which Kalie recognized as a kind of curse.

Then they began sifting through the baskets and skin pouches they had brought with them, pulling out tools that looked like mortars and pestles.

While Kalie knew better than to hope for food or water, she also knew that they would have to get some soon. She hoped she would not be reduced to begging from these women. She watched cautiously, trying to guess at what the women had been ordered to do, and how best to handle it.

The oldest woman was scraping bark from some kind of resinous wood with a small knife. The smell released as she did so was pleasant but Kalie was far more interested in the knife. It appeared to be made from a single piece of bone, blunted on one end, sharpened on the other. *If I could get hold of one of those…* She shook the thought away. *Not yet.*

The other two women were grinding herbs

together, adding bits of the bark the eldest provided until they formed a fragrant paste. Kalie saw Alessa watching them with unguarded delight. She moved closer. "Cedar and frankincense!" she said in her own tongue, pointing at the herbs. "What do you call this one?"

The women remained silent, but were beginning to look at least interested.

When they had a large amount of a whitish paste, they turned to their guests and began pulling off the strangers clothing. Startled, the newcomers resisted, which resulted in rougher treatment and the ripping apart of the last sheds of home Kalie and the others had left. Larren shrieked as her once blue linen tunic was torn from her and thrown into the rubbish heap by the largest of the women.

Kalie didn't care much about her clothing, but she'd had enough of rough handling of her body. Her tormenter was the oldest; the one who seemed to be in charge. With a simple twist of her own body and a brutal shove, Kalie knocked the woman on her back. Raising her fist, she brought it down to her opponent's throat, pressing just enough to block the flow of air.

"If you want our clothing, then ask us!" she commanded in their tongue. "If you touch any of us again this way, I'll kill you!" Strange, how quickly both the words and the movements came back to her. At a nod from Kalie, the others removed what remained of their clothes, folded them neatly and set them in a pile.

The horsewomen crouched frozen in place. Kalie released her grip on the leader who sat up slowly, glaring at her through hate-filled eyes.

"Why did you do that?" Sarhene demanded.

"Are you trying to get us killed?"

"The rules of survival in this world," Kalie said simply. "There is no protection against the men, beyond the use of sex to control them. But among the women—if you're willing to fight, they'll respect you. If not, they will use you as brutally as their men do."

The two groups stared at each other for a long moment. Finally, the eldest brought the bowl of paste to Kalie. "We are ordered to groom you. You refuse our help, then groom yourselves! I hope you fail badly enough to displease the men. Then they kill you."

Kalie stared at the paste and tried to remember what it was for, but found nothing. Suddenly Alessa spoke. "It's for bathing!" The others looked at her blankly. "Cypress! That's the third ingredient. I knew I'd smelled it before!" She scooped up some paste and turned to the three local women. "Like this?" She began rubbing it onto the skin of her arm.

Warily, the youngest nodded, and then came forward to help. "I should have realized," Alessa said in the Western tongue. "As scarce as water is here, they can't afford to use it for bathing. So they do this!"

"And what, exactly, is this?" Kestra asked, cringing as the next oldest woman began to apply it to her body.

"I'm not exactly sure but I think…" The rest of Alessa's words were cut off as the nomad woman began smearing the paste on Alessa's face, and warning her not to move her mouth.

The others followed suit, applying the paste to themselves.

By the time their bodies were completely covered, the paste had begun to harden. Kalie felt a kind of tingling that might have been pleasant under different circumstances. There was nothing to do now but wait for instructions from the nomad women—one of whom Kalie had just assaulted and threatened. Still, no attack came while she and the others sat rigidly encased in plaster.

Kalie sighed. If they couldn't hold their own against three women, they were truly doomed. But they would survive and follow their plan. They would have to. And considering all that had stood against them, how much new and different thinking was required of the people of Riverford, just making it this far was victory enough.

Just when the paste was becoming truly uncomfortable, the eldest horsewoman nodded, leaned forward and began ripping the dry paste from Alessa's body. The other two did the same with the other women. It was rather painful, but after the first few pulls—which took body hair along with the plaster—it wasn't that bad.

When all the plaster had been removed and thrown into the fire—improving the smell in the tent considerably—the youngest woman gave them each a piece of felt and instructed them to rub their skin with it. That part didn't hurt, and the women soon found their bodies clean and glossy in a way that was new to them. The grime of the hard journey, and even the stench of the men's bodies were gone.

The process they were shown for cleaning their hair was less pleasant. It involved combing rendered sheep's fat through their hair, with little time to work through the tangles. Kalie had to admit it did a fine job of stripping the accumulated filth from their hair, but she would have preferred the feeling of hair washed with water and lavender to the greasy brown locks that

now hung down her back. Looking at her friends, she
saw, for the first time since they left their homes in the
west, the rainbow of tresses that had once so
captivated their enemies: Alessa's raven black,
Larren's golden brown, Dara's honey blonde, Kestra
and Traea, both vibrant shades of red. Only Sarhene,
who wore her thinning brown hair short, failed to
shine.

A command from outside caused the three
horsewomen to grab their veils, wrap them tightly
around their heads and leave the tent. The tent flap
opened again, and a different horsewoman entered.
But what she carried made Kalie forget about the
others: a quartered section of a recently butchered
goat. *Food at last!*

Alessa offered to help prepare it, but was
rudely pushed away, so she settled for watching.
Kestra and Dara were curled together off to one side,
lost in restless sleep. Kalie envied them. She turned to
watch the nomad woman roasting the meat over a
brazier, and preparing cakes of flat bread, which were
in turn cooked in the goat fat, which dripped onto a
flat ceramic griddle below.

The food, when it was ready, did not amount to
much when divided among seven hungry women, but
after days of far less, it scarcely mattered. The meat
was greasy and tough compared to what Kalie was
used to. The bread, while strange at first, was
something she thought she could get used to. When the
food was gone, the nomad woman took a leather bag
from the folds of her robe and drank from it greedily.
After Sahrene begged for a while, she grudgingly gave
it to the foreigner. Sahrene took a gulp and gagged.

"What is this? Horse piss?" she demanded.

The nomad woman looked genuinely puzzled.

"Let me try." Kalie reached out and took the familiar looking container made from the bladder of a horse. She gingerly tasted the contents and grimaced as the name returned to her. "Kumis," she said. "Fermented mare's milk."

The nomad grabbed the bag with a curse and held it protectively.

"They prefer it to water," Kalie explained. "Of course, given what life is probably like for her, I can see why an intoxicant would be valued. The stuff the men drink is much stronger."

"She can have it!" Sahrene said. "I just want water."

After some negotiation, a skin of tepid water was provided. The newcomers had just finished off the last drops when the tent flap was pulled back and a man stuck his head inside. The nomad woman grabbed for her veil and shrank back trying to cover herself, clearly disconcerted at having a man enter the tent. Or maybe it was the identity of the man.

Haraak shoved a torch inside and peered at the women, who were nearly blinded by the sudden light. He gave a grunt of approval and ordered them to come with him. Kalie and the others reached for the ragged remains of their clothing, but Haraak growled angrily and shook his head. "You come now! As you are!" he commanded.

All at once, Kalie understood, but her fists clenched around an imaginary knife. "Come," she said, moving to the tent opening, and beckoning the others before they could get hurt. "Their king must be ready to see the prizes Haraak and the others brought back. Apparently, he wants to see us without our clothes."

Kalie caught Haraak's eye just before she crawled through the opening. *I will make you beg for death*, she promised silently. It was only an instant, but she thought she saw him flinch.

# Chapter 15

The dark night took Kalie by surprise. How long had they been in that tent? Torches were carried by men who hurried to a huge open area in front of the largest tent of all. It was here the captive women were led. Men leered openly at them while the women who crouched in tent doorways hissed and spat, until being ordered back inside by the men.

Alessa held her head high and made no attempt to cover her nakedness. Sighing with admiration, Kalie tried to do the same. After all, what had any of them to be ashamed of? The shame belonged to those who had done this to them.

Men were gathered before the large tent. In the flickering torchlight the crowd of warriors—Kalie guessed at least three hundred stinking, greasy beastmen were packed into the open area—looked like monsters out of a nightmare. Their faces bore garish tattoos; many had scars as well. Some had hair spiked upon their heads, held in place with grease or mud. All of them looked at the women with undisguised lust.

A space of about ten paces by twenty was kept clear in front of the big tent. Kalie and the others were pushed through the grasping, prodding men into this area, where they were told to kneel before the tent. Traea nearly landed on a basket before she knew it was there. As the women settled themselves in the open space, they realized that they were seated among the baskets of tribute that had been paid to make the beastmen leave the Land of the Goddess: knives of copper, gold and silver jewelry, bolts of fine linen—and the women themselves.

All of the warriors who had been at Riverford were present and, Kalie noticed, dressed up—as far as that went for beastmen. They wore new leather pants and boots, and were bristling with sharp weapons. Silver and gold jewelry sparked from arms and throats. Haraak was decked out most elaborately of all. Over a shirt of white linen, he sported a blue woolen cape, lined with the fur of a silver wolf. An elaborate copper knife rode on his belt. Kalie recognized the work of a talented young smith she had known briefly in Riverford. She wondered what Haraak would say if he knew the smith was a woman.

As hot as the days were on the steppes, the nights were cold. The seven captive women huddled together for warmth and courage.

"What if the king recognizes you?" Dara whispered beside her.

"Ahnaak was not king of the tribe who captured me while I lived there. It was while the two tribes fought that I think I must have escaped." Kalie caught her breath as from some hidden place inside her, memories surged forth.

Not now! I need to be focused on the present, not lost in the past!

When Kalie came to herself again, her friends were looking at her with concern, while the noisy beasts around them grew even louder and more frightening. She gave them a tremulous smile meant to reassure, but which probably fell short of its intended purpose. "Ahnaak won that battle—and I suppose, so did I. I gained my freedom and returned home, while he made himself king of the Twenty Clans of Aahk— that's the name of their chief god. What has kept our people safe all this time is the fact that these tribes are always fighting among themselves. Culling their own herds, as it were."

"That and the fact that they didn't know we existed," said Larren.

"But now they know about us," whispered Alessa. "And if one of their tribes becomes large enough, and motivated enough—"

"The treasures of our world will be enough to motivate them," said Sahrene. "And if Ahnaak is strong enough to lead a whole gathering of tribes to the west—"

"Yes," said Kalie. "That is the danger—but also our solution. Ahnaak is a brutal man, feared by all. Hated by many. Without him, there will be no gathering of the tribes. And once he is dead, his two oldest sons will fight each other to take his place. And each of them will have followers to fight for them."

"What if—" Alessa began, but then a man struck her from behind and ordered the women silent. Alessa flung out her arms to protect the women next to her before turning to face her attacker. Kalie saw a moment of naked shock on the man's face as he regarded the women. *You are not used to people who respond to an attack by seeking to protect those around them*, she thought as she looked brazenly into the man's eyes. *Good. It will be your undoing.*

Then the gathered men fell silent, and there was an air of hushed expectancy.

The tent flap opened, and a large, gray bearded man strode into the night. A stout woman who seemed to be all gray beneath her robes and veil followed. A boy of about ten followed with a stool made of spindly wood—a rarity in this land—and set it before the tent.

All of the men knelt.

"Arise, my son!" said the man who still stood.

Kariik rose to his feet, looking uncomfortable. "I have returned from the west, my king and my father."

"So I see," said Ahnaak. "And with many fewer men than you left with. Yet, I think you bring treasures and stories that may help make up for that loss!"

With that, Haraak and the others stood. "Indeed it is so, Ahnaak, my king. Behold the riches of the West!" He gestured to his men, who brought forward the baskets. "Knives and spearheads of copper! Ornaments of gold and silver! Fabrics and furs to adorn your wife or favorite concubine—or your mighty self. Slave girls to serve in your tent and warm your bed. Even such delicacies as honey and fruits unknown in this land!"

"But not unknown for much longer, I think." Ahnaak kept an expression of mild amusement on his face, but Kalie could tell he was impressed. "My son tells me that it was you who rescued him from the barbarians, and made them pay heavily for their treachery."

"It is so," Haraak began proudly. "We traveled beyond the western edge of the world." Kalie, a storyteller herself, was impressed by his practiced cadence, and listened carefully for any information that might help her. "There we met men like no other. In truth, they cannot be called men, for they own neither tents nor horses. Instead they squat each day in the dirt, and grow food from the ground. And they bow to women!" Roars of disbelief greeted his words.

"The cowards fell to our spears like new-weaned lambs, and we rode over them as easily as grass. We took much plunder. Prince Kariik wisely divided us into groups, placing myself in charge of one, with Merik and Utaak commanding the others, that we might more quickly claim all this land in the name of our great king."

Haraak paused, turning to Kariik, clearly expecting him to take up the tale. The young prince only shook his head, and waited for Haraak to continue. "Here, our prince and his band reached an abomination: a kind of rabbit warren built of mud, stretching across a plain that should have contained nothing but good grass for horses. Inside dwelt more barbarians than our entire tribe. But when their enemy approached, did they stand and fight like men? No! They crawled inside their warren and cowered like women!"

Kalie was impressed by the way Haraak held the crowd spellbound with his words.

"With only three hands of men, Kariik rode forth boldly, to punish those who would dare build such a thing, and then hide inside it. But we were unprepared for the treachery of such cowards..."

Ah, now he comes to the part where those idiots tried to cross the footbridge on horseback, Kalie thought.

"They were cunning enough to set a trap for us," Kariik spoke up through shut teeth.

Haraak hastily took up the tale once more, failing to elaborate on the "trap. Through their greater numbers, the weaklings were able to kill nearly half the war band, and subdue the rest. But only briefly, my king."

Now Haraak glared at Kariik, demanding that he finish the tale. Nervously, the young prince took a deep breath and plunged into his rehearsed speech. "After only a few days in the hands of our enemies, Haraak arrived with all our remaining forces. Though still outnumbered many hundreds to one, he boldly demanded the release of the hostages—" Kariik, not nearly as good a storyteller as Haraak, struggled to finish the tale. "Haraak secured, not only our freedom, but all the tribute you see before you." He swept his hand to indicate the baskets and the women, which now belonged to King Ahnaak.

Ahnaak thanked his son gravely and began, with great ceremony, to make gifts of the spoils to his clan chiefs and various other warriors. Kalie scanned the eager crowd for the faces of men who had come to her land to take what was not theirs, and who took pride in murdering unarmed strangers.

How had they felt, she wondered, when they became the prisoners of people they had so horribly abused, and found themselves treated with compassion and kindness? Did that change anything inside them? Or did they simply take it as a sign of weakness?

One by one, she found them. One was the man who had shown an interest in carving while he recovered in the temple of healing. Riyik, she thought his name was. As Kalie gazed at him now, she noticed he looked uncomfortable, as if he couldn't wait to be gone from the crowd. *That makes two of us*, she thought. *But guess which of us will be free to leave when the ceremony is over?*

Another man, seated close to the king, had actually been rather friendly—to the men of Riverford, at least—and had taught the city folk a game played with carved pieces of bone, stained red on one side and black on the other. Kalie couldn't remember his name, but he had been as eager to learn his captors' games of chance and forms of wagering, as Riyik had been to carve.

Throughout the whole journey east, Maris had insisted until the day she died that if they had only had more time, the people of the Goddess would have won the beastmen over to the ways of the Goddess through the sharing of things as simple as games and crafts.

Seated farthest from the king, a position Kalie knew to be one of disfavor, was the still heavily bandaged man whom Shara had fought and maimed. Kalie allowed herself a small smile in his direction before once again lowering her eyes.

The night grew even colder, and the torches did little to warm the naked women. The jewelry, tools, fabrics, and foods had been handed out. Now it was the turn of the women.

One by one, Larren, Dara, Kestra and Traea were given by the generous king to warriors who had served him well. Alessa was given to a man named Tarnaak, while Kalie was given to a man named Maalke. Kalie twisted her fingers together as she waited for a sign from a Goddess she no longer believed in. With only one woman left, Ahnaak made quite a show of keeping only ugly, disfigured Sahrene for himself, apparently as a gift to his wife. This caused much laughter among the men.

The king's stout, gray wife was already pulling Sahrene into the great tent, but she resisted long enough to find Kalie in the torchlight and meet her eyes with a look of grim determination. If a way existed, Sahrene would find it and kill King Ahnaak.

Kalie returned her attention to the men and caught a reference to Maylene. She would be staying

with Kariik as they had expected. Kalie heard the word
"concubine" and tried to remember what it meant, but
the cold and the noise of the crowd made it difficult to
think in her own tongue, let alone the beastmen's.
Naked and shivering, Kalie was actually grateful when
a veiled woman arrived and led her to the stinking—
but warm—tent of her new owner.

# Chapter 16

Kalie stepped out of the tent, and drew in deep breaths of clean, cold air. Her breath made frosty clouds as it left her body, and she pulled the mangy sheepskin more tightly around her felt robe, grateful for what little warmth they provided.

Hard to believe that when she arrived here just a moonspan ago, the land had been hot and dry. Now the grass was coated with frost, and heavy clouds blocked the light of the rising sun. Yet there had been little rain. In this world, it seemed, searing hot summer went directly into bitterly cold winter, with scarcely a day to catch up to the change.

"What are you standing there for, you lazy bitch?" Kalie wasn't fast enough to dodge the blow that caught her on the side of the head. Altia, senior wife to Maalke, loomed above her, red faced and glowering. Quite a trick, Kalie reflected, for someone so much shorter than herself. Shorter, but much fiercer.

"Get dung," Altia commanded, thrusting a basket into Kalie's hands. Kalie silently joined the other slave women at the early morning task of gathering dung from the animal pens. In a land without trees, dried dung served as fuel. It was ingenious, Kalie had to admit. Just one of many adaptations these people had developed which allowed them to live in a place Kalie would have dismissed as unlivable.

It was a pity they couldn't do the same with their behavior.

She spotted Alessa across the camp, already bent to work on the same task. Kalie moved towards her, gathering dung as she went, trying to make her movements seem unplanned. While she had been prepared for many aspects of life as a slave among the beastmen, there were still so many things that took her by surprise. The rules against a woman consorting with anyone from any household but her master, for example.

But a few moments with a friend was worth the risk. Apparently, Alessa felt the same way, for when Kalie straightened, depositing a particularly vile smelling lump of goat dung in her half filled basket, Alessa was by her side.

"Blessings of the Goddess." Alessa did not press her palms together in the gesture that normally accompanied the greeting, for that was sure to draw attention. "How do you fare?" The young healer's gaze lingered on Kalie's face, where a bruise was probably forming.

"Still breathing. And you?"

"Well enough. I'm glad we have a chance to speak; it might be our last for awhile."

"Why? What have you heard?"

"The tribe will be splitting up and moving to their winter camps," Alessa said, gently moving aside a young goat and bending down for more dung. Kalie followed suit. "The men will be leaving in a few days for some kind of horse sacrifice. When they return it will be time to leave."

It took Kalie a moment to see the full implications. While she had only a rudimentary understanding of the twenty clans that made up the Tribe of Aahk, she knew that her master, Maalke, fought under Kahlar, while Alessa's owner fought for one of the others. She thought of each of the other surviving women: none of them, she realized, lived in Kahlar's clan. She was about to lose her last link with her past.

Alessa touched her gently on the arm. "It will be all right. Perhaps splitting up among the various groups will allow us to work more effectively among the women. From what I can tell, they treasure the time when the men are gone. Perhaps we can bring the Goddess to them, if we are gentle about it."

Gentle? thought Kalie. They'd first have to explain the concept to the women who lived here. "Did you hear about Sahrene?" she asked.

Alessa looked away. "I was there when it happened. She saw a woman beating a child, and ran to stop her. I couldn't tell if she died from the blow the woman struck, or when her husband put his spear through her."

"So it appears our plan and the Goddess's were not one and the same. Sahrene died uselessly without ever having the chance to—" Kalie broke off, afraid even here, of being overheard. Then she and Alessa would die like Sahrene had—without accomplishing anything.

Alessa reached for Kalie's hands, clearly ready to offer comfort and hope, but Kalie stepped back and shook her head. "Haraak was, perhaps, embarrassed," Kalie said a little too quickly as she sought to keep her voice from shaking. "So some good may have come of it. What about Maylene? I haven't seen her at all."

"Kariik has just been made chief of one of the clans. Maylene came to see me—without an escort, not that either of us knew what that meant or why it was needed. She's pregnant, did you know? But when Kariik learned she had gone, he became quite enraged, and she hasn't been allowed outside his tent since. And I haven't been allowed inside, though several older horsewomen who I suspect are midwives have been in and out of the tent."

"I wonder if he's beaten her into a miscarriage," said Kalie. "Or killed her."

Alessa's grip tightened on Kalie's arm. "Please, Kalie. Don't dwell on the worst possibilities. It's bad for all of us."

In the silence that followed, they watched as some warrior's wife standing at the door of her tent began beating a girl of about ten years. Alessa sagged as if defeated; as if the Goddess had chosen that moment to show them both how much of "the worst" was daily fare in this place.

"Do you know who she is?" Kalie asked.

"Tia. She used to live where I live now. Her mother is a slave, so Tia is, too. Her father sold her to another warrior, but she keeps sneaking back to see her mother. When I first arrived, it was Anya, the mother who was being beaten for trying to see her daughter."

"Why do they do it?" Kalie asked suddenly. "How did hatred become a religion in this place?"

Alessa, staring out past the herd of horses and across the endless grass, seemed not to hear at first. Then she said, "Because it's the only thing they have in plenty." Shaking herself as if coming out of a trance, Alessa explained. "Look at how these people live. This land is barren. Things you and I take for granted—water, shade, any kind of food, clothing or shelter that didn't start out with hooves—are scarcities that have to be fought for. They live through bitter cold in the winter, searing heat in the summer; no one is spared. These people must grow up thinking Mother Earth hates them!

"As for how men came into all the power, I'm not yet sure, but I can see why they want to keep it. They get to enjoy the most of what little there is to have and, more importantly, they get to decide who gets what's left. It's as if…as if once you take enough away from a people, they'll just redefine what's good or worth having to match the environment. And here, what's good and worth having is power over others, and control over the sources of life."

Kalie, who had had more than seven years to think about it, had never thought of it quite that way before.

"We have to find out what the men are planning," she said. "How soon they plan to bring this *new environment* to the land of the Goddess."

"It is as you have said, Kalie," Alessa said with a certainty Kalie found surprising. "Not before spring. So we have all this long winter to unravel whatever plots these men have woven."

"We should try to meet while the men are away at their blood letting," Kalie said. "All of us, if we can get away."

Alessa smiled. "The night the men leave is the first night of the full moon. I take that as a sign from the Goddess."

Kalie, who had never admitted to anyone how little faith she had left, felt a surprising rush of strength. She gazed across the flat, treeless expanse of steppe, suddenly aching for the sacred groves where she had worshipped as a child.

"Perhaps the lack of trees means only that the power of the Goddess will flow unfiltered into us when we need it most," Alessa said, as if hearing Kalie's thoughts. "Or perhaps She means for us to be a beacon to the women who this land has bound, who only need to see that another way exists to make themselves free."

Kalie shook her head, knowing it was futile to wish for Alessa's unwavering faith. "Tell who you can about the meeting, and I will do the same."

The other slaves were struggling to carry their laden baskets back to the shelter of the tents, their bodies bent against the howling wind. Kalie and Alessa embraced quickly and moved to follow.

By the time Kalie reached Maalke's tent her face and hands were raw with cold. The one sheepskin she had been given did little to protect her body in these temperatures. She pulled aside the felt tent flap and crawled into the relative warmth of burning dung and unwashed bodies, too cold to even take an extra gulp of clean air before the tent flap closed behind her.

She set the basket by the fire, where Varena, Maalke's young daughter by a slave—and therefore slave herself—began to set the dung out to dry on a flat leather tray. Two younger girls sat between Varena and the fire, combing wool with nettle switches in preparation for making felt. They were also daughters of Maalke, but by his senior wife, and therefore not slaves—although Kalie could see precious little difference. Tasine, a foreign slave like Kalie, and the oldest woman in the tent, stirred a porridge of starchy roots, grain and goat meat over the fire.

Altia sat on her stuffed felt cushion and supervised the work in progress. Her legs were crossed in the manner of the nomads. While Kalie supposed it was comfortable enough, and practical in the limited space of the tent, she knew it also allowed Altia to show off her slippers. They were soft leather, lined with wool, and very warm. They were also beaded in intricate designs—on the soles. Such delicate work would be destroyed if the slippers were actually walked in upon hard ground, so their main purpose was to demonstrate the status of the wearer as one who could spend large amounts of time sitting in a tent and doing nothing.

While hunger was a constant, and the smell of the porridge made everyone's mouth water, Kalie knew they would not eat until Maalke had appeared and eaten his fill. The grunting noises that emerged from his sleeping area told them why they weren't eating yet. But, Kalie reflected sourly, knowing Maalke, it wouldn't be that much longer.

"What took you so long?" Altia demanded. "Maalke wanted you this morning and you weren't here."

Laughter came from a dark corner of the tent where Irisa reclined in a pile of warm furs, rubbing oil from rendered sheep's fat on her huge naked belly. "He's with Cassia now. Already he begins to lose interest in you, Kalie."

"I pray to the Goddess that he does," Kalie said, smiling at Irisa in a way that was all teeth. "That I may never feel his vile touch or inhale his stench again."

She felt a moment's satisfaction as Altia nearly fell off her cushion and Irisa drew her arms across her belly, making a sign to ward off evil with both hands.

"Be silent, or I'll cut out your tongue!" Altia hissed.

"Why do you say such things?" Irisa yelped.

"What else should I say?" Kalie shot back. "That this crazy world of yours is normal? That after watching your men murder my family I should then fall in love with the animal that beats and rapes me? Or compete with you for the pleasure of his favor?" She looked at them all with a contempt that made even Altia flinch. "That may be your way, but it will never be mine."

"It is the only way there is," Altia said coldly. "Do you think anyone here believes your wild stories about a land where women rule and every day is summer?"

Kalie bit back a sigh of frustration. If they didn't believe her, couldn't they at least remember her stories correctly? "That still does not explain why you fight each other over men who hurt you—and hurt your children! Even the lowest she-wolf in the pack will protect her children with her life. But you..." she glared at Irisa. "If Maalke finds your baby unacceptable, you will do nothing while he feeds it to his dogs—other than spread your legs so he can fill you with another. What does that make you?"

Irisa screamed. "I will kill you for threatening my baby!" she hissed, but she was shaking in terror, frantically making every sign of protection she knew over her pregnant belly.

"If you had the brain of a flea, Irisa, you would know that I would never harm a child," Kalie said. "A pity the same can't be said of your baby's father—or his wives!"

Altia leapt at Kalie with her fists doubled, but Kalie was ready this time and leapt aside, tripping the older woman in the process. "I speak the truth and you know it! Why do you strike me for naming your madness, and not the men who make these horrors a reality?" Her anger boiling over, Kalie longed to feel her hands around Altia's throat, though it would mean her death. At this moment, she was ready for it.

The crisis was averted when the tent flap flew open, bringing in a freezing wind that nearly doused the flames that danced in the brazier. The women fluttered like angry geese, wrestling the tent closed and twisting themselves away from the cold. A fury bundle rolled across the carpeted floor, righting itself and emerging as a boy of about twelve summers, clad in a heavy sheepskin jacket, close fitting leather trousers and fur lined boots. Tarak, Altia's son and Maalke's heir had come by to greet his mother—and get himself a hot meal.

Altia hurried to embrace her son, the rage that had contorted her face a moment ago gone. "My young warrior! How big you have grown," she said with pride.

Tarak stiffened and rolled his eyes. "A woman does not speak so to a warrior," he reminded her. "Is there any food left?"

"We have not yet eaten," Altia said, but she hurried to dish out a large bowl of meaty porridge for her son. Her two daughters edged forward hopefully, but she ignored them. Tarak had just begun eating when the leather curtains which separated Maalke's sleeping area rustled and Maalke emerged, followed by his second wife, Cassia.

He spoke no words of greeting, only squatted by the fire and waited to be served. Altia stepped out of her slippers, leaving them in a corner of the tent, and quickly scooped a large serving of porridge into a costly wooden bowl. Irisa stood by with a heavy skin of kumis and filled Maalke's drinking vessel—a human skull; one of several he kept for the purpose.

Once Maalke had all he required, he spoke to his son. "What have you learned this season in the young warriors' tent?"

Tarak swallowed a large mouthful rather too quickly, and nearly choked in his eagerness to answer. When he recovered, the boy began to recount his recent adventures. From what Kalie had been able to gather, boys left their father's tents at about eight or nine years, to live in their own community where they did nothing but train to be warriors. They were taught and supervised by seasoned fighters, away from the softening influences of women. When he was about fifteen, a boy would pass through some sort of manhood ceremony—timed to coincide with an upcoming fight whenever possible. But he was not fully a man until he had slain an enemy in battle.

"Riyik is giving me extra training with the bow," Tarak was saying. "He says I have potential. And Kuraat says he will take the best of us to hunt wolf this winter!"

*It isn't winter yet?* Kalie shuddered. Then she saw how Altia paled visibly. Wolf hunting was a dangerous sport, never more so than in winter. She could only pray her son would not be among those chosen to participate—but she would never say such a thing aloud.

But Maalke only nodded proudly, and began to recount a tale of when he had hunted wolf when he was Tarak's age. Kalie's interest sharpened, for here was a chance to learn how beastmen told stories. If she could learn what they liked hearing, she could begin to tell them. Women were allowed to serve as entertainers for the warriors. Kalie already knew of singers and dancers, though so far, no storytellers. Perhaps she would be the first. The information she could gain that way would be valuable beyond anything she had so far, and just possibly, bring her close enough to the king to end his reign.

"...Pure demon, he was, but now we had him," Maalke was saying. "First Haraak, then me, we opened up wound after wound on him, red like his eyes. I felt my strength rise as he weakened..." Kalie savored her meager ration of food, while she listened. She had changed, she realized. Once, Maalke's sickening account of slaying an animal for sport, and enjoying his suffering would have rendered her unable to eat. Now, it did not even slow her down.

By the time Maalke had finished his tale, the food was gone. Tarak took his leave to return to the warriors' tent.

"Tomorrow, the men will leave for the sacrifices," Maalke told Altia. "Have my flocks ready for the journey to winter camp. Is my household fully supplied?"

Altia bowed her head demurely. "Yes, husband. As always."

"Slay two goats and prepare them as you do, with the mint gravy, for my contribution to the feast. And go to Garik's tent. There will be the fur of a western creature called a lynx waiting." Maalke grinned. "He lost it to me in a throw of knucklebones last night. He will regret his ill luck when he sees the cloak I will have from it this winter."

Altia nodded, and waited until Maalke wrapped himself in his thick sheepskin cloak and left the tent. Then she began assigning the day's duties to the others in the tent.

"Irisa, see to making the last of the kumis and cheese. Tasine, bring out the herbs I will need to cook the goats. Kalie, help my daughters with the felt. We must have five more pieces before we leave. Varena, go to Gariks's tent for the fur."

Kalie saw Varena cringe at the thought of going outside. The howling wind had increased since she had been out earlier, and Varena, a thin and scrawny child, had less hope than Kalie of surviving this winter—even within the warmth of the tent.

Kalie felt a moment's rage that Maalke—well fed and warmly dressed—could not bother to do his own errands. If he wants a cloak of stolen lynx fur, let him collect it from the other thief himself! For that matter, let him sew it into a cloak himself! She looked at Varena and tried not to care how frail she was, and how little her worn leather cloak would protect her on the long walk through camp to Garik's tent.

She gave up. She couldn't kill all feeling within her, no matter how hard she tried. And why should she try? Alessa didn't. "Wait, Varena," Kalie said. "Take my cloak as well." She wrapped the old sheepskin around the startled slave girl.

"Why do you do this for me?" Varena asked. "I can do nothing for you."

"You can live," Kalie said lightly. Then, more softly, "Perhaps you can be my friend."

Varena scowled. "You wish to befriend Maalke's daughter?" She pointed to her two half sisters. "They are right there! I am bastard. I mean nothing to him, so I can do nothing for you." She began to take off the sheepskin.

"None of us mean anything to Maalke," said

Kalie. "So perhaps we can look after each other. I'm not loaning you my cloak for what I might get from you."

"Then why?" Varena asked, truly puzzled.

"Because where I come from, it's what anyone would do. Maybe some day, I can take you there, and then you'll understand."

"Varena, hurry up!" Altia yelled.

The slave girl ducked a vicious blow and scurried outside.

At a glare from Altia, Kalie went to the fire, where Maalke's two "legitimate" daughters—Kalie tried to remember the word and why it was important —were giggling over the wool they were pounding into felt.

"Stupid barbarian!" the older one said. She was about nine; two or three years younger than Varena, but still considered Maalke's eldest daughter. "What will you do with no cloak if my mother sends you to work outside?" She grinned at her sister, probably hoping Kalie would expect the loan of a cloak from one of the others.

"Don't worry," Kalie said. "My hatred of this place will keep me warm."

# Chapter 17

Kalie stepped carefully over the sleeping bodies in the tent. Working loose the knot that held the tent flap closed, she slipped outside, blinking in surprise. A sable sky filled with cracked ice covered the land like a huge inverted bowl. Never had Kalie seen such a sky! Were there that many stars above her home in the west? She would never have thought so.

The ever-present steppe wind blew mildly tonight—at least by the standards of this land. Perhaps enough to allow the women time to actually accomplish something before the freezing cold drove them back inside the tents.

If anyone besides Kalie showed up.

The snow was piled high beyond the tamped down area of the camp. Kalie slid her snowshoes— another ingenious invention, she had to admit—over the boots she already had on, and began to tramp across the camp. She reached clean, new snow and was nearly at the place they were supposed to meet before she saw anyone.

Larren and Alessa were standing together on a sheet of snow that threw the moonlight back into the sky. Between the full moon, the countless stars and the reflective power of the snow, it was nearly as bright as day. But it was an alien brightness: magical, to be sure, but not her kind of magic.

Kalie greeted her two friends. "Are we all?" she asked.

"Traea will be here if she can," said Larren. "She will have to wait until all the women of the tent are asleep. Unlike Alessa, here, who told the women of her tent where she was going and invited them to come along!"

Kalie turned wide eyes to Alessa. "You didn't!"

Alessa shrugged and flashed an embarrassed smile. "There are only three other women in my tent. Zarah, Tarnaak's wife, has been ill, and very appreciative of the medicines I brew. Since she plans to sleep the whole time the men are gone, I thought I would ask the slave woman and the daughter to come with me. They declined, but they are becoming more and more interested in the stories I tell. Perhaps next time..." She broke off as a fur covered figure approached. Traea. They greeted her warmly.

"I may not be able to stay long," she said. "I had to, uh, *persuade* Goat-dung to let me leave. When she's able to move again, she'll probably come after me and drag me back, and I don't want any of you getting hurt."

"Goat-dung?" echoed Larren.

"That's what I call her. She hasn't bothered to learn my name, so I thought I'd return the favor."

"Did you really hurt her?" Kalie asked, wondering if it wasn't just wishful thinking on Traea's part.

But Traea nodded, looking very slightly ashamed. "A nasty trick I learned my first day here. A hard thrust, right here." She indicated her belly, and then mimed a clenched fist punching into it.

"But you are a slave, she is a wife," said Alessa. "What will you do when the man—what do they call them? Husband—gets back? Won't she demand that he punish you?"

Now Traea actually smiled, though without

warmth. "I can handle him. For a while longer at least. These men know nothing about joining. I don't think Gorik had ever been with a willing woman in his life. Let's just say he was unprepared for how much pleasure he could get from a partner with knowledge and skill. For the moment, at least, I have power in that tent. Until he tires of me, at least."

"Goat-dung must be terrified," said Kalie.

Traea shrugged. "She has two sons. Her position is secure. If she wants to fight me over that swine's 'affections', let her. Maybe she'll grow so angry she'll burst a lung, and I could, perhaps, make things better for the other women in that stinking tent."

"Any word from Kestra or Dara?" Kalie asked.

Traea's manner changed abruptly. "Kestra won't be coming. She said she dare not displease her master."

"She won't sneak out even when he is away?" Larren sounded worried. "She must be terrified of his wife."

"Kestra *is* his wife!" cried Traea. "Or at least she's the only woman in the tent! I don't understand it! She's alone in the tent! There's no one to stop her— she just won't leave! I went there on my way here, and she was just sitting in the middle of the stinking tent, with her feet crossed, staring off into space, rubbing these awful beaded slippers her owner gave her. She wouldn't even look at me!"

"Did she say anything?" asked Alessa. "Other than that she was afraid?"

Traea looked at each of the other three, then away. "She said we shouldn't come out here tonight. That the Mother is an abomination and the gods will punish us all."

Kalie, who thought she was prepared for anything, suddenly grew very cold.

Larren tried to laugh. "That's ridiculous! Does she think she's a beastwoman…?" She broke off as the answer slowly sank in.

"How could this happen?" Alessa asked Kalie. The others seemed to expect an answer as well.

"Perhaps we should ask the Goddess," Kalie replied. "This is Her sacred time, after all." But she wasn't expecting an answer.

Now all eyes turned to Alessa, the only priestess here. If they were to worship at all tonight, it would be for her to lead them. Alessa, however, was looking toward the camp, as another figure, moving awkwardly, came toward them.

"Maylene!" Kalie cried, finally recognizing her. "How did you get out? We heard you couldn't even leave the tent to relieve yourself."

Maylene was breathing hard, and sweating more than was normal for such minor exercise as walking across camp. Then again, thought Kalie, it was more exertion than she'd had in some time. Maylene rubbed the growing mound of her belly, just visible beneath her fine linen tunic.

"I told Kariik's mother, who rules the tent, that I feared a miscarriage, and had to offer a sacrifice to my gods beneath a full moon. And that if she stopped me and I lost it, I would swear to Kariik that it was her fault—and call every women in the tent to bear witness that on this night, I had sought the only means that might have saved it!"

Kalie choked on her laughter, as much as at Maylene's naiveté as at her boldness. "Do you think for a moment any of those women would speak against one of the king's own wives?"

Maylene looked older than her fifteen years. "I think they fear the gods of this place at least as much as they fear the other women."

"It seems to have worked," said Traea.

"I hope so," said Maylene. "When I left she was shrieking curses at me. Something about the baby not being Kariik's. Apparently, that's the worst insult anyone can offer a woman around here." The women exchanged puzzled looks, and then shrugged.

"Is that her?" Everyone turned to where Alessa pointed. An old woman, wrapped in the richest furs this land had to offer stood out of the wind between the last tents in the camp.

"Yes," said Maylene. "Baraha, fourth wife of Ahnaak, mistress of his third son's tent. She dreads the day her son takes a wife who will displace her, but dares not let any harm befall his favored concubine."

"I would think a foreign wife would be the perfect solution to her problem," said Kalie. "You know nothing of how to manage a prince's tent. You would be wife in name, but she would give all the orders."

"I suspect that may be the only reason I'm still alive," said Maylene. "Come, we haven't much time and there is much to discuss."

"What have you learned?" Kalie asked.

"Ahnaak is growing weak, both physically and politically. Kariik has no ambition to be king—and would be incompetent if he tried—but his two older brothers are already preparing to fight for leadership of the tribe once their father is gone."

"Any chance someone is planning to help him die sooner than might be natural?" Kalie asked.

"Ahnaak seems to think so. He came to Kariik's tent complaining about treachery in the hearts of those closest to him and the many sorrows of kingship. Apparently, he doesn't see his third son as a threat, so he speaks freely to him. But so far, I can't tell who might be planning murder—besides us, I mean—or what that will mean, once the power shifts."

"Does anyone else know?" Kalie asked. "We came here thinking that one of us would slay Ahnaak, but if one of his own men wants to do it for us…"

"It could go worse for us," said Larren, "if Haraak takes control."

"Haraak?" Kalie echoed.

"He's come to visit Tarnaak a few times," Alessa said. "But from what I overheard, no one sees him as a threat. He's a younger son of a minor warrior who died when Haraak was still a boy. Until the attack on our people, he had never come to the attention of the king. Or anyone else for that matter."

Larren nodded. "After the attack, he thought his fortune was made, and indeed, it was, for awhile. He received many invitations to hunt and train with warriors close to the king, and share meals in their tents. Everyone wanted to hear his stories of the west."

Kalie remembered his skill at storytelling that first night in this land, and could well believe it.

"But when he began pushing for a full scale invasion of our world," Maylene said, "people stopped listening. Or, at least the king did."

"Ahnaak is not preparing for an invasion?" Kalie cried, surprised. For all that this mission was her idea, she had learned far less than the women who had followed her here.

Now Maylene was nodding. "I know it's not

what we expected, but these people are very
superstitious, and they fear change more than almost
anything. Haraak has been in Kariik's tent as well,
flattering him, trying to get him to influence his father
to lead the whole tribe west in the spring. But Ahnaak
fears his gods will desert him if he leaves the steppes.
So do many of his warriors."

"We could play their fears against them," said
Kalie. "Especially if I succeed in becoming a
storyteller for the warriors." She decided not to
mention how badly that plan was going.

Maylene was glancing nervously at Kariik's
mother. "She can see this is no religious rite," said the
young woman.

"Then by all means, let us have one," said
Alessa. "Whether she can recognize it or not."

Kalie thought about arguing: she would have
liked more information. But this might be her last
chance to worship with others of her kind, and who
knew? Perhaps the Goddess still existed, even in this
place. And even if She didn't, coming together one last
time in Her name might turn out to be as important as
their more secular scheming.

The women began shedding their veils and
outer clothing. They would have liked to strip away all
the clothing that so denigrated them in this place, and
perform the rite naked, as they would have back home.
But the freezing weather overrode that desire.
Standing beneath the moon in felt or linen shifts and
leather shoes, the women shook out their long hair,
and joined hands to begin the dance.

As they moved in a circle, Kalie felt strength
she had forgotten she had flowing back into her. The
moon overhead—always a source of power for women

—was the same one that shone over their homes in the west. Alessa began to chant, somehow managing to combine a song of praise with a plea for help.

The circle broke apart as each woman found her own rhythms and danced with only the earth and moon as partners. The snow-crusted earth, cold and hard beneath their feet, still pulsed with the power of their Goddess. Kalie felt it flow up through her feet, spread throughout her body, and fill her with light. More and more she drew it inside her, until it demanded to be released. Finally she sent it upward through her fingers, flinging her arms wide as she spun in her own circle, intersecting with those the other four women spun, but never actually colliding.

At last they were spent, the dance finished, the power safely grounded back into the earth. They collapsed on the ground as they always did after such dancing; only to hurry back to their feet as the freezing snow threatened to suck the warmth from their bodies. Awkwardly, they began to dress, and prepare to resume their lives as slaves.

"Look!" Larren cried suddenly. Kalie turned back to the settlement, expecting to see Baraha and perhaps Goat-dung march menacingly across the snow to retrieve their missing property. Instead, at least a dozen women were gathered at the edge of camp, staring at the foreigners from the west. None of them made any move toward the Goddess worshipers.

"Do you think they will tell the men?" Larren asked fearfully.

Traea laughed ruefully. "What we just did probably carries a death sentence here!"

Kalie shook her head. "They would never trouble the men over something as unimportant as women's religion—if they even have a word for it! And so what if they tried to explain what they saw? Would the men know what they were talking about? Would the women themselves?"

"Look!" said Alessa, as two of the skinniest, filthiest women Kalie had seen in this place ducked back behind one of the tents. They wore only rags despite the freezing temperature. "Those are Shadow Woman!"

"Goat-dung told me about them," said Traea. "But I thought that was just some nonsense she was making up to scare me."

"No, they're real," said Alessa.

"What are they?" Larren and Kalie asked together.

"Women who are cast out of their tents," said Maylene.

"Why?" asked Kalie. "If the man who owns them grows angry with them, he can simply kill them!"

"That happens often as well," said Alessa, her silent *as we all know* hanging in the frozen air. "This is something different. More merciful, perhaps, since it can be reversed. It is like our concept of banishment, but in plain sight. In this place, if a woman is cast out of her home, she must find someone in another tent to feed and shelter her, since she leaves with nothing. But few men in this land will interfere with a man's decision to cast out a woman."

"Of course," snapped Larren. "After all, he must have had a good reason!"

"Or they simply wish to stay out of it," said Maylene.

"If no one takes them in," Alessa continued,

"they must eat out of the midden and sleep in the elements. Eventually, they are either permitted to return home, or they die."

"So either way, the punishment is temporary," said Traea. "In this weather, I doubt those two will last more than a few days."

The warmth Kalie had found in the ritual dancing just moments ago turned very cold.

"Why don't the men just kill them?" Larren asked, a desperate edge to her voice.

"Much more effective at frightening the other women into obedience this way," said Alessa. "Come," she said, drawing a packet of carefully hoarded food from her robe. "Let's greet all of them in the Goddess's name, but share the food only with the Shadow Women. Perhaps they will have some questions for us."

# Chapter 18

Kalie and Varena struggled through the freezing wind to the rough shelter where the animals were kept during the winter. The wind cut off abruptly once they had passed the wall of the leather and felt lean to. With a sigh, Kalie slid the heavy bundle of dried grass off her back and began feeding the sheep and goats whose brands marked them as belonging to Maalke. Behind her, Varena did the same. Both watched carefully to make certain that only Maalke's animals ate from this carefully horded store of feed. All around them, other slave women did the same.

Goats and sheep of the steppes could forage on their own, even in winters as harsh as these, but fodder supplied by humans allowed more of them to live to bear young in the spring, and provide the humans with milk through the winter. Kalie had to smile at the snow-covered humps of wool, bunched together for warmth. Other than the shelter for the animals, the winter camp seemed no different from the summer camp. The tents and everything in them—most of which had been carried on the backs of the women—were all the same. The bleak and barren landscape was the same. And so was the endless round of work, deprivation, and cruelty.

Still, it was better than it had been. Maalke had lost interest in raping his newest slave, and Kalie hadn't gotten pregnant. Whether she was barren from the attacks of seven years ago, or simply lucky, she didn't know, but was she grateful just the same. And this morning before sunrise, most of the men had left on some grand winter hunting expedition, from which they might not return for several days. Kalie was openly delighted, but to her surprise, many of the other women were as well. Some of them—Irisa, especially —worried for their safety, but generally, there was a more relaxed air in the winter camp.

Varena had finished spreading the fodder and was already gathering dung. Kalie joined her, hoping they could finish quickly and return to the warmth of the tent. About half way through, Varena was seized by a coughing spell. Kalie caught the girl and kept her from falling in the snow as her body shook with spasms. Varena would probably die this winter, and there was nothing Kalie could do about it. That was the hardest part. She had spent enough years among healers to know how easily such an illness could be treated if one only had the right herbs. And no one here did—nor did they seem concerned about the lack.

At last, Varena recovered enough to continue working, but Kalie wouldn't let her. "I'll get the dung. You rest." Varena seemed grateful enough for the respite, though still puzzled by the kindness. Kalie would have preferred to send the girl back to the warmth of the tent, but Altia would surely beat her if she came back alone and without her share of dung.

Kalie finished filling her basket and turned to give it to Varena so she could return sooner to the tent while Kalie filled the other, but found the younger girl pushing her way through the munching sheep. One of them wasn't eating. In fact, as Kalie moved closer and peered at it, her eyes—only just learning how to see the nuances of this alien world— told her the sheep wasn't moving at all, though she was standing upright.

"She's dead," Varena said, her voice barely audible above the howling wind.

"Already frozen," Kalie said in disbelief.

"Quickly!" gasped Varena. "Help me carry it."

It took all their combined strength just to drag the awkward load back to the tent. Kalie worried about what this exertion, not to mention prolonged exposure to the freezing temperatures would do to Varena's illness.

Just as they reached the first tents, with still a long way to go to get to Maalke's, Kalie noticed a low, scrubby weed growing in one of the less traveled areas outside the camp. She stopped suddenly, causing Varena to loose her grip on the precious cargo.

"What are you doing?" Varena shouted, sounding the closest to angry Kalie had ever heard. Kalie smiled, realizing that, just as she hadn't recognized a frozen sheep, so Varena couldn't recognize a weed with healing properties. Her hands were cramped almost into twisted claws from carrying the sheep, but if she could just force them to dig up this plant, she might be able to make a tea that would help Varena's cough. And it had been such a long time since she had felt useful!

The weed—Kalie knew it as elecampane from the healers at Hot Springs—was like everything else in this place: strong, tough, and not yielding without a fight. By the time she had it from the ground, Kalie had scratches all over her arms. Her body was too numb to feel them now, though they would later. She didn't care. Life was getting better.

Altia's angry rebuke at their lateness died on her lips when she saw what they brought. Kalie had no time for satisfaction. Varena was near to collapsing. She carried the girl to the fire and stripped off her wet clothes, grabbing all the blankets she could from the women's sleeping area and wrapping Varena in them.

"What are you doing?" Altia demanded as Kalie began melting a chunk of ice in a bone bowl over the fire. "Come help us with the sheep."

Since everyone else in the tent was already working on the sheep, Kalie saw no reason. "I am making medicine for Varena. Unless you wish for her to die. Maalke might forgive you the loss of one of his sheep, but perhaps not the loss of one of his daughters." Although even as she said it, Kalie knew which Maalke valued more.

Altia and her own two daughters hissed at that. Altia narrowed her gaze dangerously. "If she is dying, she must be left outside, to keep the Soul Gatherers away from the rest of us. Is she dying?"

Kalie felt the girl's fevered skin and the swelling in her throat. A skilled healer and the right herbs could so easily cure her! But all the girl had now was Kalie. "Not if I can help it!" With that, Kalie closed her mind to everything but the work at hand.

When she had the water boiling, she sliced the plant's largest stem lengthways, coaxing the milky sap into the water. With one of Altia's least prized knives, Kalie chopped the nettle-like leaves into a fine paste before adding them to the brew, knowing that if she wasn't careful, one would scratch Varena's throat and make her feel worse—not to mention destroying any credibility Kalie might gain as a healer.

She was also pleased to note that no one stopped her from using the knife.

While Kalie waited for the tea to steep, she considered other helpful ingredients. Could any be found in this place? She thought of willow. There had been trees near the summer camp, and everyone she had ever met knew the use of willow bark to relieve pain and fevers. Still, these were beastmen...

She glanced at the other women. Altia would refuse her even if she had an entire tent of it, as would Irisa. Tasine had no authority. Cassia was the one she least understood. Maalke's second wife had never been cruel to her, nor any of the other slaves as far as Kalie had seen. She had no living children, but at what? Eighteen summers, she must have been pregnant sometime, or the others here would be treating her worse than a slave.

Varena began to cough again, this time moaning with pain as well.

"Shut up you lazy girl!" Irisa looked up from feeding her three-year old son. "You're no use to us ill, and you know what happens to useless slaves!" Varena whimpered once, and then fell silent.

Kalie sighed. "Cassia," she said. The other woman looked up from cutting the sheep carcass. "Do you have any willow bark?" At Cassia's blank look, Kalie realized she didn't know the local word for it. She described the tree. "People sometimes scrape the inner bark and dry it to relieve pain and fever..." Her voice trailed off. It had been stupid to think these savages knew or cared about such things.

"You mean healing magic?" Cassia asked. "Why of course not, Kalie. What would people like us know about healing? When someone is ill we just sprinkle dried bat wings on them and howl at the moon."

Kalie gaped, while the other women exploded into raucous laughter. Cassia rolled her eyes in a way that Kalie knew she herself had done countless times

since arriving here, and went to the cluster of tiny
baskets where spices and seasonings hung from one of
the tent poles.

"Here," she said, holding out a leather pouch.
Kalie took it, half expecting something foul to leap out
at her. Instead she found willow bark, prepared as any
healer would have.

She considered several responses, and finally
chose to say thank-you. Cassia smiled and
acknowledged her thanks with a nod of her head. But
Kalie found the exchange unsettling, and knew she had
a lot to think about.

While Kalie fed the medicine to Varena in little
sips and sponged her forehead and neck with scraps of
cool damp felt, a feast took shape around her. The
women of this tent, she began to realize, were
connected to Mother Earth—just not in ways she had
ever thought of.

They knew, for example, that the men would
not return tonight. The sound of the wind and the feel
of the air told them that there would be no more snow,
and that the wind would be mild—at least by their
standards. So the men would build a snow lodge and
sleep out on the steppes and perhaps return with fresh
meat tomorrow. If not, Altia at least, would be able to
offer her husband roasted mutton and rich soup, which
might well forestall the rage he would probably feel--
and take out on his women—if the hunt went poorly.

The women seemed more relaxed than Kalie
had ever seen them. They sang as they worked, and
spoke more freely than usual.

Only Irisa seemed nervous. While Kalie had
wished their owner dead every moment she lived in his
tent, she had learned that the death of a brutal man

could be even worse for a woman than living with him. Widows without grown sons had almost no status here. Their only option was to return to their families —fathers or brothers who would either take them into their own tents or arrange another marriage. This could be good, but more often it was not. Kalie began to suspect that when someone had no control over her life, change was rarely a good thing. A new tent meant new women to compete with, or worse, a loss of status with no hope for improvement.

For a concubine like Irisa, it would likely be worse.

There was something else she had heard of; some honor reserved for senior wives or favorite concubines that the women spoke of hopefully in regard to a warrior's death, but Kalie had not yet learned what it was.

Tonight, however, there was little concern that Maalke would either die or return, and the unexpected gift of a sheep in her prime that could not be allowed to go to waste. Maalke's tent became a festive place as delicious aromas filled it and Altia built up the fire so that warmth and anticipation raised everyone's spirits.

Cassia began a song that everyone seemed to know, about a warrior courting a maiden. Each verse described a new gift he brought her. The gifts grew more elaborate as the song progressed. The women sang together for the chorus, taking turns with each of the verses. For the first time, Kalie felt a pang of something almost like longing, and found herself wishing she could join in.

She shook the feeling away, and concentrated on Varena. While the girl drifted in and out of sleep, Kalie massaged her feet.

"What are you doing now?" Cassia asked.

"Just a technique I learned in one of the places I lived. The healers there believed that every part of the body could be influenced from the feet. I am trying to help Varena's breathing." She waited for Cassia to laugh at that, but the nomad woman only looked more interested.

Varena tried to shift into a more comfortable position and Kalie moved to help. She rearranged the furs, using them as bolsters so Varena could see her feet and participate in the conversation. "What else did your healers do?" the child asked.

A gust of wind struck the tent, shaking everything within and dropping the temperature further. Kalie wrapped the furs more tightly around Varena and thought longingly of the wonderful water that had given the village of Hot Springs its name.

"If we were in my home right now," she said, striking the cadence of a storyteller, "you would be soaking in a magical spring of hot water."

"Hot water?" Irisa asked, coming closer. "From the ground?" She snorted.

"Yes, from the ground," Kalie continued. "And it was always hot, even in the coldest days of winter— although winters there are nothing like they are here."

"What happened when snow touched the water?" Varena asked.

"The spring was inside a cave, sacred to the Goddess, so snow rarely touched it. But when it did, there was popping and sizzling, as if you had dropped a snowball into a boiling cauldron."

Irisa laughed. "And when you dropped a slave in it and she boiled too, right?"

"It wasn't that hot, although it was hotter than

any bath I'd taken. And it was never harmful to anyone. The water held a kind of healing magic. People came from great distances, often carried by friends or relatives, to soak in the waters. I saw many miraculous cures with my own eyes. A Temple of Healing had been built there, and it attracted some of the finest healers in the land. It got so that even if the water did not produce a cure, one of the healers could usually find something that did."

Tasine brought Kalie a large bowl of steaming broth, and then sat down nearby, seeming eager to hear more. Kalie tasted the broth. It was delicious, but more importantly, it would be better for Varena than any medicine she could produce herself. That, and a lot of rest, might allow the girl to live through another winter.

"The wealthy of your land must live very long lives," Cassia said.

Kalie blinked at the sudden change of subject. Then she realized it was no change. "The temple was for everyone," she said, clearly enunciating her words in the foreign tongue.

"Even slaves?" Varena whispered. She drank deeply from the bowl, then gave it almost reverently to Kalie, who sipped from it, then passed it to Tasine. The other women in the tent each drank from their own bowls.

"My people do not keep slaves. We don't even have a word for it. The healers of my land take a vow to the Goddess to help anyone in need. It was this reason Kariik and the others who came to murder us were able to return to you. Our healers cared for them." Kalie sighed, for it was usually at this point that her attempts to tell stories broke down. Now, however, no one jeered or argued, and with sudden inspiration, Kalie pressed on.

"Of course, those who were helped gave what gifts they could to the temple. People who you would call wealthy— who had good fortune at hunting or fishing, or the skills to make fine things—often gave lavish gifts.

"I remember furs so soft and warm you could sink into them like, like sleeping on a cloud! There was a man who made leather in such a way that it would cast off water. He traveled far every year to bring some to the temple, after one of the healers cured his brother of blindness. I remember a woman who made honey cake so rich, no one could do aught but sleep after they ate it."

The women in the tent were spellbound. Even Altia's two daughters and Irisa's young son were listening. Her tales of enchantment and speeches about the Goddess had gotten her nowhere, but descriptions of hot baths in winter and fine food during famine held the nomad women in thrall.

Altia went to check on the mutton, roasting in its own juices in a leather bag hung over the fire. "It is time to feast!" she cried. Everyone hurried over to await her share. When Varena tried to rise, Kalie shook her head. "Stay here and rest. I will bring the food to you."

"Why are you being so nice to me?" Varena asked, still suspicious.

Kalie thought about the question for a long moment before she replied. "Because most of what I told you about my world was true," she said at last.

As Altia carved the meat, distributing pieces to members of the household based on their rank she said, "It is a fine feast. We must have music and stories! Tasine, show this barbarian from the west what a real story is!"

Kalie settled down beside Varena, eager to hear. She bit into the meat and felt her whole body respond to the rich taste. She was warm and fed and was learning her enemy's stories. And best of all, Maalke was nowhere near her. It was the closest to happy Kalie had been since returning to this land.

"Once there was a beautiful maiden named Mala," Tasine began. Kalie, who had scarcely heard the old woman speak before now, was surprised by the strength of her voice.

"Mala lived in a rude tent with her father and his second wife and her daughter. And though her mother had been first wife, life was hard for Mala, because that worthy woman had died, and Mala's stepmother was cruel, and always placing her own daughter first. Their father was a weak man, besotted by his beautiful young wife.

"One winter morning, nearly as cold as this night, the wicked woman cried to her husband, 'take this useless brat away, old man! Take her to the empty fields and let the frost have her!"

"The man refused at first, but his wife kept at him until, finally, he took his daughter up on his horse, and rode beyond the last tent, through the open steppes and into the forest, and left her there to die."

Kalie stared in wonder as everyone else in the tent nodded, obviously familiar with this perversion of folklore and waited in eager anticipation as Tasine chewed a bit of meat, and sipped broth.

"Suddenly, Mala saw a man. He was white from head to toe, but dressed in rich furs and dyed cloth. 'Maiden!" he shouted in a voice that shook the trees, "Do you know who I am?'

"'You are King Frost,' she whispered, bowing her head.

"'Yes,' said King Frost, coming closer. 'Maiden, are you warm?'

"'Quite warm, King Frost,' she said, although she shivered from the cold.

"The air chilled around them, and King Frost called up a freezing wind.

"'Maiden, are you warm?' he asked again.

"'Quite warm,' she said again, although her lips were blue and the breath nearly frozen within her."

"Why does she keep saying that?" Kalie whispered to Varena. "Why doesn't she ask for help?" Tasine paused and ate some more food, glancing with annoyance at the interruption.

"Quiet, fool," Irisa hissed.

Tasine continued. "One last time King Frost asked Mala if she was warm, and this time, the breath had nearly gone from her body. But still she answered, 'Quite warm, Great King.'

"And her gentle, courteous words, and uncomplaining ways quite won the king's heart. He wrapped her in warm fur and declared that Mala should be his wife. He set her behind him on his magnificent white stallion, and rode to Mala's home to ask her father what price he had set for her.

"And when Mala's stepmother and half sister saw her riding into camp as the bride of a king, they shrieked and wailed and tore their hair.

"And when Mala's father saw the wealth and status his firstborn daughter had brought him—after he nearly cast her away—it was his wicked wife and her shrewish daughter he sent into the cold. Of course, they froze to death at once. But Mala and her king lived happily ever after."

The other women in the tent slapped their thighs in appreciation, and Altia gave Tasine a choice piece of meat. Then, to everyone's surprise, she unstopped a skin of kumis, drank from it, and passed it to Tasine. "We have enough," she said, and the women applauded again.

When Kalie's turn came, she took a small sip and nearly gagged on the rancid tasting mare's milk. She passed it on to Varena, and considered the many questions she wanted to ask. Did they really consider a woman and child dying of cold to be a happy ending? And what kind of life was Mala going to have with a man who nearly let her freeze to death while she pretended that all was well? Was he testing her for— what had Tasine said? —"Courteous words and uncomplaining ways?"

Kalie ate the rest of her meat, and felt her head swim from its richness after living on a near fast for so long. The others too were feeling the effects of the food, and more so, of the kumis.

Perhaps this time she could ask some questions without starting a fight. Or perhaps she should ask Tasine for another story.

While Kalie was trying to decide, Altia called to her in words that were beginning to slur, "Give us another of your stories, Kalie!"

Inspiration came like a lightening bolt. Kalie sat up and sipped from the water skin. "I would be honored."

# Chapter 19

"Once there were three travelers on their way to a Summer Festival." Kalie chose her words carefully, altering the old tale as she went. The travelers, for example, all had to become men if she wanted her audience to take the story seriously.

"They were a sculptor, a weaver and storyteller." Tasine's eyes widened, but she said nothing.

Irisa frowned. "What is a weaver?" she demanded.

"Someone who makes cloth," said Kalie. "The fine linen that you people prize so much? That is made by weavers."

The women in the tent nodded and Kalie continued. "When night fell, they were far from any settlement, so they stopped in a clearing in the forest and built a fire, then shared such food as they had each brought with them.

"The sculptor suggested they keep watch during the night, one after the other, to guard against wolves, and offered to take the first shift. While the others slept, the sculptor found himself growing weary, so he gathered some clay from the riverbank and began to fashion it into the shape of a fanciful creature, that he might remain awake." As she spoke, Kalie drew an imaginary lump of clay through her hands, demonstrating what the sculptor was doing.

"By the time the weaver awoke for his shift, the sculptor had created a fine being from clay, with the shape of a man, but the ears of a dog, eyes of a cat, and wings of a swan. 'What is this marvelous creature?' asked the weaver.

"Only something I made to pass the time,' answered the sculptor. 'Perhaps you can make it some clothes.' With that, the sculptor lay down to sleep.

"Why would anyone make clothes for something that isn't even human?" Irisa demanded. "Only people wear clothes!"

Kalie was thrown so far off her course by Irisa's outburst that she nearly stopped her tale then and there. But when both of Maalke's wives glared at the annoying concubine, she saw that they were actually listening—and becoming involved.

"Listen and you'll find out," Kalie said. "The weaver added more wood to the fire and sat down to examine the strange creature his companion had fashioned. It was, he saw basically human, but with greater power than mortal man. 'Such a being must have garments suitable to his station,' thought the weaver, and he rummaged through his pack until he found some scraps of blue-dyed linen that had been too fine to throw away. He then set about fashioning a shirt and cloak fit for a king." Amazing, Kalie thought, how easily the foreign words and concepts folded into her tale.

"When the storyteller awoke for his shift, the weaver showed him the creature, now looking quite regal and said, 'since your skill is in words, perhaps you can teach him to speak.' Then he lay down to sleep, not really expecting the storyteller to have much success.

"But, behold! When dawn broke, and all three travelers arose to continue their journey, the creature was no longer cold, stiff clay, but warm flesh, flying about on his wings, and laughing and speaking." Kalie paused, for it was here that she was about to make a radical departure from the story as she had once told it.

"As they watched the creature's antics, each man wished to take it home with him, and they began to quarrel over who, in truth, owned it." Kalie winced at the words, but kept her voice steady.

Then she turned to her audience. "So tell me, women of Aahk, to whom does the clay-man belong?"

This particular storytelling device, while unusual among Kalie's people, appeared to be quite common here. Tasine smiled and nodded with appreciation, Varena looked at the other women with interest, while Cassia and Irisa waited patiently, each clearly thinking of her own reply. Altia leaned forward with a ready answer.

"That's easy. The creature belongs to the sculptor! He made it, therefore it belongs to him!" Varena and Tasine nodded in agreement.

"But it wasn't alive until the storyteller gave it speech," said Cassia. "I say it belongs to him."

"But what use would it have been without clothes?" snapped Irisa. "He wouldn't have become anything worth keeping if the weaver hadn't given him status!"

Kalie grinned—and it wasn't feigned. "Excellent, all of you!"

As one they turned to her. "But what is the real answer?" asked Cassia.

Kalie saw Altia's smug look of certainty—and immediately changed her plan. For once she saw that diplomacy was called for, and not another rant. "Of course Altia is correct: the sculptor made him, so the creature would belong to him. At least, among your people."

Then she took a deep breath and plunged ahead. "But among my people, we would say that no one owned the creature: he belonged only to himself."

"How could that be?" asked Cassia. "You said yourself, he was only a lump of clay before the sculptor made him."

"True, and if it had remained lifeless, it would have been a statue, and therefore someone's property, and the three men who cooperated on its making would have most likely sold it and divided up whatever they got in exchange."

Altia snorted. "Here, they'd have fought for it, and whoever was left alive would have kept it for luck!"

"Yes, I've noticed that," Kalie said dryly. "But things are different where I'm from. A statue can be owned—a human being cannot." She held up a hand, forestalling the argument she knew was coming. "Even someone who looks different, who may not even be human. If he—or she—can speak and think and live among others then he cannot be owned—ever. The three travelers gave the creature wonderful gifts, and he in turn would honor them as parents, but just as parents do not own their children..."

"What do you mean, parents don't own their children?" cried Cassia. "What do they do? Throw them into the snow for the animals to find?"

Again, more your style than mine, thought Kalie, but she said, "Parents raise their children, but all for the purpose of seeing them choose their own path and find their own way in the world." She thought of Tia, sold by her own father. "A father who killed a child or sought to take it from its mother would probably be buried alive—but I don't know, since I've never heard of such a thing happening."

"Enough stories," Altia said, though not unkindly. "Cassia, give us music!"

Cassia crawled to her sleeping place and returned with a stringed instrument, similar to a harp, made from bone and horsehair. It was a shock for Kalie to learn that these people actually had musical instruments. Cassia strummed it gently, and began a mournful song about a young bride, waiting for her husband to return from battle. Kalie could appreciate the tune, if not the story, and wondered if such music might accompany her stories one day.

The party lasted late into the long winter night. When Kalie awoke the next morning, her first thought was that she felt almost comfortable: her stomach was full and she was warm and Maalke was not on top of her. Her next thought, as she looked around, was that she was glad not to have indulged in the kumis. The others, still asleep, looked as though they would be decidedly uncomfortable when they awoke.

She moved to add fuel to the dying fire, and then saw that she would have to disentangle herself from Varena. Kalie moved carefully, tucking the furs back around the sleeping girl, who seemed greatly improved. With continued rest, more medicine and enough food she would recover. But to wake her now and force her out into the cold would undo all that Kalie's ministering had done.

Kalie resolved to tend the animals and gather the dung herself this morning. Maybe she could get it done before anyone forced Varena out of the tent. She built up the fire, feeling it struggle against the cold air. Then she dressed herself, first in the shapeless felt robe worn by all slave women. Next, Kalie wrapped herself in her sheepskin cloak, followed by fur scraps she had been given for her head and hands. These people knew how to make mittens—they just didn't bother making them for slaves. Ironic, thought Kalie, since it was slaves who spent the most time outside in these Goddess-forsaken winters. Perhaps, she could find a way to make some for herself and for Varena as well.

She was just adjusting her top layer—the fur she had slept in—when a sleepy voice said, "Wait. I'll go with you."

Startled, Kalie turned to see Cassia pulling on her blue linen shift. Dressing far more quickly that Kalie had, Cassia moved silently to join her at the front of the tent.

"What are you doing?" Kalie asked, baffled.

"I will help you this morning." Her voice seemed strained from what was probably a kumis-induced headache, but she moved easily and with determination.

Kalie frowned. "You are a wife. Such work is beneath you."

"I am a wife, so it is my duty to see that the work gets done," Cassia replied in a milder tone. "Who else could go? Tasine's old joints would freeze solid the moment she left the tent. Irisa's pregnancy spares her. Varena is too ill."

"Irisa didn't seem to consider that important."

"Irisa was born without a heart," Cassia said bitterly. "Not all of us were. Shall we go?"

Kalie led the way out of the tent and held the flap open for Cassia.

She gasped and stood motionless when she

stepped into an almost magical land of sculpted ice and powdery new snow. It took Kalie at least ten heartbeats to realize what was different: there was no wind.

Cassia frowned beside her. "There will be a storm tonight. A big one. Let us pray the men return before then."

Kalie did not offer to share *her* prayers with Cassia, and set out for the animal pens. The eerie silence created by the lack of the ever-present steppe wind was punctuated with the lowing of animals and the crunching footsteps of slaves. It also allowed Kalie and Cassia to speak to each other without shouting.

"That healing you did for Varena?" Cassia asked casually as she spread the feed for the sheep. "Is that the limit of your knowledge?"

Kalie struggled to free a young goat whose own droppings had frozen it to the side of the pen. "I was never consecrated as a Healer," she said, throwing a wary glance toward Cassia. "I simply picked up some knowledge while I lived at the temple at Hot Springs."

"You mean that place was real? No, don't tell me; it doesn't matter. All I want to know is this: do you possess the magic that would allow me to bear Maalke a child?"

Ah, yes, that would explain why a lofty wife would gather dung with a slave girl, Kalie thought. "Have you ever conceived?" she asked Cassia.

The nomad woman nodded, eyes shut against pain. "Twice. The first time, I lost it so quickly, it was barely more than a delay in my courses. The second time, I carried for more than three moons. It was harder that time."

"How long ago was that?" Kalie asked, curious in spite of herself.

"It will be a year with the coming of late winter."

"How far apart were the two pregnancies?"

"Nearly two years." Cassia's voice broke, but she quickly regained control.

"Not impossible, then." Kalie muttered, her thoughts turned inward.

"What do you mean?"

Kalie came back to the present and explained. "If you had never conceived at all, that would have been beyond my skill to remedy. But if a woman can conceive, and the problem is carrying the baby to term, there are potions that can help the body hold on to it." Kalie saw the raw, desperate hope that lit Cassia's face and hastened to add, "I can try. I make no promises."

Cassia nodded soberly. "I would not have believed you otherwise. But if you can help give me a child, I promise I will reward you well."

Kalie laughed, the sound echoing weirdly in frozen stillness of encampment. Other slaves looked toward her, then quickly away.

"You doubt my word?" Cassia said, sounding dangerous for the first time.

"Not your word, mistress. Only your power to give me what I truly desire. It may surprise you, but where I come from, not every woman dreams of living as a slave for the rest of her life—not even a slave to one so great as yourself."

Cassia's face remained still, but she looked at Kalie with a new…could it truly be respect? "With all your fanciful tales, it's hard for me to know exactly what you were before. But it's clear enough you were no slave. Highborn apparently, and ambitious." Cassia sighed, creating with her breath a cloud of frost so white it seemed a solid thing in the still air. "So…you wish to be a wife."

This time, Kalie choked on her laughter and ended up in a coughing fit so loud and harsh that Cassia became concerned. When she had her breathing under control, the absurdity of the situation, combined with the crystalline cold that enshrouded them was making Kalie giddy. "Oh, I could never aspire to such lofty ambitions!" Kalie said, not even trying to keep the sarcasm from her voice. "Not to so great a man as Maalke, who already has two high-born wives!"

But Cassia seemed to have missed the irony, and was, in fact, thinking hard. "I don't know if I could…it's for Maalke to decide of course, but…" She looked Kalie in the eye. "Are you pregnant?"

"No. As you probably know, my courses came about half a moonspan past, and Maalke has not used me since then."

"It is not likely, then, that you will ever be more than a slave in this tent. I am sorry, Kalie, for I think you are someone I could welcome as a sister wife." *Not like the one I currently share the title with.* The words, unspoken, were clear nonetheless. "But there are things I can do for you. A new cloak of good winter sheepskin. The second cut of meat, rather than last. And if you are handmaid to a wife, it will not matter that you do not give Maalke a child."

Kalie's ears were numb, but her brain wasn't. This was an opportunity. "Promise me nothing yet," she said. "For I do not even know if I can find the right herbs in this land. And there is something you must know before you decide to proceed. There is a risk—"

"There is always a risk in bearing a child," Cassia said dismissively.

"Perhaps more so than usual in your case. I cannot see how you are made beneath all your clothing —and I will have to examine you closely for this to work…" Cassia nodded impatiently, and Kalie continued. "Often when a woman does not carry a baby to term, it is for a good reason. If bearing a child would kill you, the customs of my people would forbid me from helping you achieve it."

"They are strange, then, your people. What good is a woman's life if she cannot have children?"

"Someday, I would like to show you," Kalie said softly, the silent cold making her words louder than she intended.

"Well, we are not among your people now, though I thank you for your warning. But I would rather die giving Maalke a son than grow old pitied or despised."

"Very well." Kalie struggled to control her chattering teeth and plunged in. "Then I will ask this as payment. I will do all I can to help you get a child. In return, I would ask you to help me learn the stories of your people."

Cassia laughed. "But you would get that anyway! By the time this cursed winter ends, you will have heard every story we know!"

"Not the women's stories—though I look forward to learning those as well. You said I was ambitious and you were right. I want to become a storyteller for the warriors."

Cassia looked at Kalie as if she had grown another head. "I know such a thing exists," Kalie persisted. "Although I do not know your word. Back home, I made my living telling stories in the temple courtyard. Here, I am told, there are women who are valued for their skills as musicians and dancers. I thought perhaps, a storyteller might…"

Understanding dawned on Cassia's face, but concern was there as well. "Yes, there are women who are greatly prized for such skills. And they often prosper well—for a time. But they are whores."

It was Kalie's turn to look blank. "What is that?"

Cassia seemed at a loss. "Well, surely you must have them where you come from. Women who are neither wives nor concubines. Women who show their bodies to groups of men; who sleep with many men."

"That is true of any slave in this camp."

"But only if her master wills it!"

"I see little difference in that. Do you think being raped by your husband holds any more or less joy for me than being raped by another woman's husband?"

"I…" Cassia staggered backward as if the wind had suddenly blown across the steppe. "I…did not know you felt that way, Kalie. But, what I mean is, yes it is true, there are women here who entertain at feasts and celebrations." An image shimmered before Kalie's frost-rimed eyes: on the eve of battle, she was telling a story to an audience of warriors. On the surface, it was about the glories each of them hoped to win. But beneath were subtle threats; things that played upon their fears, until every man there went to his bed convinced that his closest friend would plant a spear in his back at the peak of the fighting…

"The best belong to the king, or his mightiest

chiefs," Cassia continued.

"I am ambitious enough that it is the king whom I dream of...serving," said Kalie.

Cassia nodded. "I can see how such a life might appeal to you, Kalie—they live very well when they are in favor. But they can never marry, and they are not allowed to bear children. And when they grow old; when their talents and beauty fade...life is not good. I would not wish that on you."

Through the biting cold, Kalie felt a chill that was altogether different. Her enemy was being kind to her, and she didn't know what to do.

"I...thank you, mistress, for your concern. But I would wish it anyway, just as you wish for a child against my warnings. I will never be any good at cooking or making felt or stitching tents. But storytelling is something I can do. It is part of who I am. And it is doubtful I can have a child anyway, so that is no loss."

Kalie realized her mistake as suspicion clouded Cassia's face. "You offer to give me a child, but lack the magic to give yourself one?"

She met Cassia's look of betrayal with one of her own. "That, mistress, was the gift your men gave to me. When they first took me, one after the other, I bled until all the life-giving powers of my womb had gone. What they left me is as shriveled and scarred and dried as that of any crone."

In the silent air, Cassia caught her breath. "Oh, Kalie! I am so sorry! I..."

"I am not." Hatred coursed through her like hot wine in the winter cold. "For that is one power no man here shall ever have. Never will they have the joy of hurting me by hurting a child I love. Never will I bear a daughter to see her sold and raped, nor watch a son grow up to murder his brothers."

"We must go inside." Cassia' voice steadied as she spoke "The cold can be even more dangerous when there's no wind, precisely because you don't feel it as much."

Kalie followed Cassia back into the tent.

# Chapter 20

"What took you so long, lazy bitch?" Altia greeted Kalie as she entered the confines of the tent. "The fire is…Cassia!" Maalke's wife looked toward her sister wife's sleeping furs, then back at the woman who was calmly tying down the tent flap. "What were you doing outside so early?"

"My job," Cassia replied coldly, while Kalie gave the basket of dung to a bleary-eyed Tasine and went to check on Varena. "How is she?" Cassia asked Kalie, turning her back on Altia without further discussion.

Kalie examined the girl, who lay in her furs, looking with frightened eyes at Cassia. Kalie guessed that attention from her father's wives was rarely a good thing for the motherless slave girl.

"Much better," she pronounced, with an encouraging smile for Varena. "A little more rest, and you'll be fine." Irisa, she noticed, was still snoring in the furs.

She heated the remains of the decoction she had used the night before, and fed it to the sick child. When she was finished, Cassia said loudly, "Attend me Kalie."

"Of course, mistress," Kalie said, starting to rise.

"Kalie!" Varena clutched at Kalie's robe. "Could you tell me more stories later?"

Kalie looked into the face of the frightened child and felt her heart melt—for all that she fought to keep it frozen. She was here on a mission—and a suicide mission at that. A successful outcome for her;

for all the people of the Goddess, more than likely meant destroying the only world Varena knew.

But as she held the girl who had no one; who had probably never known a moment of real love or safety, Kalie knew there was no help for it. For better or worse, her fate had become entwined with Varena's.

"Kalie?" Cassia was more puzzled than impatient as she stared at the slave who did not jump at her word.

Kalie gave Varena a reassuring squeeze and rose gracefully to her feet, ducking her head from long habit. She followed Cassia, who untied a felt curtain that rested in pleats above their heads. When it fell in graceful folds around them, they had privacy from prying eyes, if not ears.

As a wife, Cassia had the rare luxury of her own space. It was barely four paces wide, but as Kalie looked around, she knew she was learning a great deal about the woman who now held sway over Kalie's future. All of Cassia's few possessions were displayed with care and taste.

The furs and cushions of the bed were soft and finely made. Nothing was dyed, but the natural colors were blended in such a way as to create an overall effect no artificial colors could. A blanket of blue gray fox fur trimmed in white winter rabbit set against another of tan deer skins gave the sense of water in the desert. An intricate cape of bird skin and feathers hung against the outer wall of the tent. Caught up in the feathers were Cassia's beaded slippers. Beside them hung the stringed instrument Cassia had played the night before.

Altia liked to flaunt the gifts Maalke gave her,

especially things like these, made by skilled slaves or stolen from strangers far away. Yet Cassia chose to keep them private. For reasons she couldn't name, Kalie found her opinion of Maalke's second wife increasing even more.

She turned her gaze to Cassia who reclined on the soft bed.

She had removed her outer clothing and wore only the linen shift Kalie had seen her in earlier that morning. *Stolen from some western trader, no doubt*, Kalie thought bitterly. She lifted the shift and examined the body of the woman who so desperately wanted a child.

Cassia's hips were narrow, but not excessively. Kalie had seen women with narrower hips give birth and live. No obvious puckering or deformities shouted danger in carrying a child. Kalie wracked her brain for any other things to look for, but nothing came to mind.

"I can help you," she said with more confidence than she felt. Cassia's body went limp with relief. "Again, I make no promises. First, we must get you pregnant."

Cassia's lips twitched with amusement. "Strange," she said as she dressed. "That used to be a matter between myself and Maalke. Now, I suppose, it involves you as well." She grew serious. "I have been a wife for five turnings of the seasons, yet have conceived only twice. How can we know when--?"

"Are your courses regular?"

"Yes, always."

"There are ways to increase your chances at the right time each month, but—" Kalie broke off, suddenly remembering where she was.

"But what?" Cassia's brow wrinkled with

concern.

"My knowledge may do you little good here, mistress, for it comes from a different place. A place where women choose the time when they join with men. I can give you a potion to drink, but it will gain you nothing if you do not lie with Maalke during the precise time I tell you to."

Cassia's brow smoothed out at once and a hint of pride came into her face. "Let me worry about that, girl. I am not so old that I don't have a few tricks left, and Maalke is far from tired of me. Just tell me when, and I will see to it that he summons me to him at the right time."

Kalie shook off her revulsion and continued. "Once you conceive, the challenge will be for you to hold the baby. The simplest way to do that would be to remain in bed throughout the pregnancy."

The laughter that bubbled up within Cassia died as she looked into Kalie's face. "You are serious aren't you?"

Kalie nodded sadly as the impossibility of the situation became apparent. "My people are not nomads. If a woman needs to lie down for nine moonspans in order to have a baby, then that is what she does."

"But...how? Surely not even the wife of your greatest chiefs could be so pampered! To do no work? To be waited on..."

"It's easier than you think," Kalie said. "For none of the women I speak of were ever *wives*! Some of them had partners, of course, but each woman made whatever arrangements were needed without having to ask a man for permission. Their families cared for them, or their entire community, and I know of at least one woman who traveled alone to Hot Springs as soon as she learned she was pregnant. She never told us who her people were or why she was alone. She only said she needed a place to stay. When the Healers determined she needed complete bed rest to carry the baby to term, that's what she got!

"But it isn't like that here!" Cassia snapped.

"Then come live in my world and have a baby there!" Kalie threw back.

She feared she had gone too far, but Cassia seemed not to have even heard her last remark. "There could be up to four moonspans left in winter," she said to the walls of the tent, while Kalie sagged with horrified realization that in this land, true winter had just begun. "We will remain here a while longer than that. If I could get pregnant right away, I could carry the baby half way to term before I had to travel. The journey to our summer camp is difficult, but if the babe survives it, I wouldn't have to travel again until after he was born!" Then she looked at Kalie with such desperate hope that Kalie could only nod.

"We will try, then."

At that moment there was a great commotion as the tent shook with wind and loud voices. Cassia quickly got dressed.

Maalke had returned.

'        Cassia hurried to him, while Kalie hid in the shadows.

.        "The hunting was bad for us, but good for the wolves," Maalke was saying as he sat by the fire on a pile of cushions. Altia and Cassia were busy removing his soaked boots and wet outer clothing. "We lost Barik and Janaak; two good men, and Janaak barely more than a boy."

The women all paled at the news. Kalie wondered if they were related to the men who died, or simply fearing that it might be Maalke next time.

Irisa brought him hot kumis and a plate of mutton from the previous night's feast. Maalke glanced at her bulging stomach with disappointment. "I had hoped to find a new son waiting for me when I returned."

"Soon, master," Irisa said. "It will be very soon."

"Good. I miss having you in my furs," he added, while Irisa blushed with pleasure.

Cassia knelt beside Maalke. "You do not need her, my husband. I have missed being in your furs as well. Let me show you how much." Her hand snaked slowly up his thigh, and Cassia threw Kalie a beseeching glance.

Kalie sighed. Did Cassia think she had the potion ready now, before she had a chance to even look for the right herbs?

Maalke sat up, staring down at the remains of the mutton on his plate. "You slaughtered an animal in my absence?"

"Of course not, husband," said Altia. "We found that one dead yesterday morning. I thought to have it ready dressed for your return—"

"So sure were you I would return empty handed?" Maalke flung his plate across the tent. "No wonder our luck was so ill! You bitches cursed it!" His fist flew out at the nearest target, which happened to be Cassia's face. There was a meaty thud, and Cassia crumpled.

The other women in the tent prostrated

themselves and Irisa's young son began to wail as Maalke shrugged back into his heavy outer clothes. "Shut that brat up!" he yelled. "Since I find no peace in my own home, I shall seek it elsewhere!" With that, Maalke flung open the tent and strode out into the howling wind and early flakes of snow. The promised storm was beginning at last.

Altia and her daughters struggled to secure the tent flap, which Maalke had left open, while Kalie and the other two slaves went to Cassia. Her face was beginning to swell, and would soon sport a bruise, but she wasn't badly hurt. With Tasine's help, Kalie got her to her bed and fixed a poultice and willow bark tea.

The tent was subdued after that, with no one speaking beyond an occasional sharp command from Altia as the daily round of work continued. Varena wanted to help Kalie tend Cassia, but her own symptoms soon forced her back to bed. With two workers laid up, not much got accomplished, but trapped within the tent, there was little enough to do.

Kalie drifted back and forth between her two patients, lost in thought. Bits of memory from her first time in captivity tangled with things she was learning now, making her present situation even more frightening. She had to get out of here, and soon.

Cassia's call broke into her thoughts. "Do you need something more for the pain, mistress?" she asked, crawling into the second wife's chamber.

"No," said Cassia, looking up from the white rabbit furs she was stitching into a blanket. She touched her face. "This is nothing, though I thank you for the poultice and tea. I only stayed here this long because I wanted to think."

Kalie lost track of what Cassia was saying as what she was doing suddenly struck her. "This is your work?" she sputtered.

Cassia looked up, startled. "Yes, of course."

Kalie looked around the beautifully appointed chamber. "All of this?"

"Most of it. Why?"

"I…did not know that your people could create beauty."

Cassia gaped at her. "The women of Aahk are the finest artists in the world! Where did you think these tents—and everything in them—come from?"

"The same place as the metal knives and the cloth and the pottery—either stolen from settled people or the work of skilled slaves!"

Cassia shook her head. "How could you live among us and understand us so little? We are a great people, Kalie, and there is much beauty in our lives."

"Yes," she said. "The truth of that is written plainly on your face."

Cassia's hand flew to her swollen jaw and spilt lip as though Kalie's words stung worse than Maalke's fist. She recovered quickly. "This is nothing. A wife must bear her husband's anger. And Maalke is often very tender with me after times like this. That is why I called you. When he returns, he will want me. Will that be the right time for conception? And can you have the potion ready by then?"

Kalie shook her head. If she were going to change Cassia's view of the world, it would not be by arguing about it. "If you bled at the same time I did," Cassia nodded confirmation. "Then the best time will begin in about three days, and last for at most, five or six after that."

"The winter festival is in six days!" Cassia said, lighting up with excitement. "Maalke is always at his…most vigorous then. And it would be a fine time to conceive! The child would be born at the end of summer and would probably be lucky as well."

"None of the herbs I need are in this tent," Kalie said. "Few will be growing here in the winter. Are there others in this camp who might have some? I would have to see them myself."

Cassia nodded. "As soon as it is safe to leave the tent, I will take you to the healers I know."

"You have healers in this land?"

Cassia rolled her eyes. "Why do you insist on seeing us as animals? Why is it so hard to believe that skilled healers dwell among us?"

A myriad of replies leapt so quickly to Kalie's throat that she nearly choked. Pushing the whole lot firmly back down, she said, "Do you really want an answer to that?"

Cassia thought a moment. Then she said, "No, I don't suppose I do."

They looked at each other then, equal for the first time. "All right, then," said Kalie. Cassia nodded.

Honesty, thought Kalie, might be better than agreement—for now.

# Chapter 21

The ice storm lasted three days. Maalke returned late on the first day, during one of the few lulls that allowed him to safely reach his tent. From what Kalie could gather, Maalke had strained the bonds of friendship by staying even that long in the tent of one of his fellow warriors. Still, he showed no remorse for his earlier behavior, accepting as his due the concerned ministrations of his women as they wrapped him in furs and brought him hot drinks and food. At least this time he didn't throw any of it at them.

While Maalke remained idle, the women kept busy making felt and leather, repairing clothing and, in Kalie's case, nursing Varena through her illness. Maalke's only activity was to clean and sharpen his various weapons and demand sexual service from both Altia and Cassia, but not, to Kalie's immense relief, herself. Perhaps her habit of acting like a corpse in the furs had finally paid off.

As soon as the storm ended, everyone went outside, though the temperature remained below freezing and the wind was only slightly calmer. Kalie stopped to gaze out at the endless plain and marveled that there could be so many shades of white.

She became aware of Altia behind her, her first raised to strike the slave who dared to stop and gawk at the sky when there was work to be done—and neatly stepped out of the way, just as Altia's fist connected with empty air. Cassia stepped between them before Altia could react.

"I have need of Kalie, First Wife," she said.

"Maalke did not give her to you as a handmaiden, Second Wife," Altia hissed. "He gave her to me."

"Actually, I believe Ahnaak gave her to Maalke. Since my use for her involves the son I may soon give our husband, I think he would approve. But you can always ask him." Cassia's sweet smile told Kalie that Altia would never dare do so.

Instead she spat at Cassia's feet. "Son? Ha! Your barren womb will never give Maalke anything! Neither will hers." Maalke's First Wife grinned maliciously, showing blackened teeth, worn nearly to the gums. "Perhaps she *should* be your handmaiden, as you both are barren—and out of Maalke's favor!" Altia turned to order the other slaves to attend to the day's chores.

Cassia began to walk through the camp, not bothering to see if Kalie was following. She held her head high, but her cheeks were white and pinched and Kalie could see the effect Altia's barbs had. Although her heart burned with questions, Kalie kept silent as she followed Cassia.

They stopped at a tent similar to Maalke's. Of course, every tent in the camp looked the same, with the exception of the chief's tent, which was much larger and needed many more poles of precious wood to hold it up.

"The older midwives have the most knowledge," Cassia said. "But I have nothing they want, and none of them owe me a thing. So we come here, to a younger woman, but one whom I trust."

Kalie nodded. "It is the ingredients I need, not the knowledge."

"Yes, another reason to come here. She has, of

late, been seen gathering and trading for all sorts of herbs. No one seems to know why, although she is known for a love of the new and unusual. That may give us something to bargain with. When we enter, sit behind me, and say nothing until I tell you to."

"Yes, mistress."

Cassia scratched on the tent flap. A female voice bid her enter. Kalie followed Cassia into the tent and settled down behind her, waiting for her eyes to adjust to the shadowy interior, lit only by a small brazier and a single lamp.

The tent she found herself in was better kept and more richly appointed than Maalke's. Luxurious furs covered the floor, while fine beadwork graced the walls. But it was the smell that dazzled Kalie the most. Fragrant herbs burned in the brazier, nearly masking the stench of dung and ripe bodies.

"Greetings, Brenia," Cassia said.

"Greetings, Cassia." The mistress of the tent noticed Kalie and her eyes widened. "Oh, is this one of the barbarians from the west?" Cassia nodded. "I've been wanting to get a look at one since Haraak brought them back! Everyone says they are so different from women of the tribes. Is it true that they lack even the simplest knowledge and are only fit to grace a man's bed?"

Cassia grinned. "Ask her yourself."

"She can talk?"

"In several languages," Kalie said in the beastmen's tongue, careful to pronounce everything right. "Which would you prefer I use?"

A dark blush spread across Brenia's face. Kalie noticed that her long, curling hair was nearly the same shade of red. She guessed Brenia to be a few years older than herself, though it was hard to tell. Her creamy skin bore the wrinkles and hardness of life on the steppes, but her teeth were white and strong, her body long and sinuous. She was truly beautiful, Kalie thought.

"I did not realize you could speak at all," Brenia said. "The only one of your kind I got near enough to hear was Kariik's new woman, and she could only mutter gibberish."

"Her name is Maylene," said Kalie. "Can you tell me how my kinswoman fares?"

Brenia recovered from her surprise more quickly this time. "She was pregnant, when I saw her last, and Kariik doting on her like she was already a wife. Though how he thinks to make a foreigner such as her a wife…" Brenia stopped and continued in softer, more measured tones. "Her child should be born before summer, gods willing." She made a gesture of protection against evil, and Cassia did the same.

"Kalie has brought us many surprises," Cassia said.

At a gesture from Brenia, an old woman appeared from the shadows carrying a flat colorfully woven basket-tray with three steaming bone cups. Brenia took the tray from her and handed cups to Cassia and Kalie. *Unusual,* thought Kalie, *that a wife would serve a slave.*

"Kalie is a healer, and a storyteller as well. We have come seeking certain herbs. Perhaps we could offer stories in exchange?

Kalie could see at once they had Brenia's attention.

Cassia explained her errand, and then indicated

that Kalie should describe the herbs she needed. It went more quickly than she expected, for rather than stumbling through long translations, Brenia simply ordered her slave to bring out the household's entire complement of herbs—both healing and cooking, Kalie noted with approval.

Brenia possessed an impressive store, all neatly organized. Kalie found most of what she would need —both for Cassia's fertility potion and for herbs Kalie hoped to store against future medical emergencies. There was no need for Cassia to know everything. In fact, Kalie thought, the more costly the herbs she demanded, and the greater the quantity, the more likely Cassia was to believe in her powers.

"This is the most impressive pharmacy I've seen since leaving my own people," Kalie told Brenia, who seemed delighted by the praise. "You must be a great healer."

"My mother was a great healer," Brenia said by way of correction. "I might have become more of one if she had lived longer. Still, such skills are useful." She might have said more, but just then there was a scratching on the tent flap.

This time, the caller did not wait to be admitted. Must be a man, Kalie thought, before her nose, then eyes confirmed her assumption.

"Brenia, have you finished my vest—" the man stopped at the sight of Cassia and Kalie.

"It is here, brother." Brenia rose gracefully and ducked into a screened off portion of the tent. As she did so, Cassia covered her face with her linen veil. Kalie followed suite with her scratchy felt. She met the man's gaze before lowering her eyes as she had been taught, and recognized one of the men who had brought her here.

Brenia returned with a neatly folded leather garment. "Riyik, Cassia has come to trade for herbs. It seems her new slave is a healer."

Riyik's dark eyebrows rose. "Really? I thought that one of the others was supposed to be a healer. The one the king gave to Tarnaak." He looked directly at Kalie, seeming to expect an answer.

Kalie, who was surprised he remembered even that much, decided to reply. "If you mean Alessa, she is certainly a better healer than I am, but since I am here and she is not, it appears I will have to do."

Riyik's brows rose even further, but he said nothing.

"Perhaps we should return later," Cassia said, though Kalie could see she had no wish to leave without the herbs.

"No, stay," said Riyik. "I will be leaving shortly." But he made no move to go. Instead, he stared hard at another curtained area of the tent. Abruptly, he rose and said, "I would like to know just how good a healer you are." He moved to the back of the tent and drew aside the curtain.

Brenia rose without her previous grace and hurried to place herself between Riyik and whatever lay on the other side of the curtain. "Brother, are you sure?" she whispered urgently.

"I have to do something!" Riyik shot back, a note of desperation in his voice. "And you have no idea how skilled their healers are."

Kalie's dread that he was looking for a cure for impotence, and had decided that a slave was a safe place to experiment, subsided when Riyik pulled the covers off a sleeping child.

The boy awoke and began to cry, in turn waking the slightly older boy who lay next to him. The second boy looked around, saw Brenia and rolled over and went back to sleep. Riyik cradled the crying child in his arms, wrapping him in fur, until only one foot was exposed. Kalie could see at once what Riyik's concern was: one of the child's legs was crooked below the knee, ending in a clubfoot. A minor deformity to be sure; it would mean little in her world. Here, she knew, it was a death sentence.

"Can you repair his foot?" Riyik asked.

The irony of the situation made Kalie reckless. "No," she said. "But I know of one who could."

"Who?" cried Riyik. "Tell me, and I'll ride back to your land in the dead of winter and bring her back!"

"I'm happy to spare you the journey," Kalie said. "Her name was Maris, and she was halfway to this land when you rode her down for sport and left her dead on the plains. I doubt you remember her, since she was old and not worth raping, but it was she who saved your life back in my city. As she might well have saved your son's!"

Riyik flinched as though he had been struck. The other women gasped and seemed ready to fall over. Kalie only waited to see what would happen next.

# Chapter 22

Riyik stared at Kalie as if in shock. Kalie stared back. She had enough to time to regret the loss óf Cassia's regard for her before Riyik spoke again.

But when he did, it was Kalie's turn to be shocked.

"No one rode her down for sport," he said quietly. "Two of the girls were fleeing and we had to ride after them. The old woman—Maris—just got in the way."

"Well, then," Kalie said quietly, "I suppose that makes everything all right." Her tongue seemed to have a developed mind of its own. She had meant to say nothing, but Riyik's words and tone had startled her into reckless sarcasm. She took a deep breath, telling herself to relax; that no beastman would even notice the sarcasm…

But apparently, Riyik did. "She saved my life. I had no wish to repay her with slavery. I told Haraak she was too old for the journey, and should be left behind, but he wanted all the wealth he could get…" Riyik suddenly struck the side of the tent with his fist. "If that greedy bastard hadn't been thinking with his balls, perhaps she would be here now, healing my son…"

The women sat silently while Riyik seemed lost in thought. Then he stiffened and looked around, as if the tent was too confining and he had to get out now. He turned to his sister.

"Brenia, please learn what you can of Kalie's abilities. If you think she can help Yarik, I give you leave to offer her anything I have as payment." From the corner of her eye, Kalie caught Cassia's look of amazement. But a knowing look passed between brother and sister. Brenia would not promise more than Riyik could give, nor would she allow some charlatan to deceive her.

He kissed his son's head, nodded politely to the women and hurried from the tent.

Brenia rounded on Kalie. "How dare you speak to my brother that way?"

Kalie met her gaze as a slave never did. "How dare he murder my friends, and then expect them to rise from the dead and offer their help when it suits him?" Kalie shot back. "Does he feel nothing that he killed the woman who saved his life and might have healed his son? Other than annoyance at the inconvenience?"

"Kalie!" Cassia did look outraged. "Brenia, forgive me for bringing her—"

"It's all right, Cassia." Brenia's calm had returned. "Kalie, I am sorry for your loss. And I know that Riyik is as well. It is only that here, men are taught not to show it."

Kalie choked back the bitter laughter that rose in her throat. Brenia had shown her compassion. It was not a gift to be squandered.

Brenia continued. "My mother was a healer. She told me that for those with the gift, it was a duty to help anyone in need, regardless of who they were or what they might have done. Was it not the same where you come from?"

Kalie stared. "Your mother...? Was she a foreigner? From the west?"

"Foreigner, yes. From the west, no. She came from the frozen wastes of the north. All the women of her line were healers."

Kalie wanted to ask if she came her voluntarily, and what kinds of things Brenia might have learned, but now was not the time. She knew she had been given a second chance—both at remaining in Cassia's favor, and in rising in status among the horsemen—in the form of the child she had been asked to help. She also knew that if she didn't learn to control her tongue, she could easily doom this mission she had fought so hard to lead.

"How is it that Yarik still lives? I had thought anyone born with such a condition was killed at birth."

"Ah, now that is quite a story," said Brenia.

"Just not one that's generally known," said Cassia, throwing Kalie a meaningful look. "And it needs to stay that way."

Kalie nodded, and Brenia continued. "Riyik and Yalina loved each other since childhood. Her father, knowing that our family's herds were the best in the tribe, set her bride price at fifty horses. Riyik would have paid it the moment he was initiated as a warrior of Aahk, and thus free to marry, but our father was a stingy man and would not give him the horses.

"Then, when our tribe warred with the Hansi, and Riyik saved the life of Meraak, father of Yalina, he gave her to my brother as a gift of gratitude. They were happy, despite the fact that Yalina gave him no children for three years." Brenia glanced meaningfully at Cassia.

"Both rejoiced when she finally became pregnant, but her pregnancy was a difficult one. When at last the baby came, Yalina nearly died. And when Riyik saw his son's foot, he grieved, for he knew his duty. But when he saw how it was with his wife, he feared that losing her child would push her beyond hope of recovery."

"So he let the boy live?" Kalie asked. "To please his wife?"

"It seemed certain that both would die soon enough," Brenia said sadly. "Why deny the poor woman what little comfort she could have? At least, that was my reasoning. I told him the babe might give her the strength to live, and then someday, she might be strong enough to have another."

"But instead, it was Yalina who died, a few moons later, and the boy who lived, despite his ailment," said Cassia

"And by then, there was no way Riyik would kill him," Brenia added.

"How have you kept it a secret all this time?" Kalie asked. "Surely others have noticed..." She trailed off, hoping the two horsewomen would supply the information she wanted.

"There was only myself and old Mara, here, attending her." Brenia said nodding toward the slave woman who sat churning butter beside the brazier. "We have no formal examination, in the way of some of the other tribes, where a baby is presented unwrapped to his chief or to all the tribe. So no one else has seen the deformity. Yet."

Kalie heard the sorrow in her voice, and the fear. This situation was bad for the whole family. She thought of something else. "Is this Riyik's tent, then? Do you keep it for your brother?" Then, remembering the second child, who was now sitting up and rubbing his eyes, "Are you a widow?"

Brenia laughed. "I think I have served my husband better than that! When Hysaak dies—many

years from now, by the gods—" Brenia spread her
fingers in one of the many wards against evil Kalie
was learning to recognize, "he shall surely allow me
the honor of traveling to paradise by his side. Not for
me the shame of being a useless old widow in her
brother's tent!"

Kalie suddenly understood the honor that was
reserved for senior wives or favorite concubines, but
she had no time to dwell on it.

"When Yalina died," Brenia continued, "a part
of Riyik went with her. He became so reckless with his
life that the gods must have something special planned
for him, or he'd have died twenty times over by now!

"But I had given birth to Beraak just a few
moons before Yarik was born, and had plenty of milk.
I offered to take him, just until Riyik married again."

"It's a common enough thing in this land,"
Cassia explained to Kalie. "And men never pay much
attention to babies until they're old enough to learn to
ride. Hysaak doesn't know."

*But he will soon*, Kalie realized. Yarik was
already past the age when most children could walk.
What would happen to Brenia, then, when her husband
discovered what she had brought into his tent?

"And Hysaak was thrilled to have the boy,"
Brenia continued. "The more battle-crazed Riyik
became, the higher he rose in the esteem of his fellow
warriors. Chief Kahlar has made him a close advisor,
and Ahnaak, too, has sought him out."

"So Hysaak has benefited by a marriage tie to a
great hero?" Kalie was thrilled as well by all she was
learning.

Brenia nodded. "Then, when Riyik returned
from the west, with all that treasure and all those

incredible stories, which no one quite believes but everyone wants to hear...well, you can guess how many men are shoving their daughters his way. Everyone wants a marriage tie to Riyik—and our family herds, since he knows more than our father ever did about horses—" Brenia blushed again, realizing she was babbling.

"The simple fact is," said Cassia, "Riyik has no interest in ever marrying again."

"Where does he live, with no wife to keep his tent?" Kalie asked.

"He hasn't had a home since Yalina died," said Brenia. "The summer she died, he slept in the fields beside his horse, as most bachelors do in fair weather."

"And more than a few married men as well," Cassia added. "Men of Aahk find tents confining. They prefer the freedom of the open steppes, and the open sky."

"Last summer, of course, Riyik was in your land Kalie, and never had to worry about a tent or a family. And now, he's spending the winter in the young warrior's tent, training the boys. It's a duty every man is expected to perform at least two or three seasons in his life. And it gives my brother a place to live, until he marries again." Perfectly composed once more, Brenia turned to Kalie, waiting for her to examine Yarik.

Kalie had the feeling Brenia could outwait anyone.

Slowly, with a false smile and soft words, Kalie undressed the little boy. She had never regained her comfort around children since learning she could not have any of her own, and it seemed Yarik could sense it. He whimpered and fussed. Wonderful, thought Kalie. This will certainly help my reputation as a healer—which she hadn't been seeking in the first place!

Brenia did not complain, however. She merely set the boy in her lap and distracted him with the long strings of amber beads that hung from her ears while Kalie learned what she could. Yarik seemed healthy enough. He had no other deformities besides the leg, which was not as complicated a problem as Kalie had first thought.

"Can you help?" Brenia's question was not a plea, but a demand for an honest answer.

"I don't know," Kalie replied with equal honesty. "Among my people, his leg would have been straightened from birth, using a series of braces made from birch bark. They would have forced his leg straight while the bones were still soft and pliable."

"Would not something so confining have stunted the leg's growth?" asked Brenia.

"They would have been changed as he grew," Kalie explained. "Walking would be delayed, but still possible. At this point in his life, our healers would have made him special shoes—like snowshoes?" Both Brenia and Cassia nodded understanding.

Brenia gently probed Yarik's leg. "He is midway through his second year. His bones are not so hard—although I can see how much better it would have been had we known early on to do as you said. But...it still should be possible, should it not?"

Kalie thought hard before answering. She knew of cases when treatment had been long delayed, due to great distances, or ignorance that such treatment existed—yet were still effective. But she had no way of knowing what Maris might have done in such a situation.

"Perhaps. If you could find Alessa—Maris' apprentice—she might know."

"There will be no way to find her before summer, when the clans gather again," said Brenia. "And if you are right, we must not wait that long."

"Proceeding blindly could damage him further!" said Kalie, pressing the only argument they might take seriously. Goddess knew, they wouldn't consider the pain such measures might cause the boy any great deterrent!

"Let us start simply, with a leg brace. Perhaps we can begin the cure now, and Alessa can finish it."

They haggled over payment, which resulted in Kalie leaving Brenia's tent with a wealth of useful herbs. Yet she was distracted. Had she really spoken so unwisely to one of the beastmen? And why did Riyik not cause her to suffer, as Haraak or Maalke would have? Could love for his son make that much of a difference in the way one of them behaved? And if so, why not all of them?

Winter, Kalie decided, would not be as boring as she had feared.

# Chapter 23

The next few days were a flurry of activity, as everyone prepared for the festival of the winter solstice. For Kalie, it was the first time since her arrival that her duties did not involve shouts and blows and cruel laughter. Cassia acted as a buffer between Kalie and the women of Maalke's tent—and sometimes, she suspected, Maalke himself.

While the other women worked to prepare food and kumis and fine new clothes, Kalie was allowed to work on her potions for Cassia and set up a treatment regime for Riyik's son Yarik. She felt the hostile looks of the other women—especially Irisa, who felt that if anyone should be excused from work it should be herself—and felt as if she was walking through a bog: gliding safely across the surface as long as she stepped on the hidden patches of solid ground, but dead if she took a misstep.

For the moment, all was well: Yarik's leg responded well to the brace, and Brenia was convinced of Kalie's powers. Soon everyone in camp was convinced as well.

For all that she had protested she was not a healer, knowledge that had filled the air she breathed back in Hot Springs had the uncanny knack of coming back to Kalie, just at the time it would be most useful.

From Brenia's stores and things she found elsewhere in and around the camp, Kalie brewed a heavy dark syrup of mandrake root and yarrow, and told Cassia to drink it ten days before she was due to bleed again, and to lie with Maalke as often as possible beginning the next day. Cassia was thrilled, for the night she was to begin would be the night of the Winter Festival. When the time arrived, Cassia drank the potion with great ceremony. The bitter taste only convinced her of its power.

On the morning of the winter solstice—a day with almost no light, and heavy clouds turning what little there was into a kind of perpetual dusk—the people of the steppes rose early. The men—dressed in their new felt tunics, leather trousers and heavy fur cloaks—left the tents to struggle though freezing winds to the empty field where they would conduct the ritual that marked the turning of the season. The women rose soon after to begin preparing what would be the greatest feast of the season.

Altia was telling her daughters the traditional tale of winter while she rubbed spices into a whole skinned goat in preparation for roasting. "—And Aahk struggled with Eternal Winter for seven days until at last even that mighty spirit was forced to beg for mercy. And when Aahk had the winter in his power he cried, 'Return to your own land, and bring back the sun to ours!"

"And so Eternal Winter became only ordinary winter once more, and the summer returned to our people. But before he surrendered, deceitful winter had stolen a lock of our ancestor's hair. And he took it to his mother, the terrible witch, and with it, she made him a charm that allowed winter to come back each year, more terrible than ever, to exact revenge on the sons of the only man ever to defeat him.

"But the People of Aahk are strong. We survive the harshest of winters, and every year we emerge stronger than before. Even now, your father stands with the other warriors at the sacrifice. He will wear the blood of the white horse this day, to show winter that we are mightier than he is. And tonight, winter's power will be broken. For tomorrow, we will hold the sun a little longer, and the next day longer still, until at last it chases the snow and wind from our land."

Kalie was surprised to find herself nodding in appreciation at the story's end. Its violent nature offended her as much as the ritual sacrifice now occurring, but she couldn't fault these people for the contentious nature of their beliefs. These were, quite possibly, the harshest winters anyone on the Mother's Earth endured. Living through the longest night of the year in such a place was no small feat.

The feast began just as the sun set, the weather actually cooperating for once. While the wind still blew sharply, the snow had slowed to just a few flakes. Between the tents and the long leather windbreak the men had set up, a kind of oasis was created, heated by many fires and the body heat of over one hundred people.

True to her word, Cassia saw to it that Kalie took her portion of the feast just after Maalke's two wives—at the same time as Irisa, and ahead of the other slaves and children. It was, she had to admit, a magnificent feast. Kalie had never seen so much meat at one meal before. True, that was nearly all they had besides the many cheeses and curds made from the milk of goat and sheep. Only a few dried roots were present to remind people that food came from any source besides than animals. But the variety—sheep, goat, deer, fowl, and bear—in such a range of preparation was breathtaking. Not to mention mouthwatering.

Only the men ate the meat of the slain horse. When everyone was served, she settled down beside Cassia for the part she had been looking forward to all day: the storytelling of the warriors.

Kalie sat through several crudely told tales of battle and rape, waiting for something she recognized as a story, and wondering if this was all they had. Then a man rose and strode over to the bonfire. When he had everyone's attention, he began to speak in the cadence of a true storyteller, and something inside Kalie leapt in recognition.

"'Long ago, before men had learned the secrets of the horse, there lived a man named Saak. Born with the mark of the sun upon his brow, all could see that Saak was destined for greatness. One day, while he was still a boy, the god Aahk spoke to him in a vision...'"

Kalie listened in fascination, impressed in spite of herself. When the tale was finished, the king tossed a gold armband to the storyteller, who caught it in midair and proudly slipped it onto his arm. Ahnaak called on another warrior to tell the story of another famous battle, and the entertainment continued.

Kalie listened eagerly, waiting for something that would tell her how to manipulate these men into fighting each other or turning on their chiefs. As the evening drew on, and Kalie found nothing helpful, she asked Cassia's leave to view the rest of the festivities.

"Yes, of course," said Cassia. "Although for now, it is mostly talking and eating. The dancing will begin later." She searched the crowd anxiously for Maalke, while Kalie walked away quietly. This festival seemed to be one of the few where men and women mixed freely—not necessarily a safe thing for

Kalie, but too great an opportunity to gain information for her not to risk it.

Children ran about, tumbling together and laughing, their faces covered with grease and their bellies full of meat. Women chatted in groups, or brought food to their men. Kalie thought of her friends from Riverford, now scattered among the Twenty Clans. How many of them were even now using the feast as she was, to further their mission? How many of them were already dead? In the dark and cold of this, the longest night of the year, it was easy to imagine herself as the only one left, the only thing that stood between her world and this hell.

Raucous laughter from a large group of men caught her attention. Covering herself as best she could, Kalie approached. A different kind of storytelling was happening here, one far more useful than kind she had just left. Apparently, while each band of warriors had been hunting meat for tonight's feast, one had met up with one of the other clans of Aahk, and together, sought another kind of prey.

"There will be trouble," muttered a gravelly voiced warrior, seated near the edge of the fire. "There was peace between the Hansi and the men of Aahk for many seasons—until you men and that fool Yuraak broke it!"

"It was a fair fight," argued a young warrior, for whom the skirmish was probably his first battle. "Besides," he eyed the warrior beside him who sat with a well-endowed blond woman on his lap. "Some treasures are worth making a few enemies over." Kalie recognized the warrior with the new captive woman as Hysaak, Brenia's husband. She also noticed that the woman did not much seem to mind the change in her situation, giggling as Hysaak played with her breasts, and rubbing herself between his legs.

Brenia sat some distance away, looking unhappy. Kalie wondered why she did not simply walk away. For tonight, at least, she was free to visit friends, or simply return to her tent and go to bed. She didn't have to endure the humiliation of watching her husband play with his new toy, while she sat ignored. Then again, perhaps she did. Could Hysaak have ordered her to remain where she was? Was there some sort of expectation that a wife watch her husband with his new concubine? Kalie wanted to say something to Brenia, to offer some comfort to the woman who had been kind to her, but feared that a slave offering comfort to a wife might be considered an insult in this world.

Then the conversation turned to something that made her forget about Brenia's troubles. "Do you think Yuraak really did as he boasted of doing, and rode his clan west?"

"Alone? In the middle of winter?" snapped a one-eyed man who was missing part of his nose as well. "Even Yuraak isn't that much of a fool!"

"Not a traitor, I think you meant to say," said a small warrior, but with a dangerous bearing. He, unlike most of his companions was cold sober, and he held a long knife with a wickedly sharp point for all to see. "To suggest that my kinsman would ride off on such an adventure without the consent of his king…"

"No one is saying that, Kelvik," said a blond giant whose size alone seemed capable of preventing a fight. "But all men could see how besotted he was with Haraak's tales of the wealth in the west. Gold and grain and women just there for the taking…"

Kalie worried for a moment about the harm that might have befallen her people in her absence, but she was cheered by the knowledge that if Yuraak had followed the route used by Haraak, anyone they met was likely prepared enough to deal with the twenty or so warriors Yuraak had. That much, she had at least seen to before leaving her homeland. And if Kalie could find a way to encourage other clan leaders to make the same mistake… If she could goad them into dividing their forces…

"All of us were," said a warrior with another captured woman on his lap. Unlike Hysaak's, this one did not look very happy, and cringed whenever he touched her. "And we're all growing impatient for the day the king will lead us to this new land!"

"The king is ill!" snapped the grouchy man who had first spoken. "We should be sacrificing horses for his recovery, not chattering like a bunch of women about a golden land beyond the edge of the world!" A pall settled over the company, and the men began dispersing soon after. But Kalie felt suddenly that the longest night of the year was about to give way to a new dawn filled with hope. She wandered through the crowd, hoping for more news, but finding none, gave up, anxious to return to Verena, who was tending the fire in Maalke's tent.

Spotting Cassia, who was trying to catch Maalke's attention, Kalie approached her. "How are you feeling?" she asked.

"I will be fine once the dancing begins!" snapped Cassia. "Maalke can never resist me when I dance for him. Are you certain I did not drink the potion too soon? It may be nearly morning before—"

"You did not take it too soon," Kalie said

patiently. "My only concern is that I made it too strong. You're certain you are well? No cramping? Nausea? Headache?"

"No, nothing like that! Just impatience."

"May I return to the tent now, Mistress?" Kalie asked.

"But the night has barely begun," said Cassia. "You will miss all the music and dancing!"

Kalie checked on the choice pieces of meat she had saved for Varena, who remained alone in the tent. Kalie had agreed that an evening of rest inside the tent would be better for the girl's health than attending the outdoor festival—until she had learned that Varena would have none of the feast, as no one was planning to bring any of it to her. "Extra sleep would be my choice of festival gifts," she told Cassia.

Cassia hesitated, and then nodded. But as Kalie rose to go, she stopped her. "Kalie, it would be better if you didn't spend so much time with Varena. And especially better if you didn't coddle her so much."

Kalie felt her face stiffen. "Why not?"

"It's only that…you have a good future here, and Varena…well, the gods have decreed a hard life for that one."

"All the more reason for a few mere mortals to be kind to her," Kalie retorted.

Cassia scowled. "That is not how things work here! Bad luck can be contagious—especially to those closest."

"I'm sure you are right," Kalie began, still not sure what Cassia was talking about. Then the music began and Cassia, spotting Maalke, leapt up and hurried to him without another word.

# Chapter 24

Varena startled from a troubled sleep as Kalie slid into the tent.

"It's only me," she said softly. "I brought you some food from the feast.

Varena's guarded look of disbelief vanished at the sight—and smell—of the rich food. "You are kind to me," she mumbled around a mouthful of goat's meat. "I will miss you when you leave."

"Am I leaving?" Kalie was instantly worried. "And slow down!" Varena was wolfing down the food as if she feared it would be snatched from her—which she probably did.

Varena slowed for a moment, only enough to look at Kalie in surprise. "Everyone talks of how you are healing Riyik's cursed son. And Cassia—if you can make her have a baby, one of the chiefs will surely buy you! Or Maalke will decide give you as a gift to some warrior whose favor he wants."

Lovely, thought Kalie. I finally start to gain some status here, but it leaves me with less control than before. Still, if she were to move to one of the chiefs' tents, she would have access to all sorts of useful information. Storytelling wasn't getting her into the centers of power as she had hoped, but perhaps healing would.

Varena had finished the food and was shooting hesitant gazes at Kalie. Every time Kalie tried to make eye contact, the girl looked away. "Something you'd like to ask me?" Kalie said gently.

"It's nothing." Kalie waited. Finally, Varena blurted it out. "Could you give me a potion to keep me from becoming a woman?"

"What would you rather be when you grow up?" Kalie teased. "A fox? Or perhaps a horse?"

Varena sighed and looked away. Kalie sobered. "I'm sorry Varena. I was trying to be funny. Why don't want to be a woman?" *Other than the obvious reason that life for a woman here is worse than death?* It was obvious to Kalie, but until now, she had seen no sign that any of the other women felt that way.

Varena remained silent, so Kalie tried another tack. "Surely you have a few more seasons before you have to worry about it."

Now Varena reacted with surprise. "No, it will be soon. See?" Tugging and unwrapping, the girl shed enough of her clothing for Kalie to see two tiny bumps beginning to swell into breasts.

"Why, you must be older than I thought, Varena. How many seasons have you? Do you know?"

"Nearly twelve, I think."

"That's still too young to grow up, at least where I come from. But from the looks of things, you still have a while before the full flower of womanhood is upon you." Kalie wished she could think of something more reassuring to say. After a long silence she said, "Where I come from, this would be a happy time. When your moon times began, there would be a great feast in your honor. The priestesses would initiate you into the Great Mysteries, and later, when you decided you were ready, there would be many young men, eager to introduce you to the Mother's Gift."

Varena stared at Kalie, as if trying to make sense of what she was saying.

Kalie gave up. "I guess here, all you can look

forward to being married off to some warrior."

"Married?" cried Varena. "Do you think any man is going to pay bride price for me? I'm not some trueborn daughter to bring suitors with gifts! If I was lucky, some warrior might buy me as a concubine for his son—until he could afford a wife. At least that way, I might give him his first son, and have status his tent. But…I don't think I will be lucky."

Something in her words echoed what Cassia had said earlier. "What do you fear may happen?" Kalie asked, trying to keep the tremor from her voice.

"Maalke has been looking at me," Varena said in a voice dead with despair.

"What do you mean he's been…you mean like…? But he is your father!"

Varena turned away, cringing. "You're probably wishing you never wasted your kindness on me," she whimpered.

"Why would I wish that?" cried Kalie, wanting to wrap Varena in her arms, but not wanting to frighten her further.

"For tempting my own father!"

"Oh Goddess!" To her horror, Kalie began to cry.

"What's wrong?" cried Varena, backing away.

Now Kalie began to laugh. "Good question! Here, let me ask you one. Do you find anything wrong with the fact that your own father might force himself on you? And instead of protecting you, as any normal people would, the beast-monsters of this place would blame you for it?"

"But it's my fault! Irisa told me so!"

"And why would you believe anything that bitch has to say?" Kalie snapped. Forcing herself to calm down, she tried again. "How about the other women of this tent?"

Varena shrugged. "No one else has said anything. But Altia has noticed. The way she looked at me the time he touched me here," Varena motioned to her nearly non-existent breasts and shivered. "I think she might kill me before he does."

"He would rape you and then kill you? That seems wasteful. Wouldn't he want to use you many times, and then increase his wealth by selling you to someone else?" Kalie wished she could take back the words, but Varena seemed not to notice anything wrong with them.

"Perhaps if no one found out, but…when I was very young—my mother was still alive—there was a girl in Haraak's tent. She was his daughter by a slave, like me. She became pregnant before she was even a woman! There was no other man in the tent and she had never been allowed to leave it, so it had to be Haraak. But he said it wasn't. He said she must have been out playing harlot like her mother before her."

"What happened to her?" Kalie hoped she was not about to vomit up the only good meal she was going to get all winter.

"Oh, Haraak had to kill her, of course. Such behavior is an abomination, and could endanger the tribe."

"And why miss a chance to terrorize all the women and girls of the tribe, right?"

For the first time, Varena seemed surprised. "What do you mean?"

Kalie thought a moment, and then asked, "How did you feel when that girl was killed?" When Varena did not respond, she prompted. "Were you afraid?"

Varena shrugged, and then nodded.

"How about the other women? The slaves and their children? Were they afraid?"

"Yes. No one spoke of it, but, yes. I guess everyone was afraid. For awhile."

"You said your mother was still alive. Did you ask her about what was going on?"

"Yes, but she told me to be quiet. Then, later, she told me to always be a good girl. To obey quickly, and keep my eyes lowered."

"So it would not happen to you?"

Varena seemed to lose interest in conversation. She just sat huddled on the floor of the tent. Kalie decided to push forward.

"I'm sure that's what she did, Varena, and so did the rest of the mothers here. They all knew that girl was blameless, but what could they do about it? So they told themselves and each other that it was her fault. That let them live with themselves. And it gave them the illusion that they and their daughters could somehow control what happened to them in a place where they have no control at all. Be better than her. More demure. More obedient. More pleasing to the man who was supposed to protect them.

"But none of that matters, Varena, because it's all a lie. The simple fact is that there is nothing any of you can do. In your world, a man does as he pleases, and if a price has to be paid, it's his victim who pays it."

Varena finally looked up. She looked like she hadn't understood a word of what Kalie had said. Then she asked, "Why tell me all this? Is it supposed to make me feel better? That there's no hope no matter what I do?"

"No. It's supposed to make you see that it's not your fault. And it's supposed to make you want a better life."

"I've always wanted a better life!" Varena laughed harshly. "Wanting it doesn't make it happen!"

"True," said Kalie, thinking she was about to give up and go to bed. Instead, she heard herself say, "So come with me when I leave here."

For the first time, Varena's face lit with hope. "You mean when you become a wife in some other tent you will ask for me as your handmaiden?" Then her face fell and the despair returned. "It wouldn't work. Maalke would never let me go."

Kalie thought long and hard in a very short moment. She knew that after moonspans of suffering, she finally had some status in this place. That if Cassia conceived a child tonight, she might actually begin to accomplish her mission. But that mission suddenly seemed dull and pointless in the face of Varena's pathetic hope for nothing more than slavery to a kinder master.

"No," said Kalie firmly. "I mean that when I finish what I came here to do, and I leave this cursed place to return to my own people, I want you to come with me."

Varena stared.

Kalie took the plunge. "I didn't come here to be a slave, Varena. I came here to destroy this world, so that a different world—a better world—will have a chance to survive.

"You can betray me to the men if you choose. With information like this, you might curry favor with a powerful man, and become his slave, rather than Maalke's. Or tell Maalke. Then, instead of raping and killing you, he might reward you."

Varena seemed to seriously consider this opportunity. Then she shook her head. "No one would ever believe such a tale. And Maalke would only beat me for spreading wild stories. But would you really take me with you?"

"Yes," said Kalie. "By the Goddess, I swear it."

"And would your people really let me live among them?" Varena looked Kalie in the eye for the first time she could remember. "What will they do when they find out I'm nothing but a bastard slave girl? What if Maalke has his way with me before we leave? What use would I be then?"

"Come with me and I will show you—" Kalie began.

Then there was a great commotion outside. Before Kalie could react, the tent flap was flung open, and several burly women helped Irisa inside.

Her labor had begun.

# Chapter 25

"She didn't need to do this on the longest night of the year," Kalie said to no one in particular. "Irisa giving birth would make *any* night the longest."

Tasine and Altia, along with two women from another tent, assisted the laboring woman. Kalie's offers of help had been violently rejected by Irisa, although Altia had looked inclined to accept.

Now, after several hours of seeking to draw the baby from the shrieking concubine, Altia seemed ready to hand the job off to any who would accept it.

"Why does she help at all?" Kalie asked Varena. "She despises Irisa, and dreads the prospect that she will give Maalke another son. Why not let her fend for herself, and hope she and the baby both die?"

"She is senior wife," explained Varena. "All the children of the household are her responsibility. I'm sure she hopes that Irisa and the baby do both die, but she wouldn't dare be seen causing it to happen, even by failing to act. An Aahkan warrior values his sons above almost everything—even his horses!"

Maalke and Cassia had returned to the tent around midnight. Cassia, looking satisfied by what was apparently a victorious outcome in her campaign to get Maalke's assistance in getting pregnant, lost some of her color at the sight of Irisa in labor. Kalie didn't know if it was jealousy over Irisa already having what she so desperately wanted, of fear that, if successful, she herself might be screaming like this in nine moons.

Maalke had at first been delighted by the news that his son would be born on such an auspicious night, but was now in a foul temper from too much drink and too little sleep. While Irisa had made an effort to be quieter since her master's return, her groans and screams were keeping everyone awake. He had finally summoned Cassia to his chamber to keep him occupied. Cassia had been only too happy to comply.

Finally, near dawn, Kalie was awakened from a brief nap by a baby's cry. Smiling in spite of herself, she went to see the new life. Irisa, looking exhausted and wrung out, nevertheless reached eagerly for her baby, grinning with triumph as the gender was revealed.

"Another son!" she cried when Maalke arrived, proudly showing him the baby.

Maalke looked the baby over with obvious pleasure, and then quickly signaled the attending women to return him to his mother. Maalke slept for a while after that, but left the tent early in the day to inform his fellow warriors of the birth of his third son.

"She'll be impossible to live with now," Varena whispered. "She's the only one of Maalke's women to give him two sons."

"Will he make her a wife?" Kalie asked.

"He might, although few men besides chiefs have three wives. But he will give her gifts. Jewelry, furs, food." Varena looked envious.

Altia had curtly ordered the slaves to prepare the morning meal and clean up the mess around Irisa, then gone to her own bed, where her two daughters had already fallen into an exhausted sleep. Once Altia was snoring, Kalie insisted that Tasine get some rest as well. The startled slave woman, struggling to stay awake as she went about her daily chores, looked around nervously, then complied, throwing Kalie a look of gratitude.

While Varena stirred the porridge, Kalie gathered up the soiled rags and leather birthing mat, taking them out of the tent and as far from the camp as the freezing temperatures permitted. Then she stopped and looked around. While it might be too slight to notice, each day after this would last a little longer; each long night a little shorter. The back of winter had been broken, and spring's return was now inevitable. Kalie had survived this turning point. She would survive many more.

Back in the tent, an exhausted but haughty Irisa was nursing her new son, and smirking at everyone. "Come and see your new brother," she called to her three year old son, Bruk. The boy obediently came and looked down at the newborn. He did not seem very impressed. "Both of you will be great warriors like your father. And one of you shall inherit all his wealth."

Kalie gasped. "How can she say that out loud?" she whispered to Varena, as she added dried dung to the fire. "She's as much as telling her sons that they will have to kill Tarak and then fight each other!"

"She knows that no one but slaves can hear her. And as long as she doesn't speak directly of killing, it's no treason. Every boy grows up knowing he may have to fight his brother one day. Irisa only wants what every mother wants—to see her son inherit his father's wealth. And then make his mother mistress of a tent full of slaves and plunder."

Kalie sat back and regarded Varena while she worked. "Is that what your mother hoped for?"

Varena shot Kalie a puzzled look. "Yes, of

course. She was Maalke's favorite for a time. Altia
says she wasn't, but I know she was. She died giving
him a son."

Kalie nodded. "What happened to him—to
your brother?"

"He came too soon. He never took a breath.
Altia said that proved my mother was weak and could
only make weak children."

"Don't these people ever get tired of being
rotten?" Kalie muttered under her breath. "Do you
know how old you were when she died?" she asked
Varena.

"No. I had been too big for her breast for many
seasons. But so long ago that….sometimes, I can't
remember her face."

Four or five years, Kalie guessed. Much
younger than she was when her own mother died. She
looked at Irisa, who loved her children only for what
they could do for her. If she had borne a daughter this
day, instead of a son, would she have cast it aside?

"I was ten summers when my mother died,"
Kalie said. "Then my aunt adopted me. Wasn't there
anyone to mother you since then?"

This time, Varena just looked sad. "Altia…
she's my step-mother. My father's first wife."

"I've seen her version of mothering!" Kalie
spat.

"Is that different too, where you're from?"

Kalie nodded. "Where I come from, when a
child loses her mother, someone always adopts her.
We could not imagine anyone growing up as alone as
you have been."

"I wish it was like that here," sighed Varena.

"Would you like me to adopt you?" Kalie

asked suddenly.

Varena looked up, eyes wide. Then she drew back, as if fearing Kalie was teasing her. "Do you mean that?" she whispered. "You want to be my mother?"

"I would never presume to replace her," Kalie said quickly. "Only to help finish what she could not. And I can't promise to be the kind of mother who raised me, who would protect you—from Maalke or anyone else. But I will try. And I can't teach you to be a good, obedient woman of Aahk, because the thought of that sickens me!

"But I can promise to love you. To care for you always. To listen to anything you have to say, and sing to you at night, and see to it that you have enough to eat—whenever that's possible at least—"

"But what if you have a baby of your own?"

"Then I would have two children to love," Kalie said softly. She waited while that sank in, watching the play of disbelief, then wonder on Varena's face. Then she said, "Varena, I am twenty six turns of the seasons. Already old enough to be your mother, and not likely to ever have one of my own. Will you be my daughter?"

Varena nodded eagerly, but said nothing. Then Kalie saw she was crying, although she made no sound. Kalie, who had not heard Varena cry in all the moons she had been here, wondered if the girl had been beaten for it. Then she wondered what she was doing, adopting a child she could never protect, nor hope to see grow into womanhood.

But as she reached out a tentative hand to stroke Varena's hair, and then felt her leap into her arms, warm and alive and trusting, Kalie knew it didn't matter. She would give all she could to this child for whatever time she had.

Just like any mother.

# Chapter 26

The second half of winter passed more slowly than the first. The greatest distraction—not to mention the greatest feast—of the season was over. Kalie had heard that the omens from the sacrifices had all been good: the People of Aahk would survive the winter, and prosper greatly in the year to come. Nothing in the omens told of the Twenty Clans leaving the steppes to conquer the land to the west, nor joining with other tribes into the confederation Kalie had so feared.

The flocks were holding their own and the worst of the winter storms seemed to be over. The pace continued to slow until it seemed the only thing to do was survive until spring without going crazy from confinement and cold.

For the men of Aahk, this meant a time of gathering in small groups, in one or another of their tents for drinking, dicing, boasting contests and enjoying the charms of slave girls. It also meant training the young men in the art of war. During rare spurts of clear weather, it meant riding across the frozen steppes for hunts and races, or just the joy of moving like the wind on a favorite horse.

For the women, it meant an unbroken cycle of cooking and sewing, of making felt and tending the animals, of collecting dung and serving the men. Only wives were allowed to sometimes leave their tent to visit friends in another tent, and only then with the permission of their men. For those who stayed inside all winter, music, storytelling and gossip were the only distractions.

As Cassia had promised, by the end of winter,

Kalie had learned every folktale known to the women of Maalke's tent. Fascinated at first, Kalie soon grew tired of stories that seemed nothing more than endless variations on the theme of a woman whose problems were solved by marriage to a powerful man. There was the one about the beautiful maiden poisoned by her jealous stepsister, but roused from death by the kiss of a mighty warrior. There was another about a girl forced by her father to marry a hideous, but wealthy, monster only to have him turn handsome—and therefore good—after she endured many trials. And more than Kalie could count seemed merely to be variations of "King Frost."

To Kalie's surprise, there were a few stories she actually found familiar—but with interesting twists. Like the settled folk to the west, the nomads of the east told stories of talking animals. One Kalie rather enjoyed told of a clever dog that helped his loyal and honest, though rather stupid master triumph over his enemies. Others were darker tales of how deception and duplicity won the day. Still, these were stories that Maalke and his occasional guests enjoyed, as well as the women. They would be useful to know.

Kalie in turn, told the story of the clever midwife who needed all her wits to trick a pair of quarreling twins to cooperate in coming into the world, and of talking animals that tricked or helped humans as the stories demanded. Her tales of enchantments always caught her listeners' attention at the start, but left them confused or unsatisfied at the end.

"What was the point of the story if the farmer got everything back at the end?" Irisa demanded after Kalie told the story of the arrogant farmer whose ingratitude to the Goddess brought trouble to his village. "That goddess should have let him stay a goat forever!"

"All he had to do was say he was sorry? And that fixed everything?" Altia snorted.

"He didn't just say it," Kalie argued. "He *felt* it. That's what mattered."

The story of the wasteful hunter who mended his ways after being turned into a deer left them equally cold. But the story of the villagers who always did the opposite of what their wise elders told them had the women laughing until their sides ached.

Varena loved them all, but that, Kalie suspected, was because Varena was now her daughter. And having a mother—even a fictive mother who was, herself an outsider and a slave—made Varena happy. Her life had improved in other ways as well. Maalke's "interest" in her, as the others called it, had vanished as quickly as it had begun. Altia no longer felt the need to punish Varena for it, and Cassia no longer warned Kalie away from her. Which was good, Kalie reflected, for what had begun as a gesture of kindness to a lonely child, had grown fully into the bond that exists between mother and child.

Kalie listened to the gossip told around the fire whenever Maalke was gone, but found little of any interest. She did marvel at just how much energy Altia could maintain on the subject of whom her two daughters might marry, since that time was still years away—and neither Altia nor her daughters would have any say in the matter anyway. Discussions of which man's affections had been stolen by some brazen new wife or concubine turned her stomach, especially since Brenia's name headed that list. Elka, the blond woman Hysaak had captured just before the Winter Festival seemed well on her way to displacing the strong, dignified woman who had shown such kindness to Kalie. And the women here regarded it as sport. As amusing to them as speculations on which young wife had taken a lover, and how soon she would die for that sin.

The biggest news for Kalie involved the women with whom she lived. Irisa's new son survived his first moonspan of life, and was duly named and numbered among the tribe. Maalke held the customary feast, and presented Irisa with many gifts, including the fur of a silver wolf and a necklace of deer teeth and bone beads. But he did not elevate her to the status of wife, nor present her with beaded slippers. She was, therefore, still a concubine, and a servant in his wives' tent.

If Irisa was angry with Maalke for this slight, she did not show it. She was as adoring as ever towards him, and eager to return to his bed. She did, however, show displeasure soon after, when Cassia's news reached her.

Cassia was pregnant. While Kalie urged silence, and the wait of a second full moonspan without bleeding before she told anyone, Cassia was certain well before that. Strangely, so were all the other women in the tent. As fearsomely ignorant as they were about things Kalie took for granted, when it came to pregnancy, they seemed to have heightened senses. They could literally smell it.

If Irisa was bothered by the potential competition Cassia's pregnancy represented, Altia remained haughtily above reaction. "She will lose it as she lost all the others," Altia assured everyone—as long as Maalke was not there to overhear. Cassia had been barren for five years. Why should that change now?

*Why indeed?* Kalie worried about what it might mean for her, if Cassia had a healthy son, and insisted on giving Kalie the credit. Altia could well decide that a slave with that much power needed to be disposed of, and she had no doubt that Altia was capable of doing just that.

But Kalie saw no sign of it as the long winter slowly dragged toward spring. Every day, she brewed up teas and potions of whatever she could get her hands on—some nothing more than willow bark and harmless weeds—and solemnly fed them to Cassia, knowing that faith could be the most powerful magic of all. Cassia bloomed with health and joy, and showed Kalie the practices the nomads used to make a baby strong. Some things made sense to Kalie, such as eating the liver of the animals on which these people fed. Others, such as tying sheep sinew around her ankles, or chanting daily prayers to Aahk, she simply nodded at and wished Cassia well.

And Kalie was both surprised and touched when Cassia kept her promises. The first time Altia had, grudgingly, ordered a sheep's liver prepared for Cassia in the manner only given to pregnant women, Cassia had presented Kalie with the skin of the largest sheep killed for the Midwinter Festival. The fleece was thick and warm and had been worked and softened with great care. To this gift she added the fur of four sables, caught in Cassia's own snares. While four sable skins would not go far to line the new cloak, the fur was unbelievably soft and thick, and the glossiest black Kalie had ever seen. Clever hands could work them into a collar fit for a chief's wife.

Kalie made a new wrap for herself from the sheepskin, but used the sables for a different purpose. Cutting away the worst of her old mantle, she used what was left to make a short hooded cape for Varena. Because the girl was so small, it fell nearly to her knees. That, combined with the tattered cloak she already had, might keep her warm for the rest of winter. But lining the ragged looking hood, which no nomad would favor with a second glance, was the rich, naturally insulated sable fur. Varena's ears and neck would be warmer than Altia's when she went outside —and no one would ever know.

When she first showed it to Varena, the girl was so excited Kalie feared she would give away the secret and bring down the wrath—and greed—of the entire household. She needn't have feared, however. Varena had lived in this place all her life, and knew how quickly it would be taken from her if anyone suspected she had anything worth stealing. Still, the secret smile she shot Kalie every time she went outside warmed Kalie's heart.

It was a fitting symbol for the all the good things she hoped to bring into the life of one mistreated child. In this, as in all others of her plans. All she had to do was keep everyone else from finding out what she was really up to.

# Chapter 27

A bitter wind was blowing. Maalke, along with most of the other warriors, was away, leading a mock battle; part of a training exercise for the older boys. Altia was hosting a small party, consisting of her two sisters and a childhood friend. All of the women were first wives, and had brought attitudes to prove it.

Kalie and the other slaves were kept busy inside the tent, hurrying to refill cups with tea, and serving what fare Altia was able to provide. Precious little, Kalie thought, this late in the winter. Spring was on everyone's minds now—it was the major topic of conversation. Already the air was growing warmer. Icicles clinging to tents and animals melted and stretched during the day, only to freeze again, longer and thinner than before during the night. All living things were restless, eager for the change that meant new life.

For Kalie, thoughts of spring brought as much anxiety as anticipation. Were any of the others from her home still alive? And if so, what would seeing them again be like? And most importantly: when would the invasion come? If it were going to happen this year, the serious planning would begin in the early summer, when the scattered clans reformed into one large tribe. How long would it take to plan? How likely was it these contentious warriors could agree on anything? Kalie knew she couldn't rely on their own belligerence to keep them from organizing. She had to find out what they were planning.

"Kalie?" Cassia's sharp whisper brought her out of her reverie. "Altia told you to serve the soup!"

Sending Cassia a grateful look, Kalie hurried to lift the heavy bowl of boiled tree bark floating with shreds of stringy meat. Under Altia's baleful glare, she set it in the midst of the four women who were participating in this "feast". Kalie could remember the feasts in her homeland, where something like what she now served the guests would barely be fit for dogs.

Cassia played her lyre and sang for the women while they ate and gossiped and painted their feet with henna. Tasine told a story, but her voice was hoarse from a recent illness, and Altia did not ask her for any more.

"She should be asking you to tell stories," Varena whispered as the slaves crouched in the shadows, waiting for what scraps might be left when the party was done. "You're much better than Tasine. And you know stories that no one else does!"

"Shh!" Kalie warned. While she had hoped to begin that very work long before now, Kalie did not wish to start with Altia. Cassia's pregnancy was continuing normally, and Yarik was beginning to walk. It enhanced her reputation with everyone except Altia. From Maalke's first wife, Kalie could only hope for anonymity.

Cassia, looking contented and ready for a nap, gazed thoughtfully at Kalie from across the tent, seeming to read the foreigner's thoughts. While Altia was busy seeing her guests out of the tent, Cassia crawled over to Kalie and whispered, "Tomorrow, Brenia will have a much better party in her tent. You will tell stories then."

Same bitter wind, different tent. Yet it felt like a different world. Brenia's tent was infused with a light that seemed to soften the harshness of this world, while Altia's seemed to enhance it. There were more people at this party: Kalie counted seven guests—and not all of them were wives.

Mara kept the children occupied in Brenia's chamber, so they would not disrupt the party, but Kalie could hear her coughing, and knew she should be resting instead. Even as she tried to prepare her first story, Kalie thought about teas she might suggest before she left. Elka sat on Hysaak's bed, looking bored and put out, and not offering to help with anything.

But Brenia seemed happy to serve her guests herself, as if each of them honored her with her presence. Though she did the work of a servant, Benia carried herself like a queen. And the meal she served was certainly fit for royalty, Kalie thought, compared to what most everyone else had this late in the season: rich mutton stew, soft cheese, root cakes sweetened with honey—Kalie couldn't imagine where she had gotten *that*—and several pleasant teas. Kalie was waiting for instructions to begin telling stories when Brenia surprised her by giving her food as well. When Kalie responded with a blank look of shock—bad form for a storyteller, she realized—Brenia only laughed and told her she couldn't tell stories on an empty stomach.

When the friendly chatter died down, Brenia nodded to Kalie. She half rose and knee walked to the space by the brazier that cleared for her as women rearranged themselves in a whisper of felt and linen.

"How would you like me to begin?" she asked Brenia.

"Tell us tales of your world to the west,"

replied the hostess.

Just the opening Kalie had been hoping for—though she reminded herself not to expect any miracles. "Like everything else in my world," Kalie began, "our stories are different from yours. I shall begin with a tale which takes place by the Black Sea." Smiling at her audience's questioning looks at the unfamiliar words she added, "a sea is a body of water bigger than any lake or river. So large that you cannot see the other side. It has mighty waves that crash on the shore, over and over, and the water is full of salt."

And just like that, she had them. As far as the women in the tent were concerned, this was already make-believe. "Once there was a poor fisherman who lived on the shore of this sea. Each day…" Kalie faltered. How was she going to explain a boat to people who rarely even saw trees? "…He floated upon the water on a bundle of sticks, and cast his net for fish. One day, he caught a fish that was all the colors of the rainbow. 'Return me to my home!' cried the fish, "and I will give you three wishes…""

All afternoon it went on, story after story. Through each one, she had their attention, and usually their enjoyment, but not the enthusiasm she hoped for. Finally, sensing this was to be her last story, Kalie decided to take a chance.

"Once there was a woman named Manka," she began, giving voice to a story she had been working on, but had not planned to tell yet. "Her husband, Garok, was a great warrior and owned many flocks, but he was a miserly man, who kept his household just above starvation, and never hosted feasts, though he enjoyed those of others well enough." Eyes were widening, and at least two women exchanged a knowing glance.

Elka yawned dramatically from across the tent. "Don't you think we've had enough stories?" she asked Brenia loudly. Several of the guests gasped at the concubine's rudeness and Brenia looked mortified. "Hysaak will be home soon and this..." she looked around the tent with obvious distaste, as if she were mistress here, "...gathering will not please him."

"Elka!" Brenia began, barely keeping her composure. But it was clear she did not know how to save her party—or her dignity—from Elka's attack.

"That's quite all right, Mistress," Kalie said quietly, but making sure her voice carried across the tent. "It's very common after many stories for someone to object—especially when they see that the character being served up so clearly resembles them. As Elka obviously sees herself in wicked Garok." Kalie smiled at Elka, while the women exploded with shocked laughter. A few of them even applauded.

Kalie enjoyed the color that flooded Elka's face, and the way her mouth opened and closed like a landed fish—but she enjoyed the smile on Benia's face even more.

"Besides his stinginess," Kalie continued as if nothing had happened, "the thing that Garok was most known for was his stubbornness. So headstrong was this man that if someone remarked on the fairness of a blue sky, he'd likely say it was snowing." Now it was a softer laughter that ran through the tent. Encouraged, she continued. "If a warrior brought home a new black horse, Garok would insist it was white!

"Now, Manka was as generous and friendly as Garok was tight fisted and contentious. She was a fine cook and could make a delicious feast out of the

meanest scraps, and her kumis was the best in all the
tribes. Still, she had little enough call to use her
talents, other than on her greedy husband.

"One fair summer day, Manka stood sat beside
her tent, churning yet another batch of milk into
cheese, gazing at her husbands endless flocks of sheep
and goats, and thought 'How nice it would be to
celebrate the coming winter with feasting and drinking
and companionship. We have more than enough to
share, and if we threw a feast for the whole camp,
perhaps others would do the same, and who knows?
Perhaps the winter wouldn't seem so long or so hard.
But there's no use thinking about it. If I suggest a
feast, Garok will declare a fast!'

"Then she had a strange thought. When Garok
came home for his supper that night, Manka sighed as
she served his food, 'Well, I for one will be pleased to
see winter come. It will be quiet and easy for me, what
with no baking or stewing to worry about."

"'What are you talking about?' Garok
demanded.

"'Well, as scant as our flocks and as poor as
the harvest, there will be little enough to do. I must
say, I look forward to the peace and quiet.'

"'Are you mad, woman? My flocks have never
been larger! And the chief himself gave me ten sacks
of wheat from the last raid! You will bake bread and
cakes—and make them your finest ever!'

Hiding her grin, Manka nodded meekly. "But
with all those baked goods, I won't have to worry
about cutting big haunches of meat and roasting them,
will I?'

"'What good is bread without meat?'
demanded Garok. 'I tell you, you will kill our largest

sheep and finest goat before the clan leaves for the winter grounds!'

"Manka heaved a mighty sigh. 'It shall be as you command, husband. Only promise me you won't bring out any of the wine you took in last spring's raid! You know what that does to the warriors!'

"'Yes—it makes them enjoy a woman's poor cooking more than they otherwise would! Of course we'll drink the wine! Maybe all of it!'

"'But you're not thinking of inviting everyone in the clan!' cried Manka, doing her best to sound terrified.

"'I suppose you'd rather have all that food go to waste?' jeered Garok. 'Yes, I think I will invite the whole clan!'" The women howled with laughter, some of them looking scandalized and covering their mouths, others slapping their thighs and cheering aloud for clever Manka. Brenia, Kalie noticed, was laughing the loudest of anyone.

"Manka went away moaning about all the work she had to do, and how it would ruin them all, while Garok enjoyed more of her fine kumis and began to plan out the gifts he would give and the entertainment they must have.

"When the night arrived and the guests came, the feasting was the finest anyone could remember. People sang and danced until dawn and Manka was the loudest and freest among them. So much so, that Garok began to suspect that she had tricked him. It made him angry to see her so jolly and carefree."

The mood in the tent changed at once, as the women glanced nervously at each other, wondering what was going to happen next. *Let them worry*, thought Kalie, pausing long while she sipped her tea.

"It was a hard winter for Manka, for while, as she had hoped, many other men sought to emulate Garok by throwing grand feasts, Manka was forbidden to attend any of them. Garok took his concubine and his slaves, but Manka stayed in her tent the whole season." Kalie gazed at her audience through lowered lashes. Some were clearly offended by her last statement, but a few were staring transfixed, sensing that something more was coming. To these women, she shot a conspiratorial wink and took a deep breath.

"Now it happened in the spring that the river which the clan must cross rose high. The old wooden bridge, which was the only way across, was soaked from below. Because Garok had the biggest flocks, he and his family crossed first." Kalie had no idea if that were true, but no one seemed bothered by it. " Manka, stopping to soothe a nervous sheep, saw the boards in the middle were badly rotted. Without thinking, she called, 'Look where you step, husband. The plank is rotten. Step lightly!"

"Step lightly!" sneered Garok. "I'll do as I please—" But for once, Garok didn't finish what he had to say, for he had jumped with all his weight right onto—and then through—the rotten timbers. He fell with a loud splash into the swollen stream." Kalie paused as nearly everyone in the tent broke into applause and laughter. She realized she could stop right there. But she was so caught up in her own story that she had to finish with a greater flourish.

"Manka and the others leapt back just in time. She stared into the stream for a moment, and then rushed upstream, yelling for help to all who were still there, readying their households for departure. 'My husband has fallen into the stream! Someone, please, help!'"

"'Foolish woman!" cried the first man to see her. "We must search downstream not up!'

"'Ah,' said Manka. 'You do not know my Garok! All his life he's been so contentious that even in death, he's bound to go against the current!'"

Kalie bowed her head to indicate the story was over—and was greeted by stony silence. In that instant, she knew she had gone too far; that the women of this land would think she had insulted their men or their intelligence, or be outraged she had killed one of their warriors, even if in just a story.

Then, like a storm breaking around her, applause filled the tent.

"I've heard stories like that where it's the woman who's killed by her own greed or stubbornness," said one of the concubines. "But never the man." She blushed and covered her mouth with her hands.

"Which is strange, now that I think of it," another said more boldly, not hiding her face at all. "For I've known many men like Garok."

"You're married to one, Lisia!" laughed the woman next to her.

A young concubine spoke up shyly. "I liked the part where she kept begging him not to do the things she wanted him to—and got her way each time!"

"You must come and tell stories in my tent tomorrow!" said the woman who had found Garok's character familiar.

"I would be honored," Kalie said demurely. "I will come if my mistress allows it."

While various guests thanked their hostess and crawled out of the tent, and the woman who wanted

Kalie to come tell stories made arrangements with
Cassia, Brenia slipped a beaded bracelet into Kalie's
hand. The beads were amber, alternating with polished
pieces of horn—probably goat.

Kalie realized that for the first time since
leaving the west, she had been paid for her
storytelling. And although she knew the gift was as
much for putting Elka in her place as for the stories,
she was delighted just the same. Perhaps even more
than if it had been just for the stories.

# Chapter 28

The rest of the winter passed better for Kalie than for most members of Kahlar's clan. Her status in her own tent soared as one wife after another called her to tell stories. Even Maalke listened with interest while Kalie practiced. Old Tasine, stooped with exhaustion and swollen with arthritis, seemed to feel a kind of pride just living there and even Irisa boasted to other women about "her" slave's skill. And Verena's two half sisters now occasionally included her in the games and talk, Kalie saw. Only Altia remained haughtily above it all.

"I don't know why she doesn't ask you to entertain her friends," Varena said while they gathered dung one morning. It was, Kalie noted with pride, no longer her job, but she frequently did it anyway, to help Varena, and give Tasine's aching bones some rest. "She's losing a chance to gain status! Here she is, the owner of a talented slave, and she never makes use of you! Even Leja, the chief's wife, has asked about you!"

Kalie smiled patiently, marveling as Varena danced on her toes with a glow in her cheeks that Kalie could not have imagined when she first met her.

"She doesn't like to admit she was wrong about me," Kalie explained. "And given how little power she has, I can't really blame her. It's about the only thing no one is going to force her to do."

Varena finished filling her basket, and turned puzzled eyes to Kalie. "Little power? She's the mistress of the tent! And Maalke is an advisor to Chief Kahlar himself. She's one of the most powerful women in the clan!"

"But that's the problem," said Kalie. "What power she has comes from being Maalke's wife—and he can put her aside at a moment's whim. Even if she does nothing but serve him faithfully."

"But…if she serves him faithfully, he would never do such a thing!" cried Varena. "She gave him his firstborn son!"

"But there is nothing in your world to protect her if he should choose to. Her father is dead. Her only brother lives in another clan. Maalke need only say she displeased him, or looked upon another man with desire. He needn't even say that if he doesn't want to. No one will question him. So the only real power she has is to carry a grudge or hurt the women or children your traditions place beneath her."

Varena nodded thoughtfully. Kalie wondered how much she really understood. But she was happy for the few things she had been able to give Varena.

Kalie now had amassed a sizable collection of jewelry. And while she would have preferred to be paid in food this late in winter, she was glad for it.

And some payment was truly valuable. One woman had given her a pair of sturdy, barely worn leather boots. They were lined with ermine and topped with sheep's wool taken in winter. Once Kalie had fixed up—and sized down—her old boots for Varena, the two of them had the best boots in the tent after Altia's. Another woman gave her actual food—leftovers from the feast. These she shared with everyone—even Irisa and Altia. No asked her why this time, but that night, she told the story of how cooperation and sharing had become part of the laws of Kalie's people.

If spring would just get here, Kalie thought, everything would be fine. The nagging fear of famine would go away and they could get out of these stinking tents, and travel to where the tribes would gather. Kalie could reunite with her friends—if they still lived—and, most importantly, learn what plans her enemies were hatching about invading her world.

But spring was slow in coming.

The warriors sacrificed many horses, as well as sheep and goats which Kalie thought would have done more good if they had been eaten by the hungry people, not burned to ashes in some useless ritual. Finally, the temperatures began to rise, and the snow changed to slush, followed by a pounding rain. Relief was in the air, but it would still be many days before the beastmen could begin their trek to their spring encampment—or even leave their tents.

Kalie thought she could endure starvation more easily than another day trapped inside the fetid felt of Maalke's tent.

While the rain brought no relief to hunger or confinement, it did manage to bring fever. Kalie and Irisa—the only two to be spared from illness—took turns nursing the others. It was apparent early on that Irisa would confine her care to Maalke and her own children—the younger of whom, perhaps because he was still nursing, showed no sign of illness yet—and Kalie would care for everyone else. Surprisingly, the system worked well for both women.

For Kalie, it was a time to be creative. Her medicinal stores were nearly depleted, and there was no way she could get more. Even Brenia was rationing what she shared with others. Fortunately, Kalie had enough experience to see that this sickness was the type that would run its course and then be gone. Some would live; some would die. Nothing in the mortal world could be done but ease the symptoms.

So Kalie brewed willow bark and chamomile into one big pot of tea each day while her supply lasted. For Varena, she secretly slipped in the last of the honey Brenia had given her. She rubbed away the aches in their muscles and told stories to takes their minds off their misery. During the worst of the three or four days the fever lasted, most of those afflicted slept, giving Kalie much needed rest, and much appreciated peace.

In fact, if it weren't for Altia and her two daughters, she would have truly enjoyed this time.

Varena and Cassia were appreciative of Kalie's efforts, and even Tasine found enough voice to thank her with real warmth. In a complete change from her earlier stiffness, the old slave woman now seemed pathetically grateful for the simplest kindnesses, from a skillful massage to stories about the Goddess and the afterlife.

But Altia and her children—when they weren't asleep—seemed to take their only relief from making Kalie as miserable as they. Altia found something to demand every time Kalie tried to catch a moment's rest. She constantly needed to have her furs shifted or refolded or beaten to get rid of the bugs. And of course, anything she or her daughters wanted took precedence over Kalie's care of the others in the tent. Once, when Kalie had to tell Altia that the tea was gone, it would take some time to steep another batch, Altia managed a diatribe of curses and threats that was impressive for one so weak with illness. Then Irisa came at a hurried crawl from Maalke's sleeping space, hissing demands for silence so Maalke could sleep. She of course directed her anger at Kalie, not Altia.

After five days of this, Kalie's patience was badly frayed. The children were all on the mend—something to be grateful for indeed, as more than half the tents in the camp had lost at least one child to the fever. But Kalie found her thoughts dwelling more and more often on ways she might silence Altia forever. So many had already died of the epidemic, it would arouse no suspicions if Maalke's old wife succumbed as well. If only she had access to some kind of poison Kalie thought. If everyone would cooperate by sleeping at the same time, she might even risk suffocating her…

Kalie snapped out of the half stupor she had fallen into to find Tasine staring at her with fevered eyes. For a moment, Kalie feared she had spoken out loud or that the old woman was reading her thoughts. Then she saw the poor slave woman was barely aware of her surroundings, but in need of water.

"Drink, Tasine," Kalie said, carefully dribbling water from the goat's horn into the woman's mouth. The healer in Kalie desperately wished for willow bark for the fever, but there was none left. Instead, she soaked a scrap of felt in cool water and placed it on Tasine's forehead.

That calmed her a little, and the old woman sighed with relief. But when Kalie tried to move away to the next task awaiting her, Tasine clutched her arm with surprising strength. "Stay a little longer, dear Zahlene," she whispered. "We had so little time together, and I've waited so long to find you again."

Kalie knew from her experience at Hot Springs it would be best just to hold Tasine's hand and not attempt to force her back into reality. In her current state she wouldn't be likely to hear it anyway. And besides, Kalie was growing desperate for a distraction from circumstances that were threatening her own sanity. She wanted to hear more.

"I knew you would be special. When Ahnaak's men came, my grandmother told me not to be afraid. That I would one day bear a child who would slay Ahnaak and redeem our people. But our tents were burning and women were screaming and the first of the warriors already tearing apart the bags of wool where we were hiding. All I could think of was what would have to happen to me to have that child she spoke of. I was only twelve years and not yet a woman. It never occurred to me to wonder why she said 'child' and not 'son'. And a moment later she was dead."

Kalie gave Tasine more water, and waited, spellbound.

"The men didn't care that I wasn't a woman. They hurt me so much that I thought they had broken something inside me, and I'd never be one. In a way I was right, for you came before I was ready and my body couldn't hold you long enough, even though I loved you from the first time I felt you move. But you died without drawing a breath, and I could never have another. But I saw you in my dreams for the rest of my life." Some of the fever left Tasine's eyes. "Or is this just another dream?"

Kalie squeezed Tasine's hand and kissed her cheek. "No, Mother," she whispered. "This time it's real."

A smile spread across the careworn face of the old slave woman, and she drifted into a peaceful sleep.

The next morning, Cassia was well enough to move about. Though not quite well enough to help Kalie with the work, she could at least kept her company.

Altia's symptoms were as severe as ever. Whether it was Tasine's story or perhaps the hand of the Goddess, Kalie stopped looking for ways to murder Altia, which was a good thing, for while searching for any overlooked herbs she might still have, Kalie found a bit of unused mandrake.

"What are you making?" Cassia asked, eyeing the roots Kalie had once used as a fertility potion for her.

"Something to make Altia sleep through the rest of her illness. That way, *everyone* in the tent will feel better."

Cassia laughed, and then grew serious. "Are you sure it's safe? You told me those roots were powerful magic, dangerous in the wrong combination."

Kalie scowled, for somewhere inside her, she was aware of just how badly she still wanted Altia to die, and how easy it might be in her own exhausted condition to make that happen—by full mistake, or only half.

"I know what I'm doing!" she snapped. "There's little enough left to do more than make her groggy. But that would at least be some relief!"

Later, when Altia fell into a deep, but clearly safe sleep, and Kalie herself had finally gotten a good long nap, she decided to ask Cassia to explain something that Kalie had been unable to explain to her countrymen for seven years. They were by the brazier, mending clothing and boots in preparation for the journey to the spring pastures.

"Why does she expect my help when she has been so horrible to me?" Kalie asked.

Cassia looked up from her sewing. "What do you mean?"

"It's something I don't understand about your people! You bring slaves into your tents, beat them, starve them, degrade them—and then expect their loyalty! Altia knew she might die from this pestilence, and she knew that my healing skills might be the only thing to save her—yet she never once changed her attitude to that of a supplicant in need of help. After all, with healing teas in such short supply, I could have easily have given them to everyone but her—and what could she have done?"

"Made you pay dearly when she recovered!" Cassia looked around nervously.

"True," said Kalie, sensing she'd better not mention that Altia might not have recovered. "But mistress, you are a violent people. And revenge is a part of your code of honor. How is it then that your warriors will bring so many people to live here, after murdering their families—and never fear that they, too, are honorable in the same way."

"But they never make *warriors* into slaves!" said Cassia. "Only women! Of course a man would seek revenge! That is why no one would ever try to make a slave of a man."

Kalie thought on that for a moment. "So men can be killed in battle, or captured and tortured, or sacrificed to your gods, but not enslaved?" Cassia nodded and continued sewing. "What about boys? I've heard children of both sexes are often taken in raids."

"But only girls are kept alive as slaves. Boys are always killed—eventually." Cassia looked like she had tasted something bitter.

Kalie wondered about that, but unwilling to be distracted now that she was getting some answers. "What about boys born to slave women? If Varena's brother had lived...?"

"Sons of slaves are bastards," Cassia explained, marveling that someone could not know these things. "They start life with a disadvantage, but our laws insist that every boy have the chance to become a warrior. Many do not survive the testing—but those who do are no less warriors than the sons of a king's wife."

Until then, Kalie had not realized how fully life —and death—were divided along gender lines. "But that still doesn't explain why hundreds of slave women—many of whom were daughters of princes and warriors—don't seek revenge. Many of them had mothers just like Altia, and learned violence and bullying at an early age." She looked at Tasine, sleeping fitfully. "And there are many harsh examples of what the future will hold for them as slaves. Surely some of them must have chosen to trade their miserable lives for one moment of satisfying revenge." Seeing Cassia's shocked face, she added, "Or the honor of avenging their families."

"But honor for a woman is different from honor for a man! She honors her family through her loyalty to her husband or master. And she is rewarded accordingly. No one wants to be a slave, but that is a woman's fate if her men aren't strong enough to keep her safe. It's a bitter truth, but what's to be gained by dwelling on it?

"Besides," Cassia continued. "It doesn't have to be so bad. You've achieved great status in a short time. It can be that way for many. I know at least two wives in this clan alone who came here as slaves."

Kalie thought of the stories told here in this tent that dwelt on that very situation. "So, the way out of slavery is always through the favor of a powerful man?"

"Well...yes. Of course."

Kalie shook her head. How could two people—both intelligent—speak the same language, and still not understand what the other was saying?

# Chapter 29

It was nearly time to leave the winter camp when Maalke returned from an unsuccessful hunt with four other men. They were all wet and cold, and the women hurried to help them off with their soaked outer clothing and hang them to dry in the smoke of the dung fire. Altia brought out kumis and what food they had.

"Kalie!" Maalke called. "Come tell us one of those stories from your barbarian homeland!"

Kalie's heart quickened. This was her first opportunity to tell stories for warriors. If she did her job right, the death of her enemies and the salvation of her people might be at hand.

She crawled to the place Maalke indicated, closer to where he sat than she was comfortable, but she tucked her legs beneath her and waited demurely for the signal to begin.

At his nod, the words came, as fluently as she could have hoped. "Once there was a young man of humble beginnings..." she began. Thanks to Cassia, she was even able to make his mother a slave woman and his father a great chief. "He was skilled in battle and very brave, but he had a problem. For he had fallen in love with the king's beautiful daughter, and the king had said that only a warrior who could bring back the skin of the Great Golden Lion would ever wed the girl. And everyone knew the beast could not be killed..."

Kalie had their attention. She settled into a comfortable cadence and was soon leading them through a maze of twists and turns as the hero tried three times to slay the lion, only to succeed by winning a star from the heavens in a game of dice with the gods, fashioning it into a spearhead and flinging it into the eye of the golden lion.

The men roared their appreciation and called for more. This time, Kalie took a chance and told a tale of a warrior who slew his own chief, but was rewarded for it, for the chief had angered the gods by swearing falsely in their names.

She finished with a version of the Fisherman and the Magic Fish, especially crafted for them. In this form, the fisherman's greedy wife kept demanding more and more things in exchange for the fish's freedom, only to be dumped into the water to drown when her husband got sick of it. The compassionate fish then rewarded the good husband by giving him all the treasure and status the wife had wanted—and a beautiful new wife as well.

The men really liked that one, and began demanding of Maalke why had not shared this talented slave with his friends sooner. Kalie accepted a cup of kumis from a resentful-looking Altia. She tongued it first, to check for the taste of anything that should not be there, and then sipped quietly, basking in the warm glow of accomplishment and listening eagerly to the men's conversation, hoping for any bit of information that might be useful.

It was only moments before the attack came that she noticed one of the men eyeing her in a way that had become sickeningly familiar, and ask a question. Maalke nodded with pleasure, the very image of a gracious host.

Then the man was on top of her prying her legs apart as a helpless scream tore from her lips. The men roared with laughter at this, as moments ago they had laughed at her stories. Kalie had gone months without being raped, and as she had no warning, had no time to prepare herself. She remained conscious through the whole thing, as each of the men in the tent took his turn with her.

Finally, a particularly brutal warrior named Grubaak, displeased with her silence and corpselike posture, swore to the others he'd make her respond like a woman should. He began strangling her slowly, apparently pleased by the results. Kalie strove one last time to leave her body and escape. This time she succeeded, as Grubaak, now enraged, tightened his hands around her throat, and everything went dark.

Forced back into consciousness sometime later, Kalie found Cassia setting a cool compress across her forehead. The compassionate look the younger woman gave her might have cheered Kalie, had it not brought back the memory of all that had happened.

She tried to move, dislodging a warm felt rag from around her neck, and sending spears of pain throughout her body, but the worst of it was inside her throat and neck like a ring of fire. The minor cuts and bruises seemed to have been dressed in some fashion, and the pain there was beginning to subside.

"What…?" she tried to speak, but only a gravelly croak came out.

"Don't try to talk yet," said Cassia. "And keep this around your neck. Once the swelling goes down, your voice should return, eventually."

Her voice? Kalie remembered being strangled during the rape. Cautiously, she probed her throat and neck, careful this time not to dislodge the rag. It was swollen, and perhaps something more. Had Grubaak broken something? With something like terror, Kalie wondered if she would ever speak again.

Then another thought came to her from someplace dark and hidden. Why should she want to speak again? All her life, the stories Kalie knew and told had been a special kind of good. They had given her a purpose and a place when her first time among the beastmen had broken her ability to do anything else. They had sustained her this past half year in a land of horror and despair. And she had been arrogant enough to think that with them she could influence the hearts and minds of these so-called *people* and even lead her to a means of salvation for her own?

Now she knew what her stories meant to Maalke and the other men here: a pleasant enough diversion between bouts of rape and murder. It wasn't enough for Grubaak to strip and degrade her in front of everyone in the tent. When she failed to provide him with proof of his power over her, he had to take the only other thing she had of value: her words. She felt dirty in a way she had never felt before. The thought of telling stories again made her want to vomit.

She looked up and met Varena's worried gaze. The girl seemed as small and frightened as the day Kalie had first arrived. Kalie wanted to reassure her; say that she would be fine. But she couldn't speak, and it would have been a lie anyway.

She turned her back on Varena and curled up into a tiny ball. She had been a fool to think that by coming here, armed only with stories and the memory of a faith she once held, she could find an exploitable weakness in these beasts, and then slip unnoticed back to her homeland with the secret of their destruction.

Kalie was, she realized, exactly what the men here thought she was: an amusing little fool.

Well, there was still one thing she could do. She had escaped this world once and she would do it again. There was still Varena to think of, and spring was nearly here. Kalie would recover enough to walk out of this place, whether her voice returned or not. And when the clan left for their spring killing frenzy, or whatever these people did to celebrate the return of life, she would take Varena and escape to the west. Let the beastmen come; there was nothing she could do about it anyway. But she could save Varena. And she would.

Kalie's recovery was slow. Unlike the time she stumbled, half dead, into the temple at Tall Oaks, she had not the luxury of madness. The moment Altia judged Kalie as able to work, she was prodded upright with blows and curses. When Kalie sought the escape of oblivion as she had all those years ago among her own people, Altia applied burning dung to her skin to snap her out of it.

It was very effective.

Cassia, to her credit, tried to intervene, but could do little. Varena wrung her hands and wept. Tasine looked away with the ease of long practice. Kalie went back to work, with the slow and deliberate pace of a sullen slave, as much to silence Varena's wailing as to stop Altia's abuse.

A few days later, the chief declared that spring had arrived, and all the men left for three days of prayer and sacrifice, to be followed by the long awaited departure from the winter camp.

*This is what they call spring?* thought Kalie,

gazing into the sodden gray skies. Only the shift in the land from frozen white to brown slush told her anything had changed at all.

There was a flurry of preparations for their departure, while Kalie surreptitiously began making her own. There was little worth taking, but Kalie took note of every knife, water bag, and scrap of food as it was packed. The warming temperatures told her that they could get by well enough with just the blankets and clothing they already had. She could only pray that the rains would continue long enough to give them drinking water and mask their trail. Foraging would be possible eventually, but some food would be necessary for the first few days. Kalie planned to take every scrap that Maalke's family had left, and felt not a twinge of guilt.

Then, when all was in readiness, and the men had still not returned, Altia announced she would have one last gathering of her friends to pass the time. And that Kalie would entertain them with her stories.

It had been ten days since Kalie had spoken. She half smiled, and turned a blank face to Altia, exactly like a sheep who had been asked to recite poetry. Then she raised one questioning eyebrow, as if daring Altia to command speech from a stone.

"Never mind your stupid act," said Altia, waving her hand. "It's been fine having you quiet for once, but now that you've been talking in your sleep these past three nights, it's clear enough you've recovered!"

Kalie dropped the bundle of wool she had been carrying. "What?" she croaked.

At that everyone, even Varena, laughed. Kalie might have minded, but she was too busy exploring her vocal cords, and wondering with sudden fear what she might have revealed in her sleep these past few nights.

"What did I say?" Her voice was gravelly, but she could already feel the strength returning.

"Who knows? You were going on in that nonsense talk you savages use instead of words. But it's clear you can speak properly again, so tomorrow you can tell those funny stories about how women live when they don't have real men to take care of them."

Whether Altia was being deliberately insulting or thought she was demonstrating an understanding of the stories scarcely mattered to Kalie. Telling her stories to anything Altia hosted would be little different that Maalke's party—minus the rape.

She considered refusing, or botching stories she knew, or—best of all—telling Altia's guests exactly what she thought of them. But none of it mattered enough to her to form a solid plan.

That night, Tasine sat down beside Kalie as they bundled the last of the provisions into leather bags, which would be divided between the horses and the women to carry to the next camp. Tasine began to speak, about the journey to the tribe's summer pastures and the brief, beautiful spring that Kalie would see for the first time. Then, when it was clear that no one else in the tent was paying any attention, she said in her same quiet voice, "Your silence protects you, Kalie, but your eyes betray you. Each day you look to the west. Especially when you're tucking a scrap of food in your robe or a knife in your bedroll."

Kalie dropped the gear she was packing, and would have bolted straight to her feet had not Tasine placed a hand on her shoulder and pinched hard—

harder than a woman in her condition should have been able. They repacked the items and Tasine continued softly.

"I can't go with you. This winter will be my last. In all my years of sorrow and pain, I dreamed many dreams; told many stories. Yet never could I have imagined having the courage to simply get up and walk out of this place. For those of us born to this world, there is no other. But for you there is. And taking that child with you, though she was not even borne to your body…" Tasine's breath caught in her throat and Kalie was shocked to see tears in the old woman's eyes. "You are just as I imagined Zharene would have been, had she lived."

"You told me about her when you were ill," Kalie replied carefully, deciding not to mention that Tasine had believed Kalie to be Zharene.

Tasine nodded, though Kalie doubted she remembered. "I dreamed about her for years. For a long time, in my dreams each night, I held her and watched her grow and even heard her speak, as if my dream world was the real one, and this world the dream."

"More like a nightmare, I'd say," said Kalie.

"Yes, though I lacked the wit to see it at the time," said Tasine. "Other times, I would dream I was in a dark place where I could hear her crying, but never find her."

Kalie shivered, and put her hand over Tasine's. "That must have been terrible."

"The happy dreams made up for them. And together, they made me a good storyteller. In my tales, I could be somewhere else, even someone else, for a time. With my stories, I could remake my world."

"And you are good," said Kalie, stirring a little from her depression. "I have learned more from you than any storyteller I've ever heard."

"Yes, I was good," Tasine said with a hint of pride. "But not like you."

"Please, don't," said Kalie, her despair returning. "Whatever gift I had was killed by Maalke and his friends. If it ever existed in the first place."

Tasine turned her hand in Kalie's and squeezed hard, as if with the last of her strength. "Yes, men are good at killing things. But it's women who bring forth life. And what you have, Kalie, no man can kill. You've brought something to this world, girl. Your stories, your strength, your goddess...I can't explain it. But something will be lost when you leave. Even if no one but me knows it was ever here."

"How can you say that?" cried Kalie, as eyes she thought finally dried forever filled with tears. "I'm no different from you!" And she realized as she said it how cruel she meant to sound.

"Did I ever think to adopt a child after mine was lost? There are children like Varena in every tent of this tribe, yet all my love was held for a dead child, while living ones cried all around me! Did I ever use my gift for stories to comfort or teach? Did I try to change the world with them? Bah! I never even imagined such things!" Tasine cackled, a laugh that ended in a coughing fit. "Not even in my wildest tales."

Kalie found a water skin and helped Tasine drink while she thought about that. Carefully, sounding out the thoughts as she spoke them she asked, "Can stories change the world?"

Tasine, too, seemed to be giving that matter

much thought as she sipped the water. "My grandmother was perhaps maddened with fear and rage when she spoke her last words. But that doesn't mean she wasn't right. Keep telling your stories, Daughter, and perhaps someday we'll find out." Then Tasine lay back on her furs, the farthest from the heat of the brazier, and drifted off.

Kalie wasn't sure if Tasine had meant her grandmother's prophesy or the power of stories when she spoke of finding out, but Kalie gently lay one of her own warm furs over her and whispered, "Good night, Mother." It was, she told herself, only a simple kindness. It didn't mean she was adopting Tasine as well.

The packing was finished. Altia was busy rewarding herself for work well done with the last of the kumis. Soon she would signal it was time for sleep, and the rest of the household would lay down for one of their last nights in this camp. All Kalie had to do was distract her from the fact that one lazy slave had already gone to sleep without permission.

Would the tribe return to this place next winter? Kalie tried to imagine herself sitting beside Varena, soaking in the magical waters of Hot Springs while this stinking tribe huddled in their freezing tents then, but instead, all she could think of was Alessa and Traea and the others who had followed her in this mad mission to the steppes.

Tasine startled Kalie out of her thoughts by speaking dreamily from her bed. "Why don't you ask that daughter that you were wise and good enough to acquire what stories you should tell tomorrow?"

And Kalie, realizing now how much her own pain had hurt Varena, did exactly that.

Varena lit up like the sun. "The one about the man who did the opposite of everything his wife wanted! Everyone loves that one. And that first one you told, way back at the start of winter, about the three men who made the doll that came to life, and you ask everyone in the tent who it belongs to! And that one about the talking cat who tricks the magician into turning himself into a mouse..." Varena, it seemed, remembered every one of Kalie's stories, and couldn't find one that wasn't worth telling.

Although she was touched by Varena's enthusiasm, and inspired by Tasine's visions, the thought of telling any of her stories for Altia and her friends still left her feeling as empty and soiled as it had ten days earlier.

As Kalie lay on her sheepskin that night, she contemplated the emptiness inside her, and all of the people around her who seemed willing to fill it, and the great work she had come here to accomplish, that was going to somehow fix everything—for her and for her people. It seemed wrong to walk away, and yet useless—worse than useless—to stay.

And then Kalie did something she had not done since coming to this place. She prayed. She still didn't believe, but somehow, praying seemed to be the thing to do when there was simply nothing else left.

"Where do I go, Mother? And what do I do when I get there? I want this nightmare to end. I want to show Varena the wonders of the life I took for granted my first eighteen summers. But if I spend the rest of my life safe in Hot Springs, does that mean that one day I will die comfortably in bed, an old woman who let her world fall to slavery and ruin because she wasn't strong enough?"

Kalie rolled over uncomfortably. "That isn't fair!" she whimpered to a Goddess who hadn't yet answered. "I'd endure all this and more if I just knew it was for a purpose. But I won't stay and suffer another day if I have to believe it's all for nothing!" *Worse*, came the cruel voice from deep inside, *all a joke*.

Then a stronger voice, from somewhere outside herself, sang a single refrain: *Not a joke; not all for nothing*.

And perhaps not an answer either, but it was something, and at last Kalie slept.

# Chapter 30

While she slept well enough, no shining inspiration was waiting for Kalie when she awoke the next morning. When the guests arrived, she still didn't know what, if anything, she was going to do. She went through the usual mind-numbing routine of waiting on the collection of high status horsewomen. Kalie supposed she was expected to be impressed. Cassia certainly was. "This is the biggest gathering she's ever had!" the second wife whispered to Kalie. "Look," she bobbed her head toward a graying, fierce looking woman with a deep scar across her face, from her left eye down to the corner of her down-turned mouth. "That's Leja, first wife to Chief Kahlar! She was once a great beauty."

"How did her face get like that?" Kalie asked, curious in spite of herself.

"From the former first wife. Leja came here as a battle prize, and soon became Kahlar's favorite concubine. His wife thought she'd put a stop to that by cutting up her face, and leaving her scared like she is now." Cassia smirked. "But things didn't work out the way she planned. Leja was already pregnant by then, and when she gave him a son, Kahlar promised to give her anything her heart desired. So she asked him for the head of his first wife!"

"Did he do it?" Kalie asked.

"Yes, of course." Cassia blinked in surprise. "That old woman was the real fool, not to see how the wind was blowing. Her family had fallen from favor, her only son had died in his first battle, and there was no one in the camp to speak for her—not that anyone would have by then." Cassia nodded toward Leja's many layers of robes and furs. "They say she wears the head as a talisman somewhere—but no one knows where."

"Maybe that's the story I should tell," Kalie murmured. Goddess knows, it's what passes for entertainment around here!

But when the women settled down, legs crossed to show off the beaded soles of their slippers, and Altia gestured Kalie to begin, it was a very different story that sprang unbidden to her lips. For Altia had flung open the door flap of the tent to welcome in the first tentative breaths of spring, and Kalie got a look at a most remarkable thing: a wedge of blue sky.

"Once there was a beautiful maiden," she began, not looking at her audience, but out of the tent. "Her name was Shara, and she lived in a land where all was sunshine, and never winter. And she was promised in marriage to a handsome prince.

"Then one day, evil men came and destroyed her land. They carried her back to the dank dark bog where they lived, where all was winter and never sunshine, and set her to live as a slave. There she toiled for many years, weeping many tears for all that she lost.

"One day, Shara came across a hole in the dark frozen ground, perhaps a gopher hole or a rabbit warren. Thinking it might have food hidden in it, she crawled down to have a look. To her amazement, a spacious cavern stretched out before her, nearly high enough to stand in. A strange glowing moss allowed her to see, and also emitted faint warmth. It was like some weirdly beautiful tent, which she might have seen in a dream.

"As she explored this place, Shara found a huge dead bird. Its plumage was scarlet and blue, and she knew at once that this bird, like she herself, had come from someplace far away. How had it come here? she wondered. Perhaps he had been trying to return to his home when this frozen land had caught the creature in its grip. Perhaps he had found this refuge, hoping to survive the winter and return to his home in the spring.

"'Poor bird,' said Shara. 'I guess no one told you there is no spring in this land.' And she kissed his brow and smoothed his feathers, thinking perhaps to give him some kind of proper burial."

Altia and a few of her guests snickered at that, but Kalie, coming out of the spell she had woven for herself, saw that the others were entranced, waiting hopefully for a sign that the bird might yet live.

"Shara jumped when she felt a faint heartbeat beneath her cold fingers. The bird was alive—but just barely. Casting her gaze desperately about the dimly glowing cavern, she sought some way to keep it alive. There were bits of grain, nearby, probably stored by the bird when he—"

"Why wouldn't she just kill him and eat him?" demanded Leja.

A few of the others rolled their eyes, irritated by the interruption, but not willing to silence her themselves.

Kalie smiled enigmatically at the chief's wife. "Perhaps she hungered for something more than food. Or perhaps he was simply too beautiful to kill. In any case, Shara took her own warm cape from her shoulders and wrapped it around the bird. Then she gathered all she could of the glowing moss and tucked it around him for more warmth. She melted ice for water and fed it to him, a drop at a time, until at last the beautiful bird began to revive.

"Shara had to return to her work before she was missed, but every night she snuck away to sleep beside her friend, wrapped in his warm, soft feathers. As the bird grew stronger, he sang to her, of his warm home in the south. Of his gratitude to the kind and courageous girl who had saved his life. And of the joy that is friendship.

"Finally the day came when the bird was strong enough to fly. He spread his shimmering wings of scarlet and blue, and Shara saw he was nearly as big as she was. The bird poked his head out of the hole, sniffing the cold air with delight. 'When spring comes,' he said to Shara, 'will you not fly away with me back to my home?'

"Shara smiled sadly as she stroked his soft plumage. 'I'm afraid that spring never comes to this accursed place. And anyway, I would be too heavy for you carry.'

"The bird cocked his head and peered at her through one eye." Kalie did exactly that with her head, and the women laughed. "'You are mistaken,' he said. 'For I have flown over this land many times. Once every seven years, spring comes for three days. When that time comes, we will fly together to my home, and there I will heal you as you have healed me.'

"'But I would still be too heavy. We would both fall to our deaths—or worse be captured again by the evil ones who dwell in this land. When this magical spring comes, you must leave.'

"'And so I shall,' said the bird. 'But I will not

leave without you.'

"And he told her to weave a basket; the largest she could make. Shara gathered up bits of straw, cords and thongs her masters had thrown out, and even thread from her own ragged clothing. Little by little, each night in secret, as she had when she tended the bird, Shara wove the basket.

"Finally, the day came when the sky opened up and sunlight poured through, melting all the snow at once. Shara's cruel masters went out to celebrate, but only after they had tied her inside the tent, with neither food nor water, and not even a crack through which she might see the glorious light." The women in the audience shifted uncomfortably. Kalie couldn't tell if it was in sympathy for her heroine, or in the sudden realization that she had modeled her villains on *them*. She took a deep breath and strove to find the story's ending.

"As the light sought to enter the tent on the third morning, Shara was awakened by the sharp pecking of beaks. She tried, as she had for days, to find a weakness in the tent, when all at once, a seam that joined two pieces together split apart with a loud rip. There, in the dazzling sunlight, stood Shara's friend the bird, and with him were seven others just like him.

"'I called, and all my kin did answer!' he cried. 'Hurry! To your basket!'

"Shara dragged the basket outside and leapt inside of it. She took nothing with her to remind her of this horrid place. Each of the eight birds caught a part of the basket in their talons, and then, with a tremendous beating of blue and scarlet wings, slowly began to rise. Gathering speed, they soared into the wide blue sky.

"An angry cry from below told them they had been spotted. Shara's enemies flung spears and rocks, trying to bring them down, but to no avail. She was free now, high above the clouds, with the world below her and all its evil less important than the bite of a mosquito.

"And finally, the basket alighted in a beautiful new land, where Shara and the bird lived happily ever after."

Kalie bowed her head, and noticed a cup of water beside her. Suddenly aware of how raw and worn her throat felt, she took it and drank it down gratefully. Only then did she notice the quiet in the tent. No one was applauding.

Fearfully, she looked up—and stared in amazement at the sniffling or silently crying women before her. Even Altia was speechless—although perhaps more from the way her friends were reacting than from any deep emotion.

Finally, Leja spoke. "That was wonderful, girl." She reached into the folds of her robes and produced, rather than the shrunken head Kalie had feared, a beaded comb that might be used to untangle hair, or adorn it.

Kalie bowed again. "Thank you," she said.

Others gave her gifts of jewelry as well. One young woman, beautiful by local standards, Kalie noticed, stopped to ask, "Were they supposed to be lovers at the end? The girl and the bird?"

"I'm really not sure," said Kalie. "Perhaps."

"Then should he not have turned into a handsome prince?"

Kalie smiled. "Actually, I think the next time I

tell it, it is she who will turn into a bird. Then she can
fly by his side and never need to be carried in a basket
by anyone."

"But do you not know?" asked another wife.
"How was it told to you?"

"It wasn't. I only created it this morning."
Sensing the discomfort that greeted her words Kalie
added, "Feel free to shape it as you wish if you ever
you tell the story."

The women seemed puzzled as they left and
Altia looked as though she had tasted something sour,
but she said nothing to Kalie. "Is she angry that I made
up a story rather than telling one I learned somewhere
else?" Kalie whispered to Cassia. "Did that reflect
badly on her hospitality or insult her guests?"

"I'm beginning to think you will never
understand us!" Cassia said, shaking her head. "Or I
you! Can't you see how jealous the old goat is?"

"Of what?"

Cassia rolled her eyes. "She's never met
anyone who can just...do what you did. None of us
have. I'm sure her guests are flattered you did
something special like that for them, but Altia...she
doesn't like knowing that foreign slaves own skills she
can't even dream of having!"

Which made Altia even more dangerous to
her, thought Kalie. But she didn't care, for she had just
received the greatest gift of all. Kalie's stories had
returned to her, as if the Goddess Herself had touched
her inside. And even if they never had the power to
change the way these women saw the world, they had
to power to make them feel.

Varena crawled into her lap that night, and for
the first time since her attack by Maalke's friends,

Kalie combed her hair, and sang her a lullaby, and did all the simple things she had promised this girl she would do, and then just as easily forgotten.

"I'm sorry I haven't been here for you, Varena," she whispered, as they lay together at the farthest edge from the fire's warmth, so Tasine could get closer to it.

"I'm sorry I couldn't help you when you were sad," said the girl.

"You helped," said Kalie. "More than you'll ever know." Then she turned to Tasine. "And so did you. Thank you both."

Kalie took a necklace of shells she had received after a telling, and hung it around Varena's neck. Then she took the warm boots she had received from an earlier telling, and gave them to Tasine. The old woman might not have many days left to walk, but at least her last ones would be in as much warmth and comfort as Kalie could provide.

Both the old woman and the young girl gasped in wonder. Kalie suddenly realized that in this world, where status and acceptance was measured in the ornaments one could display, Varena had never owned a piece of jewelry, and Tasine probably hadn't since her childhood. She was ashamed it had taken her so long to grant either of them such a simple gift.

But Varena was looking as if Kalie had given her the moon. "I'm so glad you're my mother!" she cried. Tasine wrapped shaky arms around Kalie. "And I am glad you are my daughter."

Kalie knew she would not be leaving now. She had a job to do, and for the first time in over half a year, felt clear about her purpose. While she hated the thought of continuing her own captivity, and worse, delaying Varena's chance at freedom, Kalie finally understood why she had come here.

From across the time and space came Maris' words: "...our greatest chance lies not in slaying these beasts, but in transforming them. You speak of tricking a beast into swallowing the knife which will kill him. I speak of tricking that same beast into swallowing medicine that will heal him."

Kalie had dismissed the great shaman's idealism as the foolish wish of one who had never seen this land. She had come here to kill the king; to pit warriors and brothers against each other, and by those actions, save her people. And perhaps those plans would yet come to be.

But somehow, almost without realizing it, Kalie had found a different plan and a new kind of hope in the form of the people who lived here. Varina, Tasine, Cassia, Brenia—and others she hadn't bothered to get to know, but probably should. Maybe even some of the men. Kalie first gagged at the thought, but couldn't dismiss from her mind the warrior who protected his crippled son and cared about his sister.

Perhaps Kalie's mistake was in thinking that she had come here only to save her own people. For now she knew with a certainty she could not explain that there was a way out of this pit—not just for her and those who followed her here, but maybe for as many people as there were stars in the sky.

This new path was fraught with as many dangers as the old one, but it held possibilities that murder and deceit never could. Could her stories change this world?

Kalie was ready to find out.

# Excerpt from: Shadow of the Horsemen

Book 2 of Kalie's Journey
By Sandra Saidak
Coming 2012 from Uffington Horse Press

Kalie lay in her furs in the darkness, wondering why she was suddenly awake. The stars told her that it was nearly dawn, but it would be some time before Altia declared the day begun with her usual round of curses and blows. All was quiet, but for the lowing of the sheep and goats, and the soft hooting of an owl.

Kalie sat up. It was too close to dawn for an owl…

A shriek split the night, and horsemen spilled into the camp. They carried torches. Suddenly, everything was burning.

Kalie sat in the middle of it all, as warriors shook off sleep and grabbed their weapons, while women and children ran screaming into the night. Some of the men who had been on sentry duty were already mounting an effective defense, but there were clearly more attackers than defenders. The battle seemed to be as chaotic as the women's attempt to flee, and Kalie could see no safe place to hide.

Then she saw Varena running straight into the path of a charging horse, and her own safety didn't matter. She wasn't aware of moving; wasn't aware of anything until the moment she landed on the hard earth with Varena under her and a horse leaping over her back.

"Are you all right?" she shouted over the noise,

while the girl screamed hysterically. Varena seemed unharmed, but before Kalie could even begin to examine her, something tightened around her neck, stopping her breath.

She landed on the back of a horse, just as she realized in was her own felt robe that was strangling her. The pressure eased as her captor released her, the better to heave a spear with the hand he had used to snatch up Kalie, blocking an attack with his other.

"Not again!" Kalie moaned while the battle raged around them. She was aware that the stench emanating from this new beastman's body was different from Maalke and the others, whom she had apparently gotten used to. She tried to sit up and figure out how she was going to get off this horse, but her captor only laughed and struck her hard enough to keep her slumped over the horse's withers.

Kalie watched as the ground moved beneath her, back and forth for a while, and murky with smoke, then more quickly as the beastman urged his horse away from the ruined camp. This new group apparently had what they came for and now were leaving—taking Kalie and who knew how many others with them.

The smoke was gone, allowing Kalie to take a gulp of clean air. She had just decided to attempt a rolling leap from the horse, when the clatter of another horse chasing, then gaining on hers reached her ears. The horse beneath her slowed, then turned, then reared up with an angry squeal. Kalie hung on, trying to choose the best moment to leap free, while the sounds of weapons clashing and men shouting filled the air around her.

Then there was the meaty thud of a spear

striking flesh, and Kalie's captor fell to the ground. The horse slowed to a stop, and Kalie slid indecorously down the other side of it—only to catch her foot in the stirrup, and find herself hanging upside down, her head just inches from the earth.

"Let me help you the rest of the way off," said a man's voice, rich with laughter. "You're safe now. He won't be bothering you anymore."

Back on her feet, Kalie looked down at the dead man. He was smaller and darker than the men of Aahk—and dirtier, if that were possible. He wore a combination of badly made felt and uncured animal skins.

She turned to the other man, and found herself staring into Riyik's laughing gray eyes. He stood beside his horse looking proud and smug; he seemed to be waiting for something. For the woman he rescued to fall at his feet in gratitude, perhaps? Kalie felt a bubble of laughter at that. Then she realized how far they were from the camp.

"If you're going to rape me, just get it over with!" she snapped hoarsely.

Riyik's expression changed abruptly, and Kalie could have sworn he actually got smaller.

"I thought I just rescued you from that fate," he said quietly.

"Yes, and from what I've seen of you beastmen," she spat the word, "that makes me your prize."

"You belong to Maalke. He may choose to reward me for saving you—although why he would want to is beyond me at the moment. But I don't assume any liberties beforehand."

"Well, aren't you just the noblest beastman!"

Somewhere inside, Kalie knew she had lost her last connection to sanity—but she couldn't have stopped herself if the Goddess Herself commanded it.

Riyik seemed more puzzled than angry. "Actually, I think I am. Most women would show some gratitude after such a rescue—and few men would have this much patience for your reaction."

"Gratitude!" Kalie was more than spitting—she was nearly foaming at the mouth. Maybe she could pass off her behavior as rabies. "You think being beaten, raped and enslaved by your people is somehow better than being beaten, raped and enslaved by his?" She gave the corpse a vicious kick. It felt wonderful.

Riyik took a step back. "You were putting up an impressive fight. I thought you didn't want to go with him."

"And since when does what any woman wants matter to one of you sick, Motherless bastards?" she demanded.

The renewed sounds of battle drew their attention. Riyik mounted his horse in a graceful leap. "Others may be more needful of my help. It seems clear you can get back to camp safely by yourself—although I pity any enemy warriors you meet on the way." He wheeled his horse and raced back to the battle.

# About The Author

      Sandra Saidak graduated San Francisco State University in 1985 with a B.A. in English. She is a high school English teacher by day, author by night. Her hobbies include reading, folk music, attending SF conventions, researching prehistory, and maintaining an active fantasy life (but warns that this last one could lead to dangerous habits such as writing). Sandra lives in San Jose, CA with her husband Tom, daughters Heather and Melissa, and cats, Cocu and Oreo.

Learn more at: www.sandrasaidak.com

30413732R00157

Made in the USA
Lexington, KY
02 March 2014